W9-BXV-956

THE
MARTIAN GENERAL'S
DAUGHTER

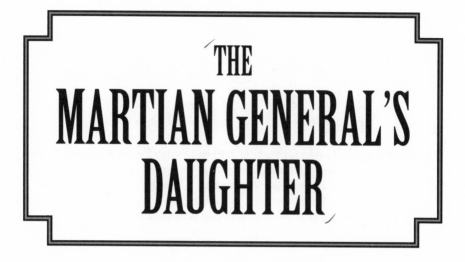

THE
MARTIAN GENERAL'S
DAUGHTER

THEODORE JUDSON

an imprint of **Prometheus Books**
Amherst, NY

Flagstaff Public Library
Flagstaff, Arizona

Published 2008 by Pyr®, an imprint of Prometheus Books

The Martian General's Daughter. Copyright © 2008 by Theodore Judson. All rights reserved. No part of this publication may be reproduced, stored in a retrieval system, or transmitted in any form or by any means, digital, electronic, mechanical, photocopying, recording, or other- wise, or conveyed via the Internet or a Web site without prior written permission of the pub- lisher, except in the case of brief quotations embodied in critical articles and reviews.

Inquiries should be addressed to
Pyr
59 John Glenn Drive
Amherst, New York 14228–2119
VOICE: 716–691–0133, ext. 210
FAX: 716–691–0137
WWW.PYRSF.COM

12 11 10 09 08   5 4 3 2 1

Library of Congress Cataloging-in-Publication Data

Judson, Theodore.
    The Martian general's daughter / Theodore Judson.
        p. cm.
    ISBN 978–1–59102–643–3 (alk. paper)
    I. Title.

PS3610.U533M37 2008
813'.6—dc22

2008005599

Printed in the United States on acid-free paper

-F
JUDSON,
Theodore

For Tim and Jean

The day will come when holy Troy shall fall
And Priam, lord of spears, and Priam's folk.

The Iliad, book VI, line 448

I.

AD 2293. Late March

When the word of Pretext's fall came to Peter Black's camp the general was seated beneath a conveyer belt on the Twelfth Level, watching a sales presentation made by the scrap men of Antioch Station. Many hundreds of workmen in small electric carts were parading past General Black and his staff officers while they displayed samples of the supposedly uninfected metal they were hoping to sell to the army. The traders had brought acrobats dressed in light armor made of silvery scales, and those agile young men jumped from cart to racing cart to impress the hopefully gullible soldiers. They looked like silver birds hopping across the backs of the ever-moving vehicles. "Bloch, Bloch, Pater Bloch!" the riders shouted each time they passed the general's retinue, for that is how these men of largely Middle Eastern descent mispronounced his famous surname. The red dust the machines were raising was becoming very thick around the conveyer belt; some of the officers—including Brigadier Harriman, the second-in-command—were choking on the rolling clouds and were frantically waving their hands in front of their faces to make patches of breathable air. One of these officers, a young Spaniard named Arango, remarked to me how well the general endured the dust; the others were making a great show of their suffering while the old veteran remained seated, his eyes held straight ahead and his body rigid. "He is an example to us all," said the young man. Not until the messengers came with the letter from Garden City did he realize that the general had gone to sleep.

"Thank you, my darling. I will treasure it always," said my father when Brigadier Harriman touched him on the shoulder and awakened him.

Father blinked at the startled man when he understood he was not addressing his wife. He motioned me to come to him and kneel at his side.

"Your mother is at home, isn't she?" he asked in my ear.

"Your wife is indeed in Garden City, sir, if that is the one you speak of," I said.

I did not think it a fit time to explain to him once again what he should know better than any man: he was my father, but the woman on Earth was not my mother.

"Of course," he said, and tapped himself on the leg. "What are we doing here?"

"Looking to buy scrap metal," I whispered in his ear.

"Do we need scrap?" he asked.

"Yes, but not this," I said. "These are mostly infected parts the traders could not sell elsewhere. They are keeping them moving so we can't examine the damage they've covered with red enamel. The entire lot is of suspect quality."

"Arabs," huffed Father. "We have beaten them."

"Many times, sir," I said. "Presently, however, they are our friends."

"Clever fellows, though," he said. "I like how they jump about. If you can't fight worth a damn, you should be able to do tricks. Could we lie down now? It's very unpleasant here."

Brigadier Harriman pointed out the messengers to him.

"Governor General, they have a letter from Mr. Golden," said the second-in-command, and handed my father a stack of sealed papers.

"Mr. Golden?" said Father, and he had to ponder the name for several moments ere he remembered Mr. Golden was the father of his sons' wives. "A slippery chap," said General Black, as he recalled. "Very rich. I wouldn't buy scrap from him, either. He talks too much. Bit of a windbag."

The general fell silent again. I could tell he was further considering Mr. Golden. The soldiers standing around him were awaiting his orders and beginning to glance at each other from the corners of their eyes.

"Sir," said Harriman, after he had awaited a word from his commander for a respectful minute, "the tradesmen from Antioch Station . . ."

"Send them away," said Father, emerging from his reverie. "They are too noisy for my liking. Send old Golden away, too. Tell him to call on me later. I don't care if we are related by marriage. I need to lie down."

"General," said Harriman, and cleared his throat, "the gentleman is not present. His messengers have brought you the letter you are holding."

"Yes, yes indeed," said Father, and was surprised to see he was holding a bundle of papers in his lap. "Well done," he added to Harriman and the other officers. "Exemplary service. You are dismissed. Not from the army—from my presence, I mean. Go about your duties. Go about your regular duties. I don't need your help," he said to me as he leaned forward to stand.

He got almost into a crouching position before he decided he was not going to get completely upright. He grunted mightily when he reached the acme of his progress, as if the sound in his throat would give him the momentum he needed to get to his feet. The sound did not help. Brigadier Harriman and I had to step forward and lift him up, which we were accustomed to doing nearly every time he stood.

"There we go. No need for help. Here we go. Once the old mule takes the first step, he can go all the way home, no matter how long the trip. Here we go," said Father.

I took his arm and led him from the conveyer belt toward the wide dome housing the military station. The officers saluted Father's retreating backside, and the general waved to them over his shoulder. He could not have used less ceremony if he were taking leave of a group of children. I noted that the messengers from Garden City were carrying other missives that they distributed to the divisional commanders and to several of the common soldiers as soon as we were a hundred paces from them.

"Good chaps, good chaps," my father said to the scores of troopers who stopped to salute him as we passed them. (I expect that as soon as we were beyond earshot many of the men commented on how the governor of Mars's mining stations needed a woman to help him walk.)

Movement always did Father good. As we walked farther, his legs became steadier and his mind clearer. On the last half of the walk home, he was able to let go of me and progress under his own power.

"Old age happens all at once, Justa," he told me. "One day I was as strong as a bull, and the next I needed an hour to wake up and longer than that to go to sleep."

The servants at our quarters scurried about like so many geese when they beheld us approaching. Mica, the Siberian butler my father had collected on a campaign in the Far East, came running to us, bowing as he went, and smiling so broadly the corners of his mouth nearly touched his ears.

"The governor general has purchased many tons of fine steel, yes?" he said. "The Arab traders have wonderful scrap. I told you so."

"We bought scrap, no," I told him. "Your friends tried to sell us defective metal that has the nano-infestation on it."

"Not my friends!" protested Mica. "Arabs are liars and thieves! They are the enemies of mankind! Never have I been a friend to Arabs! God bless the noble soldiers of the Pan-Polarian Empire for defending civilization from those evil people!"

He was indignant I should remember he was the one who had approached the general on behalf of the traders. As a member of the religious sect known as the Pristine Ones, a group that was not supposed to consort with criminals, Mica resented anyone who disparaged his moral character. He put a smile over his anger and pulled the door open to let us enter. My father instantly cast off his armored jacket and his long plastic topcoat, and laid himself upon his field cot. While Mica undid the old man's laced boots, Father gave forth a deep, appreciative sigh.

"Read me the letter, Justa," he ordered me. "What could Golden want to plague us with now? It's something to do with money, I'll wager."

Those who have spoken ill of my father—or were more afraid of his enemies than they were true to him—have said the governor general of Mars Station was an uneducated man, and that was why he had others read aloud to him. In truth he was born to a wealthy military father who saw to it that Father was proficient in both English and Syntalk while he was still a boy living at home. Father's problem when he grew to be an old man was not lack of education; it was his failing eyesight. The same blazing tunnel lights and eastern sky that had burned Father's face and neck as dark as his name had baked his eyes until everything beyond the end of his nose was a little blurry to him. In the declining years of his life he could no more have read handwritten script than he could have won a footrace. Unless he heard my voice, he was unable to identify his daughter when I was standing at a distance.

I tore open the seal on Mr. Golden's letter and began to read:

"'My warmest salutations to my lord Peter Justice Black—'"

"'Lord'?! What is this 'Lord' business?" asked my father. "The rascal definitely wants more than I can give him!"

I read: "'—the hero the Pan-Polarian people have chosen to be—I cannot stop myself from writing it—emperor!'"

"What is the fool saying?" asked Father.

Mr. Golden's declaration caused Father to prop himself onto the edge of the cot.

I continued: "'Do not, for humility's sake, forbid me to call you by that title, and order not the scholar reading this to you to tear apart these lines written by the most insignificant of your supporters. I beg your indulgence: I well know no one would dare to demand it of you. Please trust me when I aver it is my love for your noble person and my faith in the salvation you shall bring to the Empire which makes me, compels me, yea, threatens me with tortures worse than death lest I call you by that title. "The Emperor Peter Justice Black," I say aloud to myself again and again, so intoxicated am I by that sweet phrase that my family and friends and those I meet upon the streets think I am mad. The Emperor Peter Justice Black. It surpasses all other pleasures to write it and then to contemplate the words that are enthroned upon the paper.

"'I have been told by certain friends that you know what happened in the Field of Diversions upon John Chrysalis's failure to pay the Guardsmen of Garden City the gold he had promised them.'"

"I know nothing of this!" exclaimed Father. "Herman Pretext is emperor! Who is this John Chrysalis?"

"Lord Chrysalis, sir," I explained. "He was a senator. Apparently, he is now emperor. Lord Pretext seems to be gone."

"They just killed an emperor!" said my father. "How long has it been since we were in Garden City when they killed Luke Anthony?"

"We were there only three months ago, sir," I said.

I read farther in Mr. Golden's letter: "'As you know, the people gathered there, inside the Field of Diversions, and they were furious with John Chrysalis, whom they rightfully considered unworthy of the title Emperor. I was present and can truthfully say that for the first hours of that daylong gathering the air thundered with insults aimed at the impudent slug who would rule the world. Here, a group shouted lewd jokes concerning Chrysalis's unmanly passions—the which I shall not repeat here for fear I offend a man whose self-restraint in sensual matters is so widely known. There, Chrysalis's dupes came forth bearing meager sacks of gold coins and tried to buy the public's goodwill. They were driven from the stadium with stones clattering at their heels. Here again, good citizens railed against Chrysalis's brazen assumption of the throne so soon after Lord Pretext's death, and they argued that the usurper had a hand in that kindly ruler's murder. Then, from somewhere in the crowd arose a rhythmic chant we at first thought was the sound of soldiers' boots on the street outside. We fell silent and listened. We heard clearly then it was some good men chanting: "Black, Black, Peter Black!" Others followed their brave example. Then more and more shouted your name, the glorious chant rising and yet rising farther in power like the wind rising from the southern deserts, until "Peter Black" was upon the lips of every man in Garden City, save upon the girlish lips set in the midst of John Chrysalis's flaccid, yellow face. Next someone—if I recall correctly, it was myself—went to the speaker's platform and gave, in the best words he could summon, a speech invoking Peter Black as the guardian of the Empire and the true heir to the sacred office of emperor. The speaker asked, most respectfully, that General Black not forget his people in these desperate times. This speech, as poor as it was, was greeted with tumultuous applause and shouts of approval. Other far more elegant men of senatorial rank came forward to make similar, but more eloquent, orations in your favor, and each speech was followed by a round of riotous cheering.

"'I have been told by friends that certain conspirators who love not you, me, or the Empire have whispered to you that those faceless men who began the chant for Peter Black were bribed by this your loyal servant to act as they did. Consider, my friend, that these same liars have before claimed that I have secretly pledged my support to Abdul Selin!'"

"Another name," said Father. "At least I know that one. Selin is governor in North America."

"It seems some want him to be emperor now," I said.

"Everyone, it seems, will be emperor sooner or later," said Father.

I read on: "'The scoundrels should get their lies to agree. If I were supporting Selin in his ill-conceived assault on the sacred throne the gods—if they exist and have a number that can be counted—have set above the reach of all ordinary men, would I be bribing riffraff to boom your cause in the Field of Diversions?'"

"I don't get that," said Father. "The man cannot write a straight sentence. Crooked words, crooked thoughts I always say. What do you suppose he means by that business about the throne?"

"He means the emperor's throne," I said.

"Since when is that sacred?" asked Father. "Some dead emperors are sacred, or so their sects and the Senate have declared them, but the place where they sit? We're worshiping chairs now?"

"He is being poetic, sir."

"Poets," sniffed Father. "A bunch of lisping little fairies. They can't write a straight sentence, not a one of them. You ask me, they're ninety percent of what's wrong with the world; them and all their songs. Well, them and this thing that infects the metal—together they're ninety percent of the problem. At any rate, they are a bad bunch for anybody to use as a model."

"'Were I the African Selin's lackey,'" I read, "'which no true Pan-Polarian could be, would I be the first to expose myself upon the speaker's platform, despite the threats these many conspirators have sent my way? Would I have married my daughters to your sons, knowing the danger to their lives should our designs fail, if I were the Turk's confidant?'"

"Turk?" said Father. "Who is the Turk? Selin?"

"Yes," I said, "Mr. Golden is referring to Selin. Selin is of Turkish ancestry and African birth. His hometown is Tunis. To Mr. Golden, Turks and Africans seem to be all the same."

"Turks, Libyans, Syrians, Iranians, Arabs—they're all wogs," said Father, and lay back down so Mica could rub his weary legs. "The sun burnt me black. Old Selin was born as brown as a loaf of bread."

"As was I, sir," I said.

He did not mean to be as cruel as he sometimes was. He actually forgot that my mother was a Syrian. At times he succeeded in forgetting I was also a bastard.

I forged ahead in the turgid letter. "'Would I have solicited money for your cause from the capital's best families—which monies I shall be sending to you when the time is more opportune—if I were not devoted entirely to you? Would I risk this correspondence with the great General Black if I were not completely his? No, says this honest man. Put me to the test: give me whatever dangerous mission your elite troopers shun; let me die for my friend, my lord, my emperor, my special deity! I am a slave in perpetuity to you; not a common slave who may one day buy his freedom, but one who will remain your property until your death—may God forestall that evil day when you are taken from us! Tell me to cut off my right hand as a sign of my obedience and the messenger who brings you my next letter will bring my severed hand with him. Order me to kill my dear brother, and the same messenger will bring his head to you, for that is the sort of upright man I am.'"

"The man is an ass," commented Father. "Skip ahead to the pertinent parts, if there are any."

"Let's see," I said. "There are another five paragraphs of self-abuse. He says he would kill his mother for you, were that lady not already dead. He says General Black will not abandon Garden City to 'the ambling wolf and the hungry raven.' That's rather good, for him, I mean. I wonder where he lifted that phrase from."

"He goes on and on and on," said Father. "Just tell me what he wants."

"He rambles on," I said, scanning through the long letter. "There are some anecdotes here about effeminate men insulting you and the Lady of Flowers. He put those in here to anger you. Oh, this is good; he says some ex-slaves who are currently pimps are calling you a coward because you haven't declared yourself emperor. Here's the nub: 'If you allow Selin to take the throne uncontested, you will lose more than an opportunity; you will lose your life. We are all slaves in this world, my lord Black, everyone except the emperor. Chrysalis is a weakling and may be allowed to live, but Selin will never allow a slave as powerful as you to serve him.' Then there are some more words of praise for you, and that's the end of it."

"That is everything?" asked Father from his cot.

"May I say, master," said Mica, "that the gentleman is a most interesting writer?"

"The gentleman would agree with you," said Father. Of me he asked, "Is Lord Pretext really dead?"

"So Mr. Golden says," I replied. "And John Chrysalis seems to be the new emperor. We will have to make inquiries."

"Explain again how that mongrel Selin is mixed up in this," said Father.

"He himself, or someone in Garden City, wants Selin to be emperor after this Chrysalis is dead," I said. "Selin, according to the letter, is marching on the capital as we speak. He would have the largest army."

"And Golden wants me to become emperor instead of Selin?" said Father. "I was a sergeant first grade, Justa. Served in the ranks for most of my life. Now this rich fool wants me to stand for emperor? Me? The man is insane. We never should have formed a connection with him."

"I expect, sir," I said, "that Mr. Golden has sent a similar letter to every provincial general, offering each of them aid and money. Selin himself probably has a letter from him."

Father got up from his cot. The governor of Mars Station looked an old man on his skinny, blue-veined legs as he paced the floor wearing only his tunic and his underclothes. He stopped and peered out the window for a long time, though I doubted he could see anything outside in the darkened tunnels very clearly. He was not frightened. Father had been through too much to fear anything any longer. Not even the prospect of his own death frightened him anymore. He was upset because he still cared for his distant family in Garden City and for the Empire, although both his family and the Empire had taken much from him and had never given him much in return.

"There is one true thing in this letter that windbag has sent us," he said. "Should Selin become emperor, if he marches on Garden City and kills this pretender Chrysalis, then the days of my life are numbered. Selin will suffer no other army commanders. He'll purge the generals and the provincial governors and install members of that dreadful family of his in most of the dead men's places. He won't kill just me. He'll take my wife, my sons, all my relatives. Selin will do the same to anyone unwilling to carry water for him. I may not know these politicians in Garden City, those senators who want to be rulers of the world and the whispering rich men, but I do know the generals, and Selin is the worst of the lot."

"We don't know anything definitely, sir," I said. "You need not worry yourself over something Mr. Golden has written. You know what a liar he is. Lie down and let Mica massage your legs some more. We will know the full story in a few days. There will be merchants in the marketplace who will tell us. Big news like this always travels with the tradesmen now that broadcast communications are compromised."

He did as I bade him, and Mica's soothing hands soon had Father asleep and snoring loudly. When the lights in the great dome over the military camp were being dimmed, he awoke and had a simple dinner of cold polenta cakes and dehydrated vegetables. Father had gone to sleep another time when we in the household heard the soldiers outside chanting his name. Mr. Golden's messengers had spread their other letters throughout the entire camp, and now everyone knew of the events in Garden City. Thousands of people—Pan-Polarian troops, merchants from the tunnel communities, camp followers from outside the walls of the military post, and some of the now drunken scrap traders—were marching around our little house, proclaiming in a dozen different languages that General Peter Black was the new lord of the Pan-Polarian Empire. Father was completely befuddled. He stood at the window and shouted at the disorderly crowd to be quiet. To every officer he saw tramping past he barked an order to the effect that the men should be gotten back inside their barracks. "Make them stop!" he told his commanders. "I'm not of royal blood! I'm not even one of the Anthony family! I'm a common soldier!" The officers were busy till long after dark getting the soldiers to return to their quarters. After that had been accomplished we could still hear the civilians shouting "Black, Black, Peter Black!" outside the limits of the camp.

"All I wanted to do today was buy some uninfected scrap," said my father as he lay back down and put an arm over his forehead. "Now I have a camp full of idiots eager to have me declare myself emperor! We have to have a better plan tomorrow, Justa."

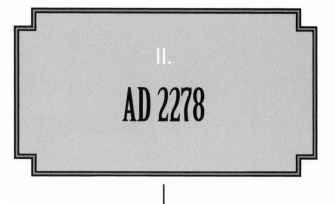

II.

AD 2278

Fifteen years before the letter from Mr. Golden came to us on Mars, we had first met the last of the Anthonys at Progress, a dreary military outpost on the Amur built of gray stone the near constant snow and wind of that forested region had striped with lines of white patina. Father was by then already a decidedly middle-aged man, vigorous and self-confident, yet as weathered from his years of military service as the stones of Progress's houses and fortifications were from the snow. My father may have never been a great strategist when at the head of an entire army, but while in the ranks, while serving at the head of a company or in command of a division, he had no equal. Tactics he left to Fate; Father knew the power of discipline and courage, and on those two pillars he had built his long career. He reasoned he had always been strong enough and brave enough to get the job done, and if he were brave and strong in the future, that would suffice to meet all challenges. His heroism in the East during the Fourth Mesopotamian War, when he led a detachment of foreign auxiliaries to glory in the siege of New Babylon, was a story known throughout the Empire, even unto the emperor. We were at that time ruled by Mathias Anthony, whom we remember as Mathias the Glistening, the philosopher-king presiding over that portion of the world between the Isthmus of Panama and the Gobi Desert. Mathias brought Father to the Amur while the gathering army there was preparing to strike across the river at the Manchurian rebels stirring on the southern shore. The emperor had placed under Father's command an entire division, the famous Twentieth, which Mathias had transferred from Britain for the sake of this one campaign. Father was so proud of his new assignment he ordered the Twentieth's wild boar insignia sewn into his personal clothing and onto the sleeves of his military tunics. In our household the image of the wild boar was stamped onto our dishes, stitched into our blankets, made the default image on our family's hologram projector, and was carved into the upright posts of our beds and furniture so that while Father was relaxing at home among his few humble pieces of property he would be continuously reminded of how high he had risen in the world.

In those brave days Father had not yet faced anything he could not defeat with his strong right arm and ten thousand troopers armed with energy weapons. He certainly never needed any assistance when he strode from place to place and from triumph to triumph. Like all men, he was ambitious. Never was he overreaching. I doubt that at the time Father thought there was any higher place to which a man of his background could rise.

Mathias's son, Luke Spacious Anthony, was with us on the Amur. His father had the year before named him coemperor, albeit the boy was a month from his seventeenth birthday and unready for the responsibilities of his office. Real administrative power remained in Mathias's hands. The whole world—and especially the soldiers amassing at Progress, who would witness young Luke Anthony's first public duty—was eager to know more about this boy destined to rule alone after his father's death. The general expectation was that the son would be a younger and more vigorous version of Mathias the Glistening, the wise and generous ruler who had kept the domestic peace and protected the Empire from foreign invasions as ably as any leader of Pan-Polaria ever had. "A lion does not sire a jackal," was my father's estimation of the boy before he met him. (My father was fond of animal metaphors throughout his life, and often shared them with those in his home, sometimes sharing them many times over.) What Father and the world would get in young Luke Anthony would be, as I will tell, something far worse than a jackal.

I was a precocious twelve-year-old when we came to cold Progress in the seventeenth year of Mathias's reign. My life up to then had been a series of stays at Father's various postings in the Middle East and in the Asteroid Belt. During my entire existence I had dwelt in the rectangular encampments the Pan-Polaric Army builds everywhere it goes, and I had seen soldiers marching outside our front door ever since I was old enough to be aware of my existence. My father never knew how to explain that existence of mine to other men: to his superiors he said the dark-skinned girl always about his quarters was the child of one of his servants, but to his brother officers of his own rank he admitted I was his illegitimate daughter, one born to a mistress long since dead. Father in those times was not a religious man. (I mean he did not participate in any of the pre-scribed religions or in any of the mystery cults that had emerged throughout the Empire during the previous century.) Outwardly he was a gruff, downright stern figure in the polished body armor he could never wear too often or shine too diligently. Within his heart he felt more guilt than he dared confess on account of the child living in his home. Father assigned failings to other men, not to himself. He knew the other soldiers, even some of the other officers, had unofficial wives living in the makeshift villages outside the military encampments. Father did not con-sider himself to be the same as other men. I was a memento of the instance he had slipped as badly as others did every day and as he had disciplined himself never to do.

Father kept a Canadian amanuensis named Clemens to read and write the orders of the day for him before I would perform those duties; this same man had taught me the two great languages of the Empire, and I had devoured every book in the English and Syntalk tongues I could lay my hands upon, which were really only those Clemens could borrow from other learned men and women who happened to be in the vicinity. As is true of most people exposed to a little learning, I was inordinately proud of myself. I did not come near my father without repeating something from Homer or Herman Bing, and I must have been a terrible irritant to him whenever he came home to eat or sleep. My father's plan was to keep me until I came of age, then marry me to a man suitable to my lowly station—meaning my future husband would at best be a worker or a common soldier, and my learning did not make me a better match for any man I was likely to wed. Father often reminded me of that fact when I showed off my abilities in algebra or my knowledge of world history. While his sense of honor compelled him to provide for me, his sense of propriety obligated him not to tell his legitimate wife in Garden City or my two half brothers that I existed; this family he seldom visited had risen in the social strata of the capital as Father rose in military rank. The three of them could barely tolerate the tough old campaigner when Father managed to travel to that great city, and they most definitely could not have endured the presence of his Syrian bastard. I therefore grew up as an only child, one surrounded by the vivid, noisy atmosphere of the Pan-Polarian Army. I idolized and feared my tall, muscular father, who appeared more muscular than he in fact was when he wore his body armor, but I lived within my treasured books and in the dreamland they inspired in my thoughts.

My father had met Emperor Mathias a year earlier, when the great man made a tour of the Middle Eastern provinces. Mathias the Glistening used a network of informers recruited from among the army's quartermaster corps and from the petty court officials, tax farmers, and provincial policemen to keep track of the important men within the Empire. Thus Mathias already knew everything about Father, including everything about me, long before he encountered Father face-to-face. Mathias would have known that two men could not have been as different as he and his General Peter Black; still he granted my father the rare honor of a private interview during his stay in Alexandria. What the emperor, one of the great thinkers of the age, and my father, famous among his soldiers for his monosyllabic speeches, could have found to discuss baffles me yet today. It baffled me more that the emperor formed a favorable opinion of my father during their brief meeting. But then Mathias's judgment of others was a mysterious facet of the great man. He was consistently more compassionate than discerning when he evaluated others. It satisfied Mathias that my father, like himself, was a veteran of a hundred pitched fights and had never flinched from his duty. Mathias appreciated the horrors Father had endured for the Empire's sake as only another soldier would. At Alexandria, on the southern rim of the Empire, Mathias had promised Father the Twentieth Division and bade him come to Progress the following spring.

Our new home in icy Siberia was a stone hovel within sight of the emperor's great hall, a massive building that stood at the very center of the military station and atop which were erected the encampment's primary communication towers. The four of us—Father, myself, Father's Greek servant Medus, and Medus's wife, Helen, who had been my nurse when I was an infant—were miserable in that cold, smoky, very crowded little house set in that wet, freezing land that may be a fit home for bears and savage men but offers only frozen ground and vast distances to civilized people. The elder Ming and the natural historian Rodriguez tell us Siberia is so very cold due to its gigantic size and to its low basins in which inversion takes place and traps the cold air close to the ground during the winter and keeps the sun from breaking through during the brief summer; these learned men say that if we laid an electronic grid underneath portions of that forbidding land and powered the grid with nuclear generators, we could make the heated portions as warm and as fertile as California. If there is a sliver of truth in what they write, my two years in Progress convinced me that the first duty of an emperor—should large-scale electronic projects ever again become possible—would be to do whatever can be done to heat that chilly corner of Pan-Polaria. While we were there we had to keep the primitive wood-burning fireplace burning day and night, as did the other souls trapped within the four straight walls of the encampment, and thus there was always a gray cloud around our houses to match the gray clouds high above us. When we did see the sun, it appeared to us a weak, silver circle that was as feeble as the light reflected in a blind man's eyes. Never did it give off enough heat; it merely illuminated the misty air during the daytime and let us behold what an ugly bog we had as a home.

My old nurse Helen had long been a believing woman. She believed in the Lady of Flowers, in the Christian Jesus, in the Muslim Allah, in the Great Mother, in Minit the god of human sacrificers, and in anything anyone ever imagined could have a power over us, including those things that move in the night and do not have a proper name. Helen knew the secret practices that lie outside religion altogether. Whenever my father was gone from the house and could not object to her nonsense, she would sit before the fire and read the future in the ashes the flames left behind, a trick she claimed to have learned in California, the home of Pan-Polarian spiritualism.

"The Pan-Polarian Army will defeat the Chinese," she told me one afternoon when she had scooped up a handful of black cinders and tossed them into the air.

"Will this be the last time we attack them?" I asked her.

She stirred the ashes with a stick while she considered my question. My love for Helen prevented me from telling her I did not have any faith in her divining skills or in any of the other superstitious notions she had.

"Yes, this will be the last time," she said.

Events would prove her prediction wrong a dozen times in the next forty years, but I never upbraided her with facts.

"One more thing," she said. "This is an unlucky place."

"I would think so," I said. "Look outside. Progress is too wet for people, too cold for the fish in the river. It is an unlucky place for everyone but the geese; they get to fly away anytime they want."

She told me to hush.

"Show some respect for the mysteries of the gods, child," she told me. "Look at how they have made the world colder," she added, which was a warning millions of elders had given children ever since—for apparently natural reasons—the Earth had become a couple degrees colder during the twenty-second century. "Look, Justa," she exclaimed, and spat into the ash pile. "The signs say you, child, are in grave danger here! You should never go outside the door without my permission, and never, never should you go spying around the emperor's residence!"

Wherever we lived, the gods of the ash heap told Helen I should not go outside. Her gods were a very anxious lot when I was a little girl. Like Helen, they feared the thousands of armed men drilling in the open spaces outside our door, and they wanted me to stay indoors and under Helen's supervision where I might learn the arts of sewing and cooking every young woman needs to know now that we no longer have the domestic conveniences our ancestors did. The gods' warnings, I regret to say, never worked on me. I would sneak out of the house regardless of the dangers they foresaw and would go places I should not have, regardless of how much they and Helen fussed. In dreary Progress, the one place the gods and Helen warned I definitely should not go was the emperor's hall, which was, of course, the one place in the entire station I wanted to give a closer inspection. Hundreds of tall, clanking soldiers came and went through that building's chromium steel doors every day, as did emissaries from the Senate in Garden City and local officials from Vladivostok, the provincial capital. I stood at the doorway of our little hut and imagined as I gazed at the gray exterior of the emperor's quarters that the interior of that four-story building must be lined with crystal and metal machines and that inside its central hallway were elegant men in pristine white suits bearing the purple stripe of nobility, and those elegant men would be holding video conferences with other important men back in Garden City as they discussed the affairs of the world with the studied honesty of the philoso-phers in the books I read. I would be utterly disappointed when I in time found the inside of the hall was as drab as its outside shell and that the men therein were mostly soldiers who looked and acted exactly like the ones I could see on the exercise grounds.

On the day Mathias announced the coming arrival via jet transport of his son in Progress he invited his generals to a banquet that would welcome the young coemperor to that frozen bit of Hades.

"You will bring your daughter, sir," he told my father in a private conference.

"I have two sons in Garden City, my lord," Father told him. "No daughters."

"I am the Empire," Mathias told him. "I see all, hear all, or so they say I do. You have an unofficial daughter living here with you, Peter. I think it commendable of you to accept your responsibilities to her. She will want to see me; I am the great emperor and so on. I might be quite impressive, to a child of her age. I am curious to see what sort of little girl lives her whole life in military stations. Indulge me, my friend. I am interested in how children develop. But then, most of us are, aren't we? We think children will explain to us how we each became what we are. Bring her to the banquet."

Helen took an entire morning to bathe me in Father's little portable tub and an afternoon to fix my hair into an extravagant pile of curls, which she said was exactly the same style as noble women in Garden City wore. (Perhaps the noble women did, just not in that particular century.) Helen patched together a white gown for me out of the bits of one of my father's old garments. Once she had checked the fit on me, she made me take off the dress, and I had only my shift to wear till it was time for us to walk to the great hall.

"Don't sit!" Helen warned me as I waited in the smoky house. "You'll get yourself dirty! The emperor will think we live like swine."

"How could the emperor see dirt on my underclothes?" I asked her. "Is he going to peek up my skirt?"

"What a filthy mouth you have, child!" she scolded me. "Come here so I may slap you. Do you think the emperor is a criminal?"

Helen's threats were hollow. She repeatedly told me she was going to slap me and never did.

"I spoke before I thought," I said. "I apologize."

Father told me I should say nothing when we got to the banquet, particularly not to the emperor.

"He has a familiar manner for a great man," Father told me as we walked through the muddy grounds toward the large building. "He may speak to you directly. I don't know why. He speaks to a lot of people he shouldn't. If he does, pretend you are deaf and dumb. Make guttural sounds and wave your hands a bit. Remember this, girl: Mathias is going to be named a god someday. You may not believe in any of that official government nonsense, but some people do. Bow when he gets near you. Whatever you do, do not look him straight in the eye."

"Is it true that when you were a boy people could just fly from place to place and never have to walk?" I asked him, for I hated wading through the mud in my white dress and having to lift up my skirt to keep it clean.

"Some people could," said Father. "Now about the emperor . . . ?"

"I will not look him in the eye," I said. "I promise." And perhaps at the moment I said it I truly meant to keep my word.

Upon entering the emperor's tall front doors I saw that his home in Progress was large, but far less than magnificent. The walls were bare stone, and the rafters were exposed beams of rough-hewn timber rather than any sort of composite material one sees inside the monumental buildings of Garden City. Several of the high windows did not even have shutters on them yet, for work on the building was not complete and never would be during our time in the camp. Rather than a central table filled with the sumptuous food one can find at any dinner in the capital, there were only rows of wooden benches and wooden chairs on which the diners were to sit. Some of the more important officers in the front of the hall had pillows to soften their stay on the hard seats; that was the highest sort of comfort I could see inside the big house. Everything looked as though it had been made on the site by military carpenters, and probably everything had been. Carpenters could also have made the food we ate. Each guest had some figs, a small loaf of fresh bread, some apples from Europe, and a glass of whiskey mixed with water to make a concoction that was so weak Father said he could have downed a couple dozen tumblers of it and remained sober. From our bench high on the steps overlooking the main floor, we could see the emperor and his party at the other side of the room, yet I did not realize which one was the great Mathias until Father pointed him out to me.

"He is the one resembling a schoolteacher," said Father.

The man he indicated wore a simple wool cloak fastened by a brass clasp on his shoulder. On the man's neck was a metal shell that ran down his spine, for the emperor, like most important men from earlier times, had mechanical implants that allowed him to communicate instantly with computers and with other men in distant locations. His very brain no doubt contained implants that supported his basic functions and allowed him to live longer than others. Mathias wore no crown, carried no scepter, had no emblem of his office other than the large gold rings on his left hand. Two bodyguards, both with implants similar to the emperor's, followed him as he walked to his dining place. I had thought the emperor would be as tall as his house and would have bigger muscles than the athletes I would one day see in the Field of Diversions; this man of fifty-seven years had thinning hair and limped when he walked because his right leg ached from an old war wound. When several of his more important guests came to salute him, he stood erect, allowing me to see him more clearly. I remember I thought he had the saddest, most weary eyes I had ever beheld.

For our entertainment that evening an actor in Garden City broadcast to us on a hologram projector stood before the emperor and recited the poet Damnmus's description of Elvis's heroic actions as told in the sixth book of the Elvisid. We soon discovered why the ham was not in the cinema making real money. In front of the learned Mathias the actor got the names of the ancient cities confused and was saying Los Angeles when meant to say Las Vegas and Miami when he should have said Memphis. I was twelve and I could tell he did not know his lines. The generals— except for my father, who had never read the Elvisid—frowned in recognition of the man's mistakes. The emperor maintained a fixed expression of approval throughout the sorry performance. Mathias thanked the actor when the dope had ceased ranting and waving his arms in what I suppose was meant to be a dramatic fashion. The emperor was so kind he ordered via his implants that the fool be given two thousand dollars and bade him visit Progress on another occasion, perhaps during the area's two weeks of summer. Because Mathias applauded the sap, everyone present gave the actor an ovation.

"Mathias is a good fellow, a good soldier, too," Father told me. "I shouldn't say he is like a schoolteacher. He's nowhere as bad as the chaps I had in school. Every master I had would beat us to toughen us up. Mathias would never do that. That is his great fault: he is much too soft."

"Sir, is that young man near the emperor his son?" I whispered in Father's ear.

I was of the age when I had recently began to look at men and just then felt a peculiar confusion later in my life I would recognize as desire. When I looked at the tall, blond, actually beautiful young man seated in Mathias's group I felt more confused than I had before in my brief life-time. Unlike Mathias, this one stood out from the other men; he had an open, seamless face that was as bright as a candle flame. He was dressed as a young noble should be; he wore polished silk and had gold chains around his neck and waist.

"That is the other emperor," said Father. "Luke Anthony."

"He is very handsome," I announced, sounding as naive as only a twelve-year-old can be.

Father laughed at my innocence.

"Don't look too long at him, little one," he told me. "I had a talk with some of the officers accompanying him from Garden City. They tell me young Luke doesn't like girls."

"He likes boys?" I asked.

Helen had explained, in her direct manner, such matters to me. I did not fully understand; I was only aware such phenomena existed.

"They say Luke Spacious likes death," said Father. "That ugly fat chap next to him is Sao Trentex. He travels with the young emperor wherever he goes. Luke Anthony has a whole group of such friends that loiter about him. Some of them are women, so I suppose I should say Luke likes a certain sort of woman as much as he likes death."

"What sort of woman would that be, sir?" I asked.

"Helen will explain it to you when you are older," said Father, and he scowled as he did when anyone close to him mentioned matters touching upon sex.

"Why do you say he likes death, sir?" I asked.

"They say he threw a poor cook onto a barbeque grill just because the wretch made his spareribs too spicy," said Father. "He has kept company with those thugs who call themselves the new gladiators. Some say he has killed unarmed men in the gladiators' practice arena merely for the thrill of doing it. He and Sao Trentex and other friends of theirs have picked up people right off the streets of Garden City and have done with them what they would."

"But he looks nice," I said, and for the sake of young Luke's beautiful face I disbelieved everything Father had said about him.

I did not note on this occasion that Luke Anthony did not resemble his father in any manner. Mathias was a slender, fine-featured man of Mediterranean and Hispanic descent, while young Luke's nose and mouth were as large as a German's. I did not know until years later that Luke was in fact the natural son of one of his mother's numerous lovers and no one knew which one. It is fortunate Nature made young girls innocent of the world, since I would not have slept for many nights after the banquet if I had known the stories Father had heard of Luke Anthony were true, and only a portion of the horrible complete truth. The handsome face I was gazing upon belonged to one of the worst monsters ever to burden the ground with his footsteps. Now when I think of Luke Anthony and how beautiful he appeared at his father's welcoming banquet, I think of the lovely black cat Arab mythology says lives south of the Sahara Desert; the beast, it is said, is so pleasing in its aspects and has such a beguiling voice that its prey will come to it whenever it calls, and so the creature may devour its victims at its leisure. To my young eyes Luke was lovelier than any beast of nature or legend. I could not have known that later in his short life he would prove himself to have a larger appetite than all the prey on Earth could have satisfied.

One of the emperor's Guardsmen making his rounds through the rows of guests stepped to our bench and informed us Mathias was ready to receive us.

"Remember: say nothing," Father warned me as we went to the other end of the hall.

"Even should he speak to me, sir?" I asked.

"We have been over this," growled Father. "You are a poor deaf girl."

We stood in queue for several moments while other officers passed the emperor's table and paid their respects to him. At our turn Mathias addressed my father by name.

"Ah, Peter, health to you," he said, and exchanged salutes with Father after Father bowed. "You've brought the little treasure. Let us have a better look."

The ruler of the northern half of the world rose from his seat and limped on his bad leg from behind the table so he might lift my chin. To both his and my surprise, there was a spark of static electricity when he touched me, as sometimes happens when people have shuffled across a bare floor, and I jumped a half-step away from his hand after he made contact. Mathias laughed at my fright. Contrary to Father's admonishments, I looked directly into his eyes that had seemed remarkably sad at a distance. Up close I could see he was amused about something; whether it was I who made his eyes smile or if he thought the onus of his position somehow ridiculous I cannot say. I can say that I was suddenly unafraid of him.

"Well, Lady," he said, though I did not merit the title "Lady." "Peter, she is very pretty," he said to my father in Syntalk. "Much too pretty to be kept a secret."

"Thank you, my lord," I said to him in the same language, which startled my father. He recovered a second later and glared at me as if to say, "You've gone and done it now!"

Mathias, contrary to Father's fears, was yet more amused and took my face in both his hands.

"So you are clever as well," he said in English. "Beauty and brains in one small body. Did you learn Syntalk in the East, little one? What is her name?" he asked my father.

"Justa," muttered Father, speaking as unenthusiastically as a dying man uttering his last words.

"You have given her a portion of your name, Peter," said Mathias. Of me he asked, "Have you read any of the great books, Justa?"

"Yes, my lord," I said. "I started at the beginning of Western civilization and read forward. I have read Plato, most of Aristotle, Epicurus—"

"Have you now, little one? At your age?" asked the emperor.

"'No one can be too early or too late in seeking the health of the soul,'" I said.

"'Whoever says that the time for philosophy has passed or not yet come is like the man who says the hour for happiness has not yet arrived or has already gone,'" said Mathias, completing my citation of Epicurus. "Very good, pretty Justa," he said, and patted my head as he again stood fully erect. "There are others here who could not say who the Philosopher of Samos was." (He cast his gaze upon his son Luke, who was tossing bits of bread crust at his friend Sao Trentex.) "You will have to visit us another day," he said to me. "Tomorrow, Peter," he said to my father, "I will be talking to some young friends. Send her to me. She will enjoy the experience. We are understood?"

"Yes, my lord," whispered Father.

The master of everything between the Caribbean Sea and the northern border of China bent down and said into my ear, "You won't have to dress up like this when you next come to see us. Wear your hair as you like. The natural way is superior to artifice, Justa." (He playfully touched the crown of my absurd coif.) "Bring your tablet and pencils. Bring a laptop, if you own one that still functions. We have much to learn, both you and I do."

The soon to be divine Mathias kissed my forehead, and Father and I returned to our bench.

"You don't listen, do you, missy?" Father snapped at me as we walked away from the imperial presence. "That isn't some damned jolly soldier of the line you were talking to! That was the bloody emperor! The one man in charge of everything. You stupid, stupid child! Do you know men have been killed for saying the wrong thing to the emperor?"

"To Mathias, sir?" I asked, for I could not believe the man we had just spoken to could be that dangerous.

"Maybe Mathias himself wouldn't kill you. You can't tell about those others about him," said Father. "And when you talk to him, you speak to a thousand others. The way you run your mouth, you are bound to say something that will provoke somebody! Then we will all be executed! You, me, the entire family! I might as well hang myself tonight! That way my sons in Garden City will at least get my house; otherwise the emperor's people will take everything in the courts. That's what they do to traitors. See what you've done, you prattling, stupid child!"

I felt such anguish at having caused my father's death I began sobbing. Already I could see Father swinging from the wooden beams of our lowly hut.

"Quit that!" Father commanded me, perhaps feeling a little guilt of his own for having overreacted to my conversation with the emperor. "Nothing has happened, yet. In the future, keep your mouth shut when you're around Mathias and the other big shots, and maybe nothing will happen to us. But not another word to him. Absolutely nothing."

I dried my eyes and managed to eat a couple more mouthfuls of the homely food. While I was looking about the vast room for what must have been the twentieth time I noticed an odd-looking little man seated two benches from us; his hair and his beard were like thick black wool, and he had dark, alert eyes that seemed to miss nothing of the activity around him. Though he ate his food vigorously—and noisily—his eyes did not glance at his meal but were kept darting about the rest of the dining room. Seated around him were thirty or so other dark, wire-haired men, each of them wearing a bronze cape clasp that was shaped like the stylized face of the sun.

"That's Abdul Selin," said Father after I had pointed out the dark man to him. "Best damn soldier in the army. I pity any Chinaman who crosses the path of that nasty little Turk during this campaign. If all the sons of Ishmael had been akin to him back in the days of the Islamic Wars, you and I would never have been born. He's smart and he's vicious. Looks like an ape trained to wear a man's clothes, doesn't he? Look sharp; he sees you staring at him. Smile back, Justa. Like smiling at a cobra, isn't it? We can rejoice he is on our side, the bloodthirsty little beast."

"Who are those other men sitting around him?" I asked.

"Relatives of his," said Father. "Selin has lots and lots of relatives. Keeps a couple hundred of them on his staff or as his bodyguards. They're from the same big tribe of Turks the Empire settled in North Africa a dozen generations back. The ones Selin can't stick in the army are back home in Tunis and Alexandria and Casablanca; they're magistrates, judges, and whatnot. You can imagine what kind of justice they dish out down there."

"What does the sun face mean, sir?" I asked, regarding the cape clasps.

"That represents a god from way back before the times of the Christian Bible," said Father. "In the African and Middle Eastern provinces they call it Heliosomething. The Selin clan members are all in the same sun worshiping cult. If you ask me, their so-called religion just gives them the chance to meet together in private when they have their secret services. They're a big gang, really. A big bunch of tax farmers, smugglers, extortionists, and crooked lawyers."

That was the first time I saw Father's eventual nemesis. We had no idea then what enmity would one day exist between Selin and our small family; nonetheless he frightened me when I first beheld him. Most of the generals at the banquet, Father included, had done terrible things on behalf of the Empire, and I did not consider them evil men; they were each a servant of the emperor and acted without malice and not out of choice. Such was the morality of the world they were born into. Selin was something more than the other generals. One look at him and a person knew he had the energy of a dozen other men compressed within his small body. He would keep that vigor through the whole of his long life and would not allow it to be diminished by the thousands of unspeakable deeds he would do with the same zest he displayed when he attacked his food at the banquet. Father said that Selin had been a financial adminis- trator—and perhaps a secret informer in the emperor's service—before he became a general, which struck me as a strange background for a man pos- sessing Selin's aggressive personality. One could not imagine him sitting at a computer and examining sets of numbers while he kept a seemingly passive eye on the accountants working in the office around him. Mathias the Glistening, again displaying his propensity for choosing unusual men to serve him, had promoted Selin from the ranks of drones slaving in the government's financial departments into the military hierarchy, where, as Father told it, the African-born Turk had displayed a fine talent for killing both the foreign enemies of Pan-Polaria and his own men.

"The emperor is a—I don't know what—a la-de-da deep thinker," said Father. "Then, for some reason only he knows, he promotes a wild- eyed killer like Selin and lets him in turn promote his bunch of money- grubbing cousins. You know why I think Mathias does it? Because he knows most intellectuals can't fight—particularly not the deep thinkers you find back in the capital. Bear that in mind, my bookworm. Intellec- tuals and philosophers are good enough when they're among themselves at their silly get-togethers and talk counts as much as money. The trouble with thinkers is they know so much and take so much time pondering what they know they get to being doubtful of everything, even of the cer- tain things every man believes. Now, if men have doubts, they won't fight. Mathias knows that Selin doesn't think a lick about anything he does; Selin just acts and knocks the pieces into some sort of shape after the dust has settled. That's why the emperor uses men cut from that hairy bugger's cloth."

"And men like you, Father," I would have said, had I been as bold then as I am now.

In those days I was barely bold enough to return to the emperor's hall on the morrow. The soldiers at the door seemed giants to me when I approached them and gave them my name. I thought them more aston- ishing when one of them led me into a smaller chamber off the main hall in which the emperor was addressing an eclectic group consisting of young officers, members of his son's entourage, and a few generals' children like myself. Unlike the elitist scholars in the Empire's universities, Mathias thought all learning should be open to everyone, regardless of the scholars' age, class, sex, or party affiliation. I was embarrassed beyond my powers to express my emotions when the emperor spoke my name as I entered the room and pointed to an empty place I was supposed to sit. More amazing than his casual manner was the extraordinary class Mathias was conducting for his pupils. Like Epicurus, the ancient philosopher I had quoted when I met him, Mathias believed a life worth living was one given to pleasure. He went beyond the Philosopher of Samos and asserted that the only true pleasure was found in leading a moral existence. A happy man, said the ruler of half the world, was necessarily a humble, kind, self-restrained, and generous man, for that was the sort of man partaking of the greatest pleasure the world could offer.

"Forgive others," Mathias said. "Forgive, forgive, always forgive. Even forgive those who hate you."

"What about the Chinese across the river, my lord?" asked one astonished junior officer. "Are we to forgive them?"

"Especially them," said the emperor.

"Then, my lord," said the confused junior officer, "should we—and I ask this with the greatest respect—should we . . . fight them? Seeing as how we forgive them, I mean, my lord?"

"Our duty as citizens of Pan-Polaria demands we fight the Manchurian rebels," explained Mathias. "They have made raids across the Amur and have killed people living under our protection. We must chasten them or they will cross the river again and slay more of our citizens. Once we have beaten them and peace is again restored, we have a second duty, as men, to forgive them and to lead them to the true path of life. They are men like us, equal to us in every aspect, except in that they live in the darkness of ignorance, as all outside the Empire do. In the better days to come, we will show them the light of understanding, of that you may be assured."

If a holy man had spoken those words, I would have long ago forgotten them. That they were said by the most powerful man alive, a man who could extinguish the life of any other human as easily as I might strike at a fly, not only seared them in my memory, it made me wonder if I were really hearing what my ears were telling my mind.

Handsome Luke Anthony and his companions were seated at the front of the room. When Mathias had turned to address the young officer they had been skylarking among themselves and making faces while the emperor spoke his solemn words. As Mathias finished his response to the officer's question, the young coemperor coughed into his hand the word "Christer."

This was a deadly insult in the imperial court. Mathias's old tutor Frons had taught him that the Christians were not good people, as they acted morally to gain heaven rather than for the sake of being good. Moreover, they, like the Jews and the Muslims and unlike the new religions, did not recognize the divine natures of the dead emperors and their Empire. During the previous summer the emperor had yet again suppressed the Christian movement by killing five hundred thousand of that antique sect in Europe and North America. Mathias was not alone in his disdain for the once-dominant religion that had been forced underground three generations earlier; Christians (and the Jews and Muslims) had loyalties that were not connected to the Empire and thus were suspect citizens. The imperial agents who spied upon the outlaw sect had spread the rumor that Christians practiced incest between brothers and sisters, as they called each other by that title even if they were married to each other. They were outlaws in an Empire that tolerated nearly everything else. Everyone knew these same outlaws proclaimed a doctrine of moral living that, except for their belief in heaven, seemed to be much akin to Mathias's theory of the good life. No one was more sensitive of that fact than Mathias himself. The emperor eyed his impertinent son, and the small room was completely silent while Mathias the Glistening fought against his anger. When the emperor's self-restraint had triumphed over his wrath, he continued speaking to the class as if nothing unpleasant had happened.

The great Mathias had written a peculiar book during the previous year, a tome that was part autobiography and part a series of high-minded statements on anything that had crossed his mind. During his gatherings at Progress he would often read to us a short passage from this book of his, expound upon the meaning of what he had read, and next allow anyone to ask questions pertaining to the reading. The words he chose to read to us on my first day in his group were: "One can live well even in a palace."

"Why do we say: 'even in a palace'?" asked Mathias. "Because the opportunity to do evil is greatest for those who live there. The stockbroker working on the exchange in Garden City can do more harm to others than can the janitor who sweeps the exchange every evening. The sergeant can do worse than the individual soldier of the line. The ruler, who makes choices that touch everyone, can do more mischief than anyone. Thus, the higher our station in life, the more difficult it is for us to be good men and women."

Mathias spoke as if he were a detached observer of the world and not one holding half the world in his hands. His objectivity made everyone present apprehensive—everyone other than his son Luke Anthony, I should say. That young man pretended to yawn as his father spoke, so familiar was he with the emperor's discourses. Mathias told the story of his predecessor, the deified Pius Anthony, the palace dweller Mathias held to be the example of one who used power wisely. Next he told of the emperor Marcellus Darko, who he said was the example of one who did not live well in a palace, one who in fact burned his palace and the city around it to the ground.

"Forty-eight years ago, the citizens of Washington, where the capital once was," narrated Mathias, "believed that the newly crowned Marcellus Darko would be worthy of the title emperor, for he was an athletic, handsome youth, and the people, being shallow thinkers, believed the inner man would mirror the outward appearance of the young man they saw each evening on their interactive screens. They did not know that long before he ascended to the throne Darko had been corrupted by his degenerate companions and, more significantly, by his indulgent, evil mother, the disgraceful Angelina. From the beginning of his reign to his last sad day, when he was murdered in the bedroom of his country estate, Darko surrendered himself to his baser inclinations; he committed murder, theft, rape, and every manner of carnal act decency forbids me to name in mixed company."

"Plus he was a lousy poet," chimed in young Luke.

For the second time in that session the father turned his eyes upon his wayward son. The officers present fidgeted in their chairs and wished they were somewhere else. I was a child and was ignorant of important matters; the officers from Garden City knew the references to Darko and his mother were Mathias's way of speaking of Luke and his corrupt mother Gloriana. The young coemperor's companion Sao Trentex giggled at the senior emperor's disapproving frown, an indiscretion for which any other ruler of Pan-Polaria would have removed the fat toad's head.

"Must you, sir?" asked Mathias of his son. "Of everyone here, you, young man, need to learn the truth concerning palaces."

"Why?" asked Luke. "We never live in one. We are vagabonds, we in this royal house, O great teacher." (Sao Trentex and some of his other young companions snickered at the son's grandiose title for his father.) "We move from place to place, from war to war on the Empire's frontiers, sleeping by campfires like savages, eating bread and corn cakes the peasants in India wouldn't touch. Constricted by such austerity, we have to be moral, sir. There are no temptations where we live. Back in Garden City there are people confronting their desires every day; some days they abstain from doing as they would, and some days they surrender themselves to what you, sir, call their baser natures. They do not pretend to be holy eunuchs, sir. They are not hiding themselves out here in the wilderness while real life goes on."

Two members of Luke Anthony's entourage shook their heads enthusiastically. They had second thoughts about their actions when the emperor glared at them.

"Young man," said Mathias, "you should not challenge me in front of others."

"Am I not emperor with you, sir?" asked Luke Anthony, the pitch in his voice rising as he rose to meet his father's challenge.

"You have a title," said Mathias. "I think, young man, the world recognizes one of us as superior to the other. Should we ask some of the soldiers inside and see which one of us they will obey?"

Luke Anthony would in time show himself to be a monster, but he was always more a coward than a monster. The possibility of his father bringing a squadron from the storied Tenth Division into the room quickly brought the more powerful aspect of his personality to the forefront. His face turned ashen, and so did those of his companions, as he and they considered what might happen to them if the young emperor continued to confront his father. Luke's friend and fellow coward Sao Trentex likewise had a change of heart and decided mocking absolute authority to its face was not the wisest course of action. The fat fellow whispered something to his young friend, and Luke Anthony said to his father, "In the spirit of debate, sir, I was suggesting some alternative possibilities to your—"

"Young man," said the emperor, "I know what you were doing. You and your companions may leave us for the day."

Luke and his friends scrambled for the exit, bumping into each other in their rush to reach safety. At the doorway they turned to bow to Mathias before they disappeared into the hall outside. A couple of them tried to speak a few words of apology to the emperor before they left, but Mathias waved them on their way.

"We are young and foolish, my emperor. This is the unfortunate inclination our formative years have given us," pled Sao Trentex. "You must not think we—"

"You are indeed young and foolish," said Mathias. "In time, you will no longer be young. Now, go or the soldiers come in."

The members of Luke's entourage literally knocked each other aside as they charged out the door.

The emperor held his hand to his forehead for a moment, much as ordinary people do when they suffer severe headaches. When he put his hand down, he continued to instruct the remaining students while he maintained the same detached mood he had before he had been interrupted. Before the session ended that day he engaged a young officer in a lively exchange concerning the origins of private property, and he seemed his normal self again.

"Did you say anything?" Father asked me over dinner that evening.

"No, the emperor talks enough for everyone, sir," I told him.

"Very good," said Father. "Let him talk. Like most bigshots, he loves to ramble on. Good. As long as he's only talking, nobody can get hurt."

"Sir, does Mathias get along with his son?" I asked.

"How would I know?" growled Father. "You are asking a foolish question. Shows you're becoming a woman. That's the only kind of question women ask. Look, Mathias made that pup of his coemperor, so he must like the boy in some way. Why would a person give a gift like that to somebody he doesn't like? You've got to think about these things, girl."

"Did the Greeks like the Trojans, sir?" I asked.

"That's from a book, isn't it?" said Father.

"Yes, a really old one."

"It may surprise you, Miss Genius, but I happen to recall that comes from a rotten long poem written by that Homer fellow."

"That's right," I said. "So tell me, sir: did the Greeks like the Trojans?"

"It's another foolish question, Justa," said Father, and set aside his fork for a moment. "You must practically be a woman to talk like that. You need to have a talk with Helen. Anyway, as I recall, the Greeks hated the Trojans. They were fighting a long bloody war, weren't they?"

"Then why did they give the Trojans a gift, sir?" I said.

"Well, they gave them that big horse full of bloody soldiers, didn't they? That is the right story, isn't it?" asked Father. "This doesn't have anything to do with that other old story about the man in the red suit?"

"Yes, it's the wooden horse story."

"Then that was not a real gift, was it?" said Father. "Honestly, Justa. You are bad as the emperor. You think so deeply you confuse yourself. You see, there are two types of things in the world: those that are simple and those that seem not to be. The simple ones are easy to understand, and the other ones are really simple matters disguised as complicated ones. It's like what happens in battle: there are brilliant generals and there are slow-witted ones; in the end it's always hit them on the left, hit them on the right, soften them up with rockets and aerial bombardment, and finally attack down the middle. You see?"

"Yes, sir," I said, and ate my chickpeas.

I attended the emperor's symposiums throughout that cold first winter in Progress. I said nothing during class time and grasped what I could. Every day Mathias was more attentive to me than I could have rightfully hoped. He addressed me by the pet name "the Most Just" and would speak individually to younger students such as myself at the end of each session.

"What did you learn today, Most Just?" he would ask me as I crept toward the door.

"I learned, my lord, that I do not know what the transmigration of souls is," I told him one day.

"No one does, Most Just," he said. "That is an idea that first appears among the Pythagoreans, although they probably borrowed it from the Egyptians, and perhaps it was current in the Indus Valley long before that. Those who believe in it lack imagination, you see. They can envision no other world other than this one. Old Pythagoras and his kind believed the soul would return again and again to this realm in different forms. The Hindus think something similar even today. They did not know the soul is made to live a thousand times ten thousand years, but only once will our souls know this world."

I comprehended a small fraction of everything he said, yet he was, I reminded myself every day, the emperor, and he must know what he was saying.

"You are very wise, my lord," I said.

"So everyone tells me," he said. He bent his head to my ear—so close was he I could see the separate segments of the flexible metal casing on the back of his neck—and he asked me, "You would not be flattering me, would you, Most Just?"

"Perhaps I was, my lord," I said.

"Don't do it, pretty one," he told me, and stood straight once more. "I have a mob of flatterers about me. I want you to give me honest answers, my dear. The emperor demands that of you."

One thing Mathias had in common with his criminal son was that he too had seen some master actors in the cinema back in Garden City, and he too could act if he wanted to—just not as well as his boy could. When Mathias pretended, the real man always shone through his pretense. On the day I mention here, he had meant to sound stern with me. I could detect the gentle smile within the hard man he was pretending to be, for he could not keep his goodness from shining through.

As much as I loved him, I do confess Mathias was a man with his faults. I do not refer to the brutal deeds he did, for his position and the chaotic state of the Empire demanded he do many horrible things. Nor do I refer to the mistress he kept in his household after his wife's death, as lust is a weakness known to humans in general. When I speak of his faults, I mean that he enjoyed his wisdom and his own sonorous voice more than a man should. Worse than that was his love of his own virtue. Mathias had condemned the Christians for being good in order to please God. I have since come to think such religious folk are at least wiser than those who love virtue in order to please themselves, and Mathias, the finest man of his age, was often too pleased with himself.

On the second day of spring, when the snows had begun to diminish, the emperor took me aside after one of his symposiums and gave me a composite hand mirror as a going-away present. He told me the time for the campaign against the Manchurians had arrived.

"Look within, Most Just," he told me as he handed me the gift. "Make your soul as beautiful as the face you see in the mirror. One day in the distant future, the face you see here will disappoint you. Do not despise your looks for being a passing circumstance. Take pleasure in everything that will not harm you; enjoy the small diversions of this physical plane, for nature put those things here to give us intimations of the perfections which forever lie beyond our reach."

On the following morning he was gone, as were my father and the rest of the army. The combat engineers had built bridges of black carbon filament across the swollen Amur to allow passage to the southern shore. The troop carriers passed two abreast across these black sections straddling the brown water and into the sparse, sandy hills on the opposite bank. Select men in silvery helmets and body armor carried the banners of the separate divisions before the ranks of trucks and armored cars while drummers from the emperor's marching band marked the even cadence as the traffic crept across the composite planks of the bridges. Mounted infantry from Mexico, recruited after mechanical problems had rendered so many troop carriers unusable, each of them wearing a long wool coat to shield his body from the cold, crossed in double lines behind the Pan-Polarian regulars. Siberian auxiliaries sporting long black beards came after the Mexicans; they shouted to the jet-streaked skies as they proceeded, and a camp follower told me the men were calling to their gods to grant them good fortune on the long trek that lay ahead of them in the hostile Chinese-controlled lands. Last to make the crossing was the grinding baggage train—the ammunition carriers and the heavy trucks with wheels as tall as a man's head. The entire procession needed a full day to exit Progress. Helen and I watched their movement during the daylight hours from the doorway of our stone hovel. While we lay on our beds at night, we could hear the engines growling on the undulating bridges during our slumbers. Whenever a truck with an infected engine ground to a halt, a group of soldiers would put the machine in neutral gear and shove it out of the army's path. I counted twenty-six such stricken vehicles within sight of the encampment on the first day of the march toward the south.

Father and his servant Medus both went with the Twentieth Division, leaving Helen and myself in the military station among the other women and children. Most of the other senior officers sent their families back to Garden City or to other places far from the lonely outpost, and in those distant spots the families awaited word of the expected victories. I was terribly alone that long summer and fall the soldiers were gone. I rarely had the company of other children during my youth: my peculiar situation was far too lowly for me to have friends among the offspring of other generals; being the daughter of a legion commander I was far too high-born to associate with the unofficial children dwelling outside the station walls. At Progress I daily wandered like a sparrow through the nearly deserted encampment, playing games with imaginary companions and dreaming of what Father and the emperor were doing beyond the southern horizon.

Luke Anthony had ridden on a personnel carrier beside his father into the Manchurian countryside, and had left his pack of jaded playmates in a cluster of drab buildings near the central hall Mathias had used. Other children left in the station made a pastime of running near to the quarters of the young coemperor's entourage and shouting the nasty expletives they had learned by listening to their elders discuss Luke Anthony's friends. The scamps would run away if one of the insulted hanger-ons emerged from a doorway to see what was happening. I stayed away from Luke's people from Garden City because Helen had told me there were witches from the secret cults among the group. I knew my old nurse was trying to frighten me away from that loud, drunken crowd that partied late into the night after every sunset. I also knew there were certain women from East Africa in Luke Anthony's group who painted their eyebrows green and wore spangled clothing and certainly looked to my twelve-year-old eyes to be the hawk-faced practitioners of the forbidden arts Helen had told me about in her stories. "Witches eat nosy little girls, you know," Helen told me. I did not linger near the strange foreign women to learn if she was telling the truth. I preferred staying close to the river and the only living foliage in the region; at least there I could see types of life I could under-stand, and observing the sparse stands of trees and rusting trucks on the other shore somehow made me feel closer to Father.

Luke Anthony returned to Progress unexpectedly in the middle of the summer. A small detachment of the Mexican horseman was his only escort through the wild countryside on his journey back to us. There had been a scrimmage in the Manchurian wasteland, and despite his reputation for ferocity and his love of staged combats, Luke Anthony had disgraced himself by running from the first enemy gunshots of the campaign. After the Pan-Polaric troopers had routed the suicidal Chinese assault, Mathias had disparaged his son as a coward in front of the entire high command. Report had it that some generals present had laughed at the humiliating quaking the young man did when he suffered the emperor's rage. I thank Providence my father was not so foolish as those laughing officers. Anyone who mocked Luke Anthony on that day died soon after he became sole ruler of the Empire.

"I didn't flee," Luke had reportedly told his father. "My carrier's engine seized up, and I had to get out and run."

"Then your carrier was a cowardly machine, young man," Mathias was said to have replied. "Take it back to Progress. I'll not have such a faint-hearted machine among these other brave vehicles. When you have found a less nervous transport, one that will carry you toward danger rather than to the rear, you may return to us."

Luke Anthony apparently had a difficult time finding a better ride in the nearly vacant military camp. He loitered for months on the safe side of the Amur, hunting day after day and reveling with his friends during the warm nights. His teams of beaters daily made wide sweeps through the forest surrounding the station, sometimes driving game right against the stone walls or into the river. These drivers and their dogs (they used real ones, rather than the mechanical hounds that had been popular a few years earlier) attempted to tighten their large arc into a slowly constricting circle that would meet at a point where Luke would kill the trapped animals with his methane and gunpowder-powered rifle. Pan-Polarian troopers have traditionally left the mastery of such conventional weapons to foreign auxiliaries while our men carried laser or particle beam rifles. Luke Anthony had mastered the use of such ancient weapons while hunting and training with Mexican peasants in the hills around Garden City. Everyone agreed he was an expert shot. Those in the station who had seen him mow down the trapped deer, bear, wild boar, wolves, and tigers say he rarely missed, though he rode a motorcycle while he fired, and that the more he killed the more he went into an ecstasy of delight. When he became lost in the frenzy of the slaughter, the beautiful young man with the long golden curls would put a titanium sabot through the heart of some doomed beast and scream, "I am Luke Spacious Anthony! I am the Empire!" After all the animals in a trapped group had fallen, he would hop off his motorbike and run into the piles of dead and find a beast that was still convulsing so he could ask the dying creature if it appreciated the great honor of dying at the hands of the emperor of the Northern Hemisphere. Those telling the story say he waited for a reply and would savage the animal with his sidearm when the beast presumed to die without giving him one.

Once, on a rare cloudless day, I was walking along the river near the remains of a disassembled bridge when I heard the barking dogs and the "clang" of the beaters beating their flails against their body armor as they moved from the north toward me. To my horror, I realized the hunting party was not only headed for the Amur; it was converging directly upon a smattering of small houses built outside the encampment walls a few rods from where I was. The underbrush suddenly flickered to life as animals crashed through the foliage and toward the water. I at once ran onto the remaining portion of the bridge, the middle section of which had been removed, and I lay flat inside one of the concrete foundations, thus hiding myself from the oncoming hunters. I peered over the edge of the concrete shielding me and beheld the beaters' circle drawing tight immediately west of the end of the bridge. Several deer leapt into the river and swam away before the beaters could get between them and the water. A frightful uproar took place as various creatures and two small boys who had been caught in the sweep dashed into the open, crashing into each other and howling in terror as they found themselves inside the ring of the beaters' shields. A large bear, its front leg wounded by a rifle shot, charged into the ring and with two swipes of its good forepaw tore open a large dog and ripped the side of one of the terrified boys, both of whom were shrieking to the beaters to let them go. Luke Anthony, looking as dashing as Alexander riding down the Persian army, rode his motorcycle to the outside of the ring and fired once into the bear's chest, killing it instantly.

He was as tremendous a marksman as everyone had claimed. From his mount he fired round after round into the animal melee before him. Every sabot he sent into the chaos went straight into a beast's vital organs; a boar, three stags, a fox, and a bull from a nearby farm were caught in midflight and fell lifeless on the ground. Luke Anthony then took a flail from a beater and chased the two small boys about the ring on his motorcycle, slapping them with the blunt weapon as he swore aloud.

"You cost me three deer!" he shouted as he struck them from his mount. "Don't you know who I am?"

The boys were covered in blood. Their screams had degenerated to less than human cries of distress and were more like the squeals of dying cattle inside a charnel house. The boy the bear had mauled soon could withstand no more and collapsed in the dirt beneath the wheels of Luke's cycle. The other one charged the beaters' wall, but the heartless men knocked him back with their flails. Unable to escape the scene, the pathetic child curled into a ball on the unprotected dirt where Luke Anthony continued to beat him.

"I am the emperor!" the brave hunter shouted. "I am the Empire!"

He might have pummeled the two hapless boys to death but for the actions of his friend Sao Trentex—of whom I have forever after thought better—for that second young man broke into the ring of beaters and declared to Luke Anthony that perhaps Emperor Mathias would learn of this incident if the two children were killed.

"Are you afraid of him?!" shrieked Luke Anthony, wild with the strange satisfaction violence gave him and raising the flail in the air as though he were about to bring it down on his friend's pockmarked head.

The boys were fortunate Sao Trentex thought quickly. The cunning fellow dropped to his knees and clasped his hands in an exaggerated gesture of supplication.

"Oh, yes, Luke Anthony!" he said in a semihysterical voice that made young Luke smile. "I fear your father will come back to Progress and give us another lecture on moral philosophy! I know you do not fear death, my lord. I quiver for the both of us when I think we might have to endure another seminar burdened by his vast piety! Please bear in mind that the rest of us are mortal, my lord! We cannot endure as much of his sancti-monious person as you can!"

Luke Anthony laughed, which cued the rest of his group they should laugh with him. Sao Trentex's joke had broken the bloodthirsty mood that had seemed to grip him only seconds before. Luke gave the flail back to its owner, and having ordered his men to dress the fallen game he rode toward the great hall. The moment he was gone, Sao Trentex had some of the bearers carry the two boys to a physician. He wrapped the most bloodied of the children in his own long coat, and cleaned the still-unconscious child's face with a loose corner of the cloth. "I am terribly sorry, little one," I heard him say before the bearers carried the child toward the encampment walls. The ugly man's kindness was more astonishing to me than Luke Anthony's cruelty had been. No one today has anything good to say concerning Sao Trentex. History remembers him as one of the fawning dilettantes about young Luke who abetted the soon-to-be emperor's corruption. History and the rest of us never knew the real man. If he was capable of showing courage and compassion in defiance of Luke Anthony's irrational fury, I expect there were deep mines of virtue within the man he normally kept hidden lest he offend the unthinking power that throughout his short life was always just a few steps from his side. If the distance between him and Luke had been thousands of miles, if Sao Trentex had been a programmer in Poland or a farmer in North America, he might have been as good a man as Mathias aspired to be. Fate thought otherwise. He was doomed never to be far removed from that evil influence, and being as close as he was he had to be a slave to Luke Anthony's whims, as was everyone else near the willful young emperor. Since history has overlooked the goodness in the man, I pray some higher power—if any exists—took note of the luckless man's act of charity beside the chilly Amur and for that deed his soul is today in some better place than that of his thoughtless master.

I did not leave my hiding place on the bridge till everyone in the hunting party had departed. The moment I could no longer hear the dogs yapping, I sped off the pontoon bridge and ran home. I told Helen what had happened by the river, and she tore her hair and threatened to take a rod to me. In the end she merely kissed my face a few dozen times and thanked her numerous gods I was well.

"You see!" she said. "This is what happens when you go near the young emperor!"

"I didn't," I said. "I was by the river. He came near me."

Helen replied that everything in creation, or at least half of it, belonged to the emperor, and he could go anywhere he wanted on his property. The only safe place in the camp was our house.

"He could squeeze you like a flea," she said, and pressed her fingernails together to demonstrate his power.

For once, I nearly obeyed her. I still went for strolls along the river, but each time I left the encampment I made certain the coemperor was not out hunting game of either the four- or two-legged varieties.

The army was gone the entire winter and did not return to Progress until the rain had changed to snow and back to rain once more. In the early spring the engineers appeared on the other shore and filled in the midsections of the bridges so the soldiers could return to our side of the Amur. The seemingly undiminished force returned largely on foot and brought in its train three thousand ragged Manchurian prisoners, most of them old people and children. There had been no great battles in the sandy hills. When report of our approaching soldiers had reached the isolated settlements in that desolate region of the globe, the majority of the clans who had been raiding southeastern Siberia simply retreated into China proper, leaving behind nothing of value for our soldiers to attack; yet somewhere in the field pack of some tired veteran the army carried home to us the sole important trophy they had won on the long and uneventful campaign: they brought to us the demon called the new metal plague. Every household in Progress sealed its doorway with caulk once the unwanted guest made itself known to us. People purified the air about them with antibiotic sprays and washed their metal possessions in soapy water and mild acids to keep the evil visitor from moving into their machinery.

Helen claimed she had felt the plague in the wet soil of this strange country when we first arrived there. She believed it had traveled up the roots and into the trees, and that was why she had seen the unlucky signs in the wood ashes. She believed this although I explained to her the plague was clearly human-made.

What we in Progress did not yet know was that this new curse was not a variation of the human-made virus we had seen corrode our metal goods during the previous forty years. That earlier plague had indeed been a virus; that is, it was a microscopic chain of proteins that excreted an acid capable of corroding metal surfaces. As nearly as the Empire's scientists could discern, some laboratory in southern Africa had created the old metal virus, which was one of the many designer germs and viruses that have afflicted humankind during the past 150 years. We in the Pan-Polarian Empire had contained the old metal virus by substituting plastics and ceramics for metals when we could, though metalloids and non-metals from the upper right-hand corner of the periodic table make poor conductors of electricity. We had to coat our metal circuitry in heavy insulation, and even protected electrical systems had to be decontaminated every three or four days, which caused interruptions in communications and interfered with the functions of most computers. What had saved us from the old metal plague was that since it was a true virus it had mutated rather quickly and most of the newer varieties it became were no danger to our metal. Nonetheless, scientists in the Southern Hemisphere continue to create batches of the original metal virus, and it has become the primary reason the Empire (and the whole world) has become poorer and less technologically sophisticated over time. The new plague the army brought back from Manchuria was not a virus or even a living organism; it was in fact a nanomachine only three molecules in size. These tiny machines feed on negative energy, as is found in electricity, which the machines consume and convert into positrons. Normally these tiny machines lie dormant in the soil, feeding on the electrons in sunlight. But when they are in the vicinity of electricity coursing through metal structures, they latch onto the circuitry the way mosquitoes do blood veins. When infected with the new metal plague, machines grind to a halt, generators shut down, and those who have metal implants in their bodies wither away as if stricken by the plagues of the Middle Ages.

That spring in Progress any neighbor with an electronic implant might in the morning be as healthy as a goat, by noon become as sluggish as someone walking in his sleep, and by evening be dead and as stiff as a carbon beam. When we first saw people die from it, we did not realize the new plague could not strike all humans, and we thought we too were in peril. Helen made me and her husband Medus wear amulets she claimed had been blessed at a temple of healing somewhere in Europe. Medus was as superstitious as his wife, and I was terrified by the bodies I every day saw being carried away for burial in the handcarts, so we did as she wanted. My father threw away the amulet she gave him. He vowed he would slay any plague demon that came for him with a flame thrower. He slept with such a weapon at his bedside, ready to strike at any virus daring to venture through our front doorway. Given our ignorance of the new affliction, we thought either the amulets or Father's threats must have worked, for when the deaths in the encampment waned and in a few weeks ceased altogether, everyone in our household remained well. Our good emperor Mathias Anthony was less fortunate.

Mathias fell ill soon after his return. For five days he lay on his bed in the great hall, fighting the affliction with all the remaining strength he had in the natural portions of his body. When his physicians told him he would become progressively weaker in spite of the decontamination work they had performed on him, he refused food and drink and prepared himself for an honorable death. On the sixth day of his ordeal he summoned groups of his generals and former students into his room to say good-bye to them.

"Why are you weeping?" he asked his lieutenants. "You should be worrying about the plague and what it may yet do to you. Each of us is condemned to die on the day of our birth. My time is now. Take care yours does not come soon hereafter. I suspect this is something the Chinese have created. It has long been obvious that technology will be eventually used to destroy itself. I should have written a book upon the subject. But take heart: our civilization is more than electric lights and thinking machines. Learning, language, the arts, our medicine, our laws, our courage—these and much more will endure, and they will sustain our Empire in the long night to come."

I was included among the students he called to his bedside. I waited in the deserted banquet hall for two hours while sobbing men entered and left his room. When it was my time, two enormous soldiers dressed in armor they had to move themselves, as it was no longer self-propelling, escorted me to his chamber. He was lying against the wall in his small cot, looking much paler and thinner than when I had seen him last. Like everyone else—including the tall soldiers—I wept when I beheld his wan, yellow face.

"Shhh, Justa," he said in his weak voice. "This is the fate of mortal things. Do not grieve over what is fated to happen."

I wanted to be brave for him. Instead I cried the more when I heard how frail he sounded.

"I should be the one weeping," he said. "I will not live to see you blossom into a beautiful woman. Don't come too close, little one. We don't understand how infectious this thing is. I have another farewell gift for you. Over there."

He pointed to a small table holding a jewelry box filled with golden combs I could wear in my long hair. On the box's casing was depicted the Judgment of Paris, showing Aphrodite, the goddess of beauty, accepting the golden apple. I imagine the present was the emperor's kind comment upon my appearance.

"Think of this old friend when you put on the combs," he said. "Most Just, you really must control yourself."

We had been in Progress for nearly two years. I had turned fourteen in the meantime and was practically grown by the standards of the day. I was nonetheless weak in that terrible moment when I should have been as emotionless as a statue and insisted on weeping before the wasting emperor when he needed me to be strong.

"What will you do when you are older, Justa?" he asked me.

"I will . . . serve the Empire . . . however I can, my lord," I sputtered through my tears.

Mathias turned his face to the wall. My answer had not pleased him.

"You have been told I do not want to hear that sort of rubbish," he said.

"I would say anything that would be pleasing to you, my lord," I told him.

He turned back to me and motioned me to take another step closer to his bed.

"Then say what is in your heart and not what you think I want to hear," he said. "An emperor hears many words intended to please him. That is our chief duty: hearing such words. People saying them do not necessarily know what I want to hear. I would have been more pleased, Most Just, if you had said you wanted to lead a good and simple life, the sort of life that would belong to you and your family. You should marry a farmer, little one. They are honest people. Some of them are, anyway. Be a good wife and a good mother to a family of honest farmers. That would please me. I would have liked to have been a farmer myself."

The import of what he was saying was lost on me in my sorrow. Nor could I stop weeping for him.

"If you had not been our emperor," I said, "then, my lord, historians in ages hence would write that Pan-Polaria was deprived of her noblest, most valiant—"

"Stop that, Justa," he told me. "Leave us for a moment, friends," he said to the soldiers. When he and I were alone in the chamber he said to me in a whisper that carried plainly to me ears, "Child, historians ages hence will write the same nonsense they have always written. They will most likely say I was a good ruler, that I saved the Empire from several invasions and did not completely destroy the economy. They will add I made my one great error when I made Luke Spacious my successor. Don't be shocked, Justa. I know better than anyone what sort of man Luke is, and I have imagination enough to guess what evil he will do after I am gone and there is no one to restrain him. His mother raised him to be exactly the sort of . . . the sort of thing he is. She and the crowd of sycophants she put about him did a thorough job. I could not improve upon her work. Know this, my child: I came not to care what he has become. There once was a time I thought I could educate him, education being the last depot the train called failure usually stops at. In later years I considered raising another man outside my family to be the next emperor, as my immediate predecessors have done. Then, four years ago I returned to Garden City and found him and several of his friends sitting on the palace steps like idlers in front of a convenience store; it was morning and they looked to have been out all night on the streets of the capital, dressed as they were in their heavy cloaks and hoods. He was only fourteen. The gang of them, they had a sack full of something they did not wish me to inspect. I had a squadron of soldiers with me, of course; they retrieved the bag for me, and inside there were the most hideous bits of animal life they had collected during the night, the whole of it cut up in a bloody mess: a cat's head, a dog's hind leg, and such. When I poured it all out on the ground, there was a child's severed hand amid the other gore. The soldiers and I were aghast. We looked at them and wondered. And they, the little murderers, they could only cower like cowards before me. 'This,' I told myself, 'is the Empire we have fought a hundred wars to preserve. Pan-Polaria's story was endured to produce this.' I walked away from him and returned to the frontier without staying another hour in the capital. Two years later I named him my coemperor. Leaving him to the Empire and the Empire to him will be the most just deed I have ever done. Pan-Polaria will have the master she has long deserved.

"Now, Justa, your father, General Black, is over fifty-five. He may retire from the army any time he wishes. Tell him to settle somewhere far from the capital. We are losing control of more outer regions every week. The farther away from Garden City he settles, the better it will be for you and for him. Someplace in the far north of America will do. You will meet your farmer husband there; there you can teach your children to aspire for nothing more than to be farmers and farmers' wives. Never, never, little one, should you or anyone in your family go again to Garden City. Never. Now good-bye, pretty one, and do not mourn for me."

I hid my face and wept as I ran from the room. I was so distraught I forgot to bow to him before I exited. The soldiers posted at the doorway were shedding tears as plentiful as mine. I knew they were weeping both for the great goodness about to depart the Earth and for the calamity that was to befall us when Luke Spacious took Mathias's place.

Mathias the Glistening died on the seventh day of his affliction. Because Luke Anthony was in the emperor's bedchamber when Mathias left us, the rumormongers have claimed the young emperor strangled his father. I know this is a lie, for Mathias's bodyguards never left his side while Luke was present. After the news of Mathias's death had spread through the encampment, Luke called the senior officers together at the great hall and addressed them and the Empire via a hazy satellite transmission.

"Our daddy," he said, putting both his hands over his heart and casting his eyes skyward, "has gone to heaven to sit among the other emperors as a god. He has left us to govern the world while he is away."

Luke told the world the army units were to return to their various provinces, and he, the sole emperor, was returning to Garden City to bury his father. The Manchurian war was officially over.

My father told us while we packed our belongings at our house that night that the new emperor had cut quite a figure for an eighteen-year-old boy.

"He's a handsome lad," said Father. "The ladies back in Garden City are going to love him. Somebody has to. Of course I will serve him as best I can. That's what his father would have wanted me to do, and Mathias is the one who lifted me up in the world. I won't betray him just because he's no longer here to keep an eye on me."

III

AD 2293

"**I** could be a leader after Mathias's example, if I trusted our friend Mr. Golden and did as he wants," said Father as Mica gave him his morning massage. "I would be a friend to the poor and a champion to the weak, and so on."

Father meant well when he said this. I could have pointed out to him he thought being a friend to the poor meant giving them positions in the army and that for Father being a champion to the weak consisted of using the combat divisions to ward off potential invaders. That an emperor might do other things, such as reform our corrupt judicial system or break the power of the commodities speculators, was beyond the limits of his imagination. Rather than contradict him, I said, "Do you remember when we last saw Selin in Garden City?"

"How could anyone forget any time he crossed tracks with that one?" asked Father. "The bristle-headed bastard was frightened then. He was in a crazy snit, like he always is, but he was scared to death of Luke Anthony. That may have been the only time anybody has seen him scared."

There had been a time when Father had feared Luke Anthony too. I did not challenge him on that point either.

The soldiers and laborers in the tunnels outside our quarters had been quiet during the night following the arrival of Mr. Golden's messengers. The men had not been chanting Father's name, but Mr. Golden's men had brought plenty of money to pay the local merchants to keep the beer flowing to the troopers and miners, and the good feelings toward "Emperor" Black lived on in the hangovers of the morning after.

"Would you return to Garden City, sir?" I asked.

He shook his head. If we could see the thoughts of others, I would have seen Father's imperial ambitions fleeing out the door while he contemplated the dangers of that distant city.

"Only if I went there to retire forever," he said, and looked into space at a scene only he could see. "To go to the capital when called is to risk death. To stay there is to decide to die. Travel across the solar system is becoming so hazardous, anyway, because of the tiny machines. Do you recall the first time Luke Anthony . . ."

He did not finish the question. Father looked at the scene before him and was lost to me for a moment. I knew what he was contemplating.

IV.

AD 2280

When Young Luke Anthony ended the Chinese campaign, Father and his household returned to the Middle East in what was once the nation of Turkey, and there he again commanded troops opposite the Iranian frontier. In addition to his military duties, the emperor in Garden City made Father a tribune of the courts, and Father had to thrust himself into legal as well as military matters. As was required of his new office, Father became directly involved in suits well-connected provincial officials were bringing against hapless local debtors. At that time and in those circumstances, there could not have been a more inappropriate choice for this new position than my father. Court cases bored him; these legal disputes involved property and financial obligations, both of which were alien concepts to Father, a habit-bound and nearly propertyless soldier. Father had never dealt with anyone other than men-at-arms since he had been old enough to shave with a laser blade. He took the job assuming that citizens obeyed rules as soldiers did, and when he decided that a disputant in a case had strayed from the letter of the law, Father would at once give judgment to the cheater's opponent, which meant that in an extraordinary number of cases he decided in favor of the lowborn debtors and against the well-connected moneylenders, tax farmers, and petty government officials appearing before him. The courts would have tolerated Father's behavior in Mathias's time; back then justice and fairness were supposed to have some weight in a tribune's judgments. During the reign of Luke Anthony, when the magistrates and other provincial officials were either favorites of the emperor's court or had purchased their positions directly from the throne, Father's actions quickly earned him the disfavor of the powerful back in the capital. The emperor's cronies had expected the courts to let them steal anything in the provinces they wanted—the same as other tribunes of the court in other provinces allowed the powerful to do; Father was so unworldly he thought he was supposed to protect the weak. "You have been charging usurious rates," he told more than one moneylender; "this poor fellow should keep his land." The wronged shysters were quick to send missives to Garden City that complained of Father's good deeds in Turkey. The new emperor might have had Father eliminated straightaway were it not for the renewed Iranian threat on the border, a threat the Empire needed experienced officers to fight in that time of faltering technology and constricting imperial power. Poverty doubly protected Father. He owned only a small house in the Field of Heroes back in Garden City, and the emperor would profit little if he killed Father and seized everything he had.

The foreign raiders then making forays across the mountainous country around Lake Van were mounted forces attacking Pan-Polarian settlements and native cities as far west as the Mediterranean coast. In the early months of their forays they used motorcycles and hovercraft, but as those too succumbed to the new metal plague they became the cavalry forces their ancestors had been in ancient times. They struck and quickly raced back to their homelands after they had stolen everything they could carry with them. Whether entering or leaving our territories they did their best to avoid the Pan-Polarian army. Armed with primitive rifles made of wood and steel and obviously more mobile than our men, the Iranians were invincible in the open desert south of Turkey's mountains. They were far more vulnerable on the broken ground and in the heavily populated Anatolian hill country, where the still-fertile soil had attracted many new farmers in recent decades. Father called the raiders "nomads" because of the rootless way they fought, though actually the Iranians are a highly civilized people living in the great cities that used to belong to the caliph of Baghdad before Pan-Polaria invaded that region 140 years earlier.

"We have to catch the nomads in places they can't jump around," Father explained to me. "Get them in the mountain passes or out in the muddy fields the farmers have along the rivers or in among the houses of the towns. Hill country and woodlands are other good spots to tear up the silver-scaled bastards. What good is their speed then, eh? If they fall on us in open country, we have to close ranks in our body armor and march to where the land favors us. The nomads can't hurt us as long as we move in unison. Their old-fashioned bullets can't penetrate our armor, you see. When they charge our ranks they can't protect themselves, you understand. They're not in armor like we are. If they stop and shoot at us from a distance, they're wasting their time. We have only to fight them in places that favor us. I was there when we burned their capitals down, missy. Did I ever tell you about that?"

I had to tell him often he had already related to me the sacking of Teheran and Qom many times before.

"The nomads need to take care," Father told me, "or we'll do it again."

The Pan-Polarian army holding the frontier against the Iranian intrusions belonged more to the frontier than it did to Garden City. Few of the men serving in the ranks under Father's command still had any blood of the Empire's founders in them. Since the time of Blando the Wayward, some two hundred years before, the soldiers of the army had been the sons of professional soldiers married to wives they had found near the military stations, and they were no longer the citizen-soldiers the military had been made of during early imperial times. The men in Turkey had, like their fathers, taken up with local women and were raising the next generation of soldiers in the unofficial families in the ghettos packed close to the military station at Van City's four walls. The men had each enlisted at age nineteen and served for thirty years; should they survive until retirement, they would wed their unofficial wives in a civil ceremony and would thereafter continue to live near their old bases and to serve the army as teamsters, farmers, or as the various types of engineers and artisans the military needs to survive in this time of reduced industrial capacity. While most of the old hands in and around the base called themselves Pan-Polarians, they had adopted local customs and spoke a language that contained some English and Syntalk words and much other vocabulary that came from local tongues or from the languages of the traders who frequented the base. A large portion of Father's army was completely alien in origin, and a large portion of those foreign men were from the various Muslim tribes—the very people the Empire had sometimes fought against. Even in Turkey and the other Asian provinces on the remote southern edges of the Empire one could find thousands of tall men in turbans serving as mercenaries for Pan-Polaria and still calling themselves Uzbeks, Tajiks, Afghans, or Turkmen. Mixed into these infantrymen were also the increasingly common Mexican cavalry, the German artillerymen, and the odd contingents of North American sharpshooters, Slavic heavy infantry, and of course the Boers, the people who had no country and took their families with them to the frontier; this last tribe went wherever the Empire sent the banners of its divisions. The Tenth, the finest fighting unit in the army and thus in the world, the celebrated mobile unit that protected the heartland of North America—the most valuable place in the Empire because of the food it produces—could not have taken the field minus its dour Boer contingents. So it was for Father's army in Turkey. If only the men of pure Pan-Polarian blood from North America, the place the Empire was born, served in the Turkish army, Father would have gone into battle with himself and perhaps ten senior officers to lead. Had his charges been limited to those men who had ever set foot on American soil, Father would have had left from the thirty thousand at Van City only himself and a few hundred others.

Whenever I walked with my father through the encampment at Van City we could take a hundred steps and hear a dozen different languages and look upon men from that many different lands. The officers and sergeants used a modified Syntalk to communicate with their men, as everyone in the East knows at least a portion of that tongue. The words they use in the languages they speak lack tenses and conjugations and articles of any sort. "Man see many house yesterday," was how a sample sentence might run, and the speaker would pat himself on the chest to show he was the man who saw the houses. Each tribe of soldiers had its own food in camp—baked potatoes and beef for those having any American blood, thick beer and overcooked sausages for the Europeans, mounds of cracked and bleached grains for the Muslims—and each group had its own collection of gods. The men set small idols of clay and metal in front of their houses to protect them from death in battle and from the new epidemics that periodically swept through every army post. The men called their squat, mud-brown idols Minit, the Lady of Flowers, Sraosha, and Llyr. They each said their particular idols were the most powerful because they, the dutiful worshipers, remained alive after so many of the others they had served with had perished. Few in the camp, and almost none among the generals, worshiped the old Christian God, the one in three their great-grandfathers had adored in ages past. Nor did any among them mention the ancient stories their grandparents had used as literary metaphors and that their earlier ancestors had lived by.

The most popular deity among the senior officers in Father's Turkish camp was the Eastern god Invictus, "the Unconquerable," and the reasoning behind their devotion to this bloody god was more social than spiritual in nature. The officers considered the savage religion of Invictus a manly cult, one suitable for soldiers, and since the men in the army had nothing else in common, their commanders hoped the troops might accept the new religion as the dominant martial faith. The recently crowned emperor in distant Garden City was of the same opinion. Luke Anthony had ordered the construction of Invictus's temples in military stations throughout the Empire, including a squat, rectangular one without windows at Father's base at Van City; the emperor had paid for priests to evangelize the men, and had let it be known that he too was a devotee of the invincible deity and would be pleased with those who believed as he did. As a female, I could not enter the cult's temple: Invictus's followers necessarily had to be men, for in our time gods discriminate as readily as humans do. From what Father told me I knew that before initiation into the group's sacred mysteries acolytes were given generous servings of strong drink while the priest told them the first secret of their religion, namely, that Invictus had emerged from the Great Egg of Creation holding the Sword of Truth and the Torch of Enlightenment, which I am sure sounds about right to men eager to believe in anything; then the priest put the new believer into a windowless room and made him stare into a barrel filled with water until the man's senses were befuddled. In the last act of the initiation rite, the older members of the sect would baptize the new man in the blood of a bull; the drunk, disoriented, and blindfolded soldier would be made to lie beneath a heavy metal grate onto which a live bull was led and sacrificed by the priest, who would slit the bull's throat in imitation of Invictus's slaying of a holy white bull in one of the religion's earliest myths. The shower of warm, reeking blood had a powerful effect upon the young man cowering beneath the grate. (It was invariably a young man. An older man would not do such things.) If the soldier did not go mad during the ceremony, he was certain to be permanently altered by the experience. My father considered the manly cult a great farce, yet he was tolerant of what went on inside the unimpressive-looking temple. The blood, he said, "scared the mischief out of the lads." The blood did not, however, scare the other gods out of them. The new believers crawled from beneath the grates and added Invictus's image to the idols of Minit, the Lady of Flowers, Sraosha, and Llyr, and added another superstition to their old ones.

Money and terror were what really held the army together as the

Empire grew weaker. Should the men not be paid on time, as happened more than once during Luke Anthony's rule, they might kill their officers and pillage the countryside to make up the lost wages. My father forestalled any rebellion among the army of Turkey with constant drill, constant movement, and the most severe discipline in the Empire. The men respected his harsh leadership as much as they respected his humble origins in the ranks of the infantry. They knew Father now made a fire in front of his house as they did in front of their homes and that he ate no better food than the lowliest soldier did. Father was to his soldiers a relic from the past, a reminder of the traditions the troopers' grandfathers had taught them when they were children living outside the military stations. When the men came to our home and demanded liquor to celebrate the New Year or the summer holidays, Father would give them vinegar instead of wine. If the men grew tired from marching and demanded water, Father would point in the direction of the nearest river. Should they demand more money on payday because the currency had been devaluated again, Father would brandish his sidearm and tell them, "You will have to go over me to get it!" The men loved his toughness. During the Iranian campaign alone there were a dozen occasions when the troops would have butchered a sympathetic general the first time he gave in to them. Father knew this single great truth: soldiers obey leaders who demand more of them than could be reasonably expected, and his men knew no leader demanded more than General Black.

During the fighting against the Iranian raiders Garden City had ordered Father not to pursue the enemy deep into their territories. Luke Anthony wanted victories; given the developing realities of the Empire, he did not want to spend the money or lives necessary to gain them. We were fortunate that the rough country on the Turkish frontier exhausts all who dare cross its mountains with heat and thirst in summer and terrible cold in winter. The land thus provides a natural defense against any invasion coming from the flatlands lying to its south. Father first tried fortifying the mountain passes on the border lands, hoping to catch the Iranian attackers from ambush. The enemy reacted to this plan by riding around the fortified positions and crossing the high ground as best they could, even if that meant going right over the highest, snowcapped peaks. From this preliminary failure to trap his opponents Father would stumble—with my assistance—onto a strategy that would eventually defeat his more mobile enemy. To cross the frosty mountain wastelands where there was no clear trail and food and fodder were hard to obtain, the Iranians came to depend upon local tribesmen to guide them along the safest routes. I realized Father could in turn bribe the native people to lead the enemy into traps we had set for them along the way. Early in the morning or late in the evening the bribed tribesmen would guide the unsuspecting and very tired enemy cavalry between two ranks of hiding Pan-Polaric infantry. At a broadcast signal (for we still had radios then) our men would shower the horsemen in baggy trousers with hundreds of carbon filament sabots, cutting them to pieces before they could react. Any raiders our infantry did not slay with the first volley could be pursued into the high ground by our Mexican horsemen mounted on fresh steeds or strafed by the handful of aircraft Father kept on isolated bases where they would be removed (for a time) from the new metal plague. After two score of these ambushes Father quickly became the most successful general on that portion of the frontier, and Turkey became the safest border province in the Empire. News of General Black's numerous small victories had to have reached the capital via the news reports made by the Portus Network, the last of the television broadcasters operating in the Middle East. Perhaps these successes were something of a counterbalance to his judicial honesty on the emperor's scales of injustice, and we were left alone for a time.

My father imperiled his somewhat favorable position within the emperor's court by writing a letter to Garden City that suggested the emperor extend the terms of every provincial judge and governor to five years. Father reasoned that too many administrators and officers of the courts made a quick fortune in the Empire's far reaches, usually by buying debts or farming taxes, and went home before they had to deal with the consequences of their actions. Father wrote he wanted experienced men, ones able to spend some time in the areas they had been assigned to, and no more of the vultures who fattened upon the poor before flying home to their villas near the capital. Father knew long-term appointments worked in the army. He never was able to understand that the ways of the civilian world were infinitely more complex than military life. Father assumed the emperor would at once see the common sense in the letter's proposals. Father had given so little thought to the dangers he was courting he did not tell anyone on his staff that he had sent the letter until the day after he had handed the missive to an airplane courier bound for the capital. He was having a conference with Harriman—then a young man in his late twenties and already my father's chief lieutenant—when he let drop in an offhanded way what he had written to Luke Anthony.

"You have killed yourself!" exclaimed Harriman.

"Stuff," laughed Father. "I'm being a good servant to the emperor. I made the same suggestion to his late father once, and he did me no harm. These highfalutin folks in Garden City need our level-headed counsel now and then, don't you know? I wouldn't be surprised if the boy didn't give me another promotion."

"Sir, please, sir," Harriman begged him, "you have to send a secure radio message to the courier! If he doesn't turn back to us, get a fighter to shoot him down! Whatever you have to do, that man can't reach Garden City. The emperor cannot read that letter! Don't you realize these administrators you are criticizing bought their positions from Luke Anthony's hand? Stealing from the provincials and hurrying home is precisely what they came out here to do!"

"Young man, I realize the emperor can be a violent lad. Some of his friends are outright thugs, I'll give you that. But you're now saying he is a common thief," said Father, who never understood anything as quickly as he should have. "I would remind you this is Mathias the Glistening's son you are slandering! There has to be some decency in him. Besides, I am only doing my duty. My experience has been that if a soldier does his duty, then everything works out for the best."

He concluded the conference by telling Harriman his treasured anecdote of the time he killed a giant crocodile on the Nile in Egypt.

"There he was," said Father, demonstrating to the bewildered junior officer how he had drawn his pistol on the ungainly beast. "He was as big as two lions laid end to end and had a mouth as wide as a theater's front door, and he was coming right into the boat for me! 'It's you or me,' I told him, 'and trust me: it is going to be you!'"

Two months later Father received a letter demanding he come to Garden City for a private conference with the emperor. His staff looked upon this epistle as a notice of Father's death. They held a banquet for him the day he was preparing to leave; each senior officer came to Father's dining table in the officers' mess to bid him farewell, as though my father were about to be executed in the morning. They were certain they would never again see him alive. The older men thanked him for the discipline and the exacting example he had established in the East. The younger ones, such as poor Harriman, wept when it was their turn to bid Father good-bye.

"None of this, boys," Father told them, and ordered more beer to lighten the mood in the room. "I'm only off to have a chat with the emperor. He probably wants me to talk to his people—I mean the administrators, the chamberlains, the whatyoucallthems and the whatnots—about this fine idea of mine. You won't be rid of old General Black yet. That I guarantee you."

"We will miss you, sir," bawled Harriman.

"Let us act like men!" demanded Father. "The son of Mathias Anthony is not the big thinker his father was. I'll allow that. I know he's fond of hunting and rough athletic stuff, like boys tend to be. I've hunted myself. I killed a crocodile on the Nile, you know. I'll tell him about that. It'll give us a common ground to stand on, put him in the right frame of mind. I don't know if I've ever told you lads that story," he said to his men. "There he was, the big, warty brute, ready to swallow me whole, and I said to him: 'As long as I have a good Pan-Polarian firearm in my hand you'll not sink your foreign teeth into me!'"

I was seated behind Father's sofa with his household servants and was able to whisper into his ear that he had told his officers this same story only a few days before.

Three years earlier, after his father's death at Progress, the new emperor
had ridden into Garden City in a golden hovercraft led by a thousand
naked Chinese in golden chains while he kissed his friend Sao Trentex full
on the lips to scandalize the populace on the first day of his reign. On the
second day of his rule Luke Anthony had withdrawn into his rambling
palace and into a personal domain of athletic contests and sexual indulgence. He left governing the Empire to Sao Trentex, whom he had named
his chief chamberlain. Anyone who had hoped young Luke would evolve
into anything similar to his father quickly had their eyes opened to his
true personality. Luke had found the treasury depleted by his father's military campaigns and by the decline in the economy the metal plagues had
caused, so he raised a quick surplus by selling state offices and by seizing
the estates of certain wealthy citizens close at hand in North America. His
method was to charge a rich man he hated with conspiracy, have the
accused killed before the man could flee to the Southern Hemisphere, and
seize the dead man's land and money as an additional penalty for his
alleged crime. As Luke Anthony should have anticipated, his methods
soon gave birth to a real conspiracy against him. A nobleman named
Fourthman, who was a grand nephew of Mathias the Glistening, and
Lucilla, Mathias's elder sister and the new emperor's aunt, met secretly
with Pedro Tarantella, the general of the City Guardsmen (the soldiers
protecting the emperor and Garden City itself), and they chose Lucilla's
stepson, one Claude Pompeianus the Fifth, a hotheaded young nobleman,
for the task of putting a bullet in Luke before the new emperor could
murder again. The young hothead made a terrible muff of the attempted
assassination. One morning while the emperor was exercising with his
athlete friends on one of the grassy fields within the palace grounds, some
City Guardsmen the conspirators had paid off allowed the bold Claude
Pompeianus to approach Luke from behind while the emperor was taking
a rest on a bench. Pompeianus had drawn his gun and was set to fire the

weapon into Luke's back. At the last moment the idiot paused to make a proclamation like an actor upon the stage. "This bullet the Senate sends you!" he announced. He must have thought it an apt, indeed a courageous statement for him to make. Luke of course heard him and sprang away swiftly while a half dozen of his beefy friends jumped on Pompeianus before he got around to doing what he was proclaiming he was about to do. After unspeakable tortures administered in the bowels of the palace, the would-be assassin gave the names of his associates. Fourthman, Lucilla, Tarantella, Pompeianus, and hundreds of others who had known of the plot were either at once put to death or exiled to distant lands and put to death at a later time. In the midst of this abortive coup, the emperor's friend and chamberlain Sao Trentex ended up lying in a slum street with his throat slit; perhaps Pedro Tarantella's men had killed him as part of the plot to seize power, or perhaps his old friend Luke Anthony had simply grown bored with the pockmarked man. No one knew for certain. The emperor found a new City Guardsmen commander in the dreadful Jerome Perlman, a man capable of committing murder as thoughtlessly as most men breathe. He had given the same thug all the powers the late Sao Trentex had formerly held. Luke Anthony had then retreated farther into his private indulgences. In the center of his palace he kept a harem of three hundred beautiful women and three hundred equally pretty young boys; when one of these lost souls displeased him, his or her body would be found the next day in the smoldering waste heaps outside the city limits. Every day Luke killed an unarmed convict in hand-to-hand combat to perfect his fighting skills and to get his blood up for when he visited himself upon his women and pretty boys. Killing with his own hands also eased the emperor's fear of the conspirators he could discern lurking in the darkened hallways and garden enclosures he wandered among during all the daylight hours and during the night when he could not sleep. This was the man with whom my father fancied he could have a constructive little chat concerning provincial government officials.

My father and his small household flew in a functioning plane to Guadalajara, as security prohibited any craft entering the airspace above the capital city. Thence we traveled on a train south to Garden City and its sprawling suburbs and slums of forty million people. As soon as he reached the inner city Father strolled across the Imperial Plaza to the palace gates without stopping to visit his long-unvisited wife at their home on the Field of Heroes. The servants and I stopped to wait for him near the palace in a small park in which a later emperor would eventually build the gigantic bathhouse that would be one of the Empire's last great public buildings.

"I'll be out in a couple hours," Father told us.

He presented himself to the City Guardsmen standing at the front gates by showing them his credentials. The soldiers would have normally run a DNA scan on him, but the government's central computers were no longer in use. The guards led him inside to an antechamber and told him to sit beside another gentleman awaiting an imperial audience.

"You don't understand," Father told the men, and showed them the rings and the insignia bearing the markings of his rank. "I am General Peter Justice Black, the commander of the emperor's Turkish army. I have a letter from Luke Anthony himself summoning me—"

"Sit!" the City Guardsmen told him.

Father realized the men ordering him about were mere City Guardsmen in fancy chromium armor and not, in his opinion, real soldiers. A couple of the men were Canadians straight from the north country, which in Father's mind showed what miscreants the whole bunch of them were. The white marble antechamber they wanted him to remain in was many rooms away from the palace's central halls and living quarters, where the emperor undoubtedly was that afternoon. Father thought the men would be showing him a smidgen of proper respect if they let him wait someplace closer to the imperial presence.

"See here," he told them, "I want one of you to go—"

Four of the City Guardsmen pulled their sidearms on him.

"Listen, Grandpa," one of the guards said to him, "sit here and keep your mouth shut, or you'll be dead sooner than the emperor wants."

Father was more shocked at their insolence than he was frightened by their threats. In his heart he wished he had these men under his command in the East; he would teach them how to talk to a general then! He knitted his eyebrows at the reprobates, and he sat on the stone ledge beside the other waiting man because he was confident he would eventually make these pretend soldiers regret their actions. The guards took the pistol from Father's side and strolled into the palace's labyrinthine interior, laughing among themselves about "hicks from the provinces."

"What the blazes is going on here?" Father asked the man sitting next to him. "The dolts didn't so much as salute me!"

The man he spoke to was a silver-haired gentleman of approximately sixty years. While he had a nobleman's clean, uncalloused hands, he was dressed down for this appearance in the palace. He wore an unbleached linen suit minus a necktie of party affiliation and had recently removed the rings of office from his fingers. Father could see where the bands had left their impressions. Upon hearing him speak, Father thought he recognized the man from somewhere.

"I do not know anything concerning these goings-on in the capital," said the man. "I am merely an olive farmer from southern Texas."

"I think I know you, sir," said Father. "Aren't you connected to Pius Anthony? You are his nephew, or grandnephew perhaps? I saw you in the court of Mathias the Glistening when he visited Egypt."

"No!" insisted the man, whose mouth had twitched when Father said the name "Pius Anthony." "I am an olive farmer, sir," said the stranger. "As I told the City Guardsmen: I have never been to Garden City before. Were the computers up today, they would see I have no DNA records on file. I'm no one."

"Then you look like somebody I once met, good sir," said Father, sounding as apologetic as he was capable of sounding. "I meant nothing. Aren't these damned Guardsmen a wonder? I will have to put a bee in the young emperor's ear about them when I get in to see him. Get these louts into apple-pie order then!"

The man was too frightened to make a reply to Father. He looked at the inlaid ceiling and the four walls and floor made of the eerie pale marble and pretended he was someplace else. The palace audio system was still in use that day. Like all modern systems, it used directed beams of sound, and if Father moved himself a few inches in the antechamber he would hear a different stream of music. At first he was amused by this bit of technology we no longer have on the frontier, but after an hour of shifting about his hard perch the changing sound only gave Father a headache.

Many more hours passed. Through the chamber's high, solitary window crept less and less sunlight as the evening came on and the shadows grew longer. Outside, an orange sun was setting on the smoggy city. No one came into the room to summon either waiting man. A couple of the emperor's Canadian Guardsmen drifted in and out of the antechamber, talking to each other in their throaty version of Syntalk. When Father called to them, using vocabulary he knew they would recognize, they made filthy gestures to him rather than attempt to give a civil answer. A third man—obviously a courier from the Senate, because he carried a bundle of documents bearing the seal of that august body—entered the room, and he too was made to sit on the polished stone bench with Father.

At dusk a group of six Canadians emerged from the interior maze and approached the three men on the bench. Without warning or pronouncement of any sort, one of them drew his pistol and shot the courier with a smart bullet that swirled about the interior of the unfortunate man's skull before it exploded. Father would describe it to me as "a nasty barbarian's round, nothing like a regular Pan-Polarian soldier would use." Blood and gore splattered everywhere, across the white marble floor, onto the white walls, and onto Father and the other man. The papers the unlucky man had been carrying fell onto the floor and sopped up a portion of the flowing puddle of red.

Father jumped to his feet, but the Guardsmen pointed their weapons at him and motioned for him to sit. "Nah, Greatfader, nah," they said till he again took his place on the bloody bench. They dragged the unfortunate messenger's body into an adjoining hallway, leaving a trail of smeared gore behind them. The right side of Father's face and his pristine white officer's dress uniform were covered with the same red mess. The man on his left, the self-proclaimed olive farmer, remained seated and kept his eyes fixed straight in front of him during the entire atrocity.

"This is madness!" shouted Father after the guards. "The emperor will hear of this!"

He would have then left the palace if there had not been armed men posted at the room's exits.

A few moments later, the Canadians and several of the regular City Guardsmen, one of them an officer, reentered the chamber. The officer was berating the northmen and went so far as to slap one of them on his shiny helmet. The great lumbering Canadians hung their heads and looked as sorrowful as schoolboys caught talking out of turn by the headmaster.

"That was the wrong one, you cabbage heads!" the officers yelled at them. "That was a bloody messenger from the Senate! You know: papers? Carry papers?" he said, and pantomimed the act of carrying paper documents under his arm. The Canadians looked at him in uncomprehending passivity. "You damned savages don't know anything!" he concluded.

The Canadians pointed to Father and to the olive farmer. They were asking without speaking: "Which one, then?"

"One is the posh you were supposed to whack and the other is some idiot general from the boondocks," said the officer. "Who can tell the difference?"

"We could kill them both," suggested one of the City Guardsmen.

"In time, we might," said the officer. "The emperor wants to speak to the idiot general first. Your hands, gentlemen," he said to Father and the other man.

The officer boldly grabbed a hand from each man and examined their palms.

"See here!" protested Father. "I am General Peter Justice Black—"

"Your name's not worth dirt here, old man," said the officer. "Shut up, or we'll give you something worth complaining about. See here," he said to his companions as he held up Father's palm, "this big-mouthed, sun-burnt chap has got paws like a lobster. I'll wager he's pitched camp from here to north China. Drilled with the range finder and rifle all the live-long day. This is our general. This other sod, old rosy fingers, he's the one we want."

At that a Guardsman stepped forward and dispatched the man beside Father with a single conventional bullet in the heart. The Guardsmen dragged his body away as they had the courier's, leaving Father sitting between two pools of blood and thinking he was having an insane dream.

The dusk turned to night. The slanted light coming through the high window disappeared, and the general sat on the bench alone. Some Canadians came and went from the palace's inner apartments; once, when they espied Father sitting by himself amid the blood, they laughed and drew a finger across their throats.

My father died his first death as he sat there waiting for the end to come from the shadows at the edges of the white room. His years of self-discipline, his military acclaim, and the strength of his good right arm were of no use to him there. He had confronted eternity many times before on the battlefield; then he had held his energy weapon in his hand and his comrades were about him. In the most dangerous straits he had always felt he would decide what would happen to himself. "Let the devils have at me," he had thought back then. "I may die or I may kill; but either way the bastards will not see the back of Peter Black." In the antechamber he was less than the flies buzzing through the slanted light beams before they were devoured by the palace's mechanical insect predators. The guards could murder him as easily as they took a sip of water or stepped across the floor. His unusable strength and courage in that moment of utter hopelessness only served to make Father yet more ridiculous. He felt a pain in his chest that was like a missile going into him as the Guardsman's bullet had gone into the man who sat beside him. While he continued to sit in the darkness, Father's mouth slowly came open and his limbs became heavy, so heavy he thought he would not be able to move himself ever again.

After midnight the City Guardsman officer and his men appeared in the chamber and told Father to leave.

"The emperor is in bed," he said. "Come back tomorrow, Grandpa. He'll have plenty of time for you then."

The officer and his men laughed at Father when the old man pulled himself onto his benumbed legs and fell to his hands and feet as he struggled toward the outside. The servants and I met him in the park, and hired a taxi to carry Father to the home of his legitimate wife. Propriety kept me from entering his house. Helen and I took lodging at a nearby inn, while Medus stayed with his master. From our second-story room we could see the outside lights burning in the peristyle around the garden behind Father's little house. In the small hours before dawn we saw his two legitimate sons come through the deserted streets to visit his bedside. When the sun had nearly risen, the wealthy fuel factor Mr. Andrew Golden arrived at the house in a limousine accompanied by four bodyguards. From our vantage point we clearly saw Medus bow to the rich man on the illuminated street and lead him through the front door of Father's house.

In the first hour of daylight the household servants and I drove Father back to the palace in another taxi. Shame prevented him from speaking to us the entire long journey. The first of the merchants from the city's outlying suburbs were moving onto the abandoned city streets that by law are free of commerce through the night because one could travel after curfew in the city only with a special permit.

"They'll be selling generators and bread and old computers in the street bazaars today," I told Father as he leaned against sturdy Medus in the backseat, for there was a weakness in his entire right side. "I promise you will be there to see it."

The City Guardsmen at the gate at once conducted Father into the central palace complex to the throne room in which the emperor awaited. Not only did Father not have to wait on that second day, the guards allowed Medus to assist Father after they had entered the front gate. Father later told me the emperor was lying on a large sofa surrounded by a host of his pretty girls; a small fountain containing red liquid narcotics and powered by a subterranean engine was sending up a steady mushroom of crimson beside his sofa. The room was made to resemble a spot in the jungle that morning, and there were realistic holograms of dense foliage and calling birds all around the emperor. Luke Anthony was amusing himself by ladling the red liquid from the fountain with a crystal bowl; he took only a few sips each time he filled the vessel and splattered the rest on the members of his harem, who had to endure his abuse without making a syllable of protest. The young ruler of the northern world was naked but for the silk sash he had draped across his loins. His hair and body were sprinkled with gold dust that made the young man's tanned body shimmer like a trout in a mountain stream when he moved his muscular limbs.

"General Peter Black," he said to Father, "I know I wanted you to do something for me. I can't remember what."

He told Father to stay in Garden City while he thought of some chore for him to perform. Having reached this decision he raised an imperial hand and sent Father away so the game of humiliating his concubines might continue.

Earlier, before the sun had risen, Mr. Golden the fuel speculator had sent a large sum of money to Jerome Perlman, the creature in charge of the City Guardsmen, thereby securing Father's safety, at least for a while. Within the course of a fortnight, Father's sons had divorced their first wives and married Mr. Golden's plain but available daughters, giving Golden a connection to a family that contained the commander of one of the emperor's field armies. It was a disgraceful bargain, but none of us could, under the circumstances, have thought of a better one.

I was not allowed to attend the weddings. Not that I regret that slight. I was thankful Father's wife let me come to the house in the Field of Heroes and allowed me to tend to the stricken general. She had guessed who I was but endured me if the rest of the legitimate family continued to think I was a servant like Helen and Medus. Her indulgence meant I could feed Father and change his bedclothes and not be turned from the door.

It was during this time of recuperation that Father became the less-aggressive, softer-spoken, and weaker man he would be for the rest of his life. While he recovered from the great fright he had suffered on his first day at the palace, he constantly needed someone at his bedside. Father lay awake most hours of the day and night, repeatedly checking his heartbeat and proclaiming "It is good" or "It is bad." The strange tingling sensation in his right side persisted for months afterward. Sometimes the feeling would become so strong that Father would sit upright in his bed and call for someone to help him. If no one happened to be near him in one of those moments of crisis, Father would cry out in panic that assassins were near. The physicians said his psychological nature had become unbalanced and they saw no chance for improvement until Father's state of reason had been restored. Helen declared that the doctors knew nothing about medicine and said Father's blood was running too hot through his brain; she showed me how to put cool wet cloths on his forehead to relieve the fever inside him. Whether her folk methods helped him or not, I cannot say. I do know I took great comfort in doing something for him, and in being close to Father's trembling body when he needed me.

"Justa," he whispered to me one night when I was seated next to his bed and holding his hand, "you are my last loyal soldier."

He must have thought I was asleep, and did not later mention to me he had said anything so tender.

A priest of the Lady of Flowers or Sophia sect, a man whom Father had known when both men were young troopers in the East, came to visit Father at the house in his time of sickness. The old soldier sat with Father and fanned him while he told him of how the goddess, who was partly the ancient Great Mother and partly the Virgin Mary and partly a nature goddess, would restore the health of those suffering in this world, if only they believed in her. In his anguished state of mind Father could not resist any kindness offered to him, and there was something in that gentlest and silliest of the new religions that promised hope to our hopeless general. Before any of us in the household were aware of a transformation in the old soldier, Father had become a devoted follower of the new cult. He took the razor from Medus's kit and with his own hands shaved the crown of his head to make the round tonsure that is the distinctive mark of Sophia's priests. To perform the sect's daily rites Father would rise from his bed clad in a long white linen robe and take up the cithara and the rattle to play his part in the slow shuffles and equally slow dances that somehow please the composite goddess. The formerly all-business soldier moved through the rituals chanting in unison with his old friend: "O Sophia, goddess of the green reed, sister and wife of the universe, mother of us all, restore me as you restored him." He made a ridiculous sight chanting and swaying in his long white gown. I as well appreciated that performing such nonsense got him from his bed and back among the living. The religion promised a rebirth in a new life after the body perished. Father chose to continue living on the chance he might see that new life someday, even if he had to spend his present one dwelling beneath the threat of imminent death.

There were prices to be paid for the improvements in Father's condition. We never again ate meat at family meals, as Sophia is said to want her followers to eat only fruits and vegetables. Besides that, no one in Father's household could use foul language, not even if we stubbed a toe or accidentally bit our tongues while eating. We had to maintain a calm, inoffensive demeanor, lest we offend the goddess' chaste sensibilities. As for strong drink, a part of dinner Father had formerly greatly favored, we could still use wine and beer to honor Sophia in certain rites or when the water was bad—as it thankfully was in many parts of the world—but otherwise Sophia and Father insisted we shun anything that could induce intoxication, for while under the spell of Bacchus one might forget Sophia's kindly laws. The most disconcerting change for me was Father's insistence that we in his household participate in the same ceremonies he did. To my maid Helen the Lady of the Flowers was another god in a world that offered many, many deities; she performed the rituals gladly. Her husband Medus did as the master and his wife wanted, but I would get the giggles when I had to put on my diaphanous ceremonial robes and shuffle behind Father chanting, "O Sophia, you have put together all the world has rendered asunder. Put together my heart."

"You will never see paradise if you keep doing that, Justa," Father would warn me when I laughed during the holy ceremonies.

He did not become angry with me, for anger was another emotion that disturbed the goddess.

"I am very sorry, sir," I would tell him. "You see, every time I walk in front of the sacred lanterns in this obscene outfit, I look as naked as a streetwalker. Your fellow worshipers can see all of me."

"There are only chaste eyes at our ceremonies," he told me. "You should not be presumptuous. The educated need paradise as much as anyone."

"I will do better, sir," I promised him, and I would bite my lips together to keep from laughing again. I still felt uncomfortable because I could tell the other old men in Father's rites looked upon me while entertaining thoughts that surely would have put a whole legion of chaste goddesses out of sorts.

Father prayed to the East, the direction from which true wisdom is supposed to come, each morning and evening while he was in the capital. His pleas and his devotion to the distant Sophia seemed to do us some good. The emperor forgot Father was in Garden City, and for many months he left us undisturbed.

V.

AD 2293

Thirteen days after Mr. Golden's first letter came to us on Mars a second group of his messengers carried another letter from their loquacious master into our camp inside the mining tunnels. This missive informed Father that Abdul Selin had indeed declared himself emperor of all Pan-Polaria and that the Army of North America had gone over to him. Mr. Golden wrote:

"'Unfortunately, Selin will reach Garden City and the military fleets at San Diego and Tampico and thence cross to Western Europe and collect the forces there before you can take action; that is, I mean to say, my beloved General Black, before we can take action. There is much to behold in the capital, where the remaining members of the emperor's City Guardsmen are slipping away in the night to join Selin's forces in the north. The cowardly pretender John Chrysalis goes from door to door in the palace seeking anyone who might stand with him. He is still trying to buy supporters at this late hour. They say he has offered money to those senators having contacts within the army. Everyone has refused to have anything to do with him; even after Chrysalis murdered two prominent men to terrify the city's populace, the people have refused to acknowledge his rule. We in the city will have a merry spectacle when that brute Selin gets his paws upon this dainty one. Thank the gods that you, my true emperor, are safe on another planet. Now you can fly swiftly to the Middle East, your old arena of operations, so you can there gather your forces to oppose Selin after he has disposed of Chrysalis.

"'As you have perhaps heard, Claude Whiteman, the commander of the divisions in northernmost Europe, has also proclaimed himself emperor. He has not started to march into other areas. The metal infection is so great in his portion of the world, he no longer has the use of computers or airplanes. My sources tell me that Selin has sent a letter to Whiteman proposing that the new pretender declare for him, and in return Selin has promised to make Whiteman his successor.'"

I had been reading the letter to Father. I stopped at this point and asked, "How can Mr. Golden know what Selin wrote?"

"He says he has sources," suggested Father.

"No," I said, "he was told. He is conspiring with Selin. With General Whiteman, too, I expect. He is playing the three of you 'emperors' against each other."

"You may be correct," said Father. "I should give some thought to that, whenever I feel better. This is in the Lady of Flowers's hands. If she lets me clear my mind and gives me the signs . . . Now I need your and the Lady's help to get up, Justa."

Father had been in his bed since observing the troops' morning exercises. Groups of soldiers came by our house to chant his name and show their support while he rested. As had happened on the day the first letter from Mr. Golden came, I expected the men had been bribed by the couriers to make shows of support. None of their activity moved

Father much. He continued to sleep fitfully, when he could, and I hoped he would awake refreshed and feeling strong enough to resist Mr. Golden's pleas.

Toward the sixteenth hour of the day a disastrous event changed the course of Father's life. A group of soldiers brought to our home in the tunnel wall a battered man Father's troopers had captured while he was attempting to approach our house from the rear. From the man's bright new armor and his clean clothes as well as the nanomachines that had infected his weapon he clearly was newly arrived from Garden City and was not one of our dusty Martian veterans. Our men had discovered on the man's person an air rifle and a vial of poison into which he could dip the darts his gun fired. After repeated beatings, the captured man had confessed he had come from Senator Chrysalis. This confession did not deceive Father. Father immediately realized this sort of violence could only come from Abdul Selin and his clan of sun worshipers.

"He's already trying to eliminate me!" pronounced Father. "This man has brought an infection that will trap us on this lifeless planet when it spreads. What choice do I have now?!"

In a fit of panic Father allowed the soldiers to hoist him onto their shoulders and take him to the exercise dome before I had opportunity to put a few words of reason in his ear. On that open ground Father mounted a makeshift dais made of overturned fuel drums and gave a speech to a throng that had rushed from the rest of the camp to hear him. He then said the words other men driven by ambition or fear have said when they began their attempt upon absolute power. He reminded his men they were citizens of a great empire and were heirs to a tradition that had lasted two and a half centuries. Mong, Rogers, Navarro the Younger, the brave Svenska, and Pius Anthony had been Pan-Polarians, orated Father, and every man within the sound of his voice was likewise a member of that same glorious Empire. The whole world cringed before their power. Then, as many would-be rulers among the Pan-Polarians tend to do, Father spoke of the beloved and long-departed Republic. Someday, he said, we would know the freedoms our ancestors enjoyed; someday, he promised, we would again be ruled by the Senate and not by a single man. (He did not speak the obvious: that an empire divided by faction, race, class, language, religion, and the competing ambitions of the elite would plunge into a hundred different civil wars the day the emperor's power diminished. The emperor's absolute power alone holds the Pan-Polarian realm together. The lowliest, most illiterate soldier present knew this; still everyone applauded when Father said the magic word "freedom," though none present could have said what exactly freedom was.) Father said to the men he and they faced a long struggle against implacable enemies. He appealed to the lingering nativism of some of his European and American soldiers by reminding them that his rivals Selin and Whiteman were foreigners from Africa. (Of course nearly every member of his audience on the exercise ground was at least partly of some other race than could have been found among the original Pan-Polarians. Most of them understood so little of the English Father was speaking that they did not understand what he was saying until their officers translated the general's words for them. No less a personage in the Martian mining force than Harriman, Father's second-in-command, was an African and a cousin to General Whiteman. Those things too went unsaid.)

"My dear martial comrades," Father told them, "as long as this good hand shall hold a weapon"—he then held up a trembling conventional rifle—"you will have a champion in me!"

Father wanted next to tell the men the anecdote about the crocodile. Before he could, some of the men near him began to shout in unison a slogan that in a few days' time would be on every wall in the mining tunnels: "Black is the best. The African is worse. The worst is White."

Some of the chanters bore Father from the makeshift stand on their shoulders at the moment he was about to retell how he had used the gun he was holding on the scaly monster of the Nile. Father so enjoyed being carried about by his soldiers that he set aside the tale and waved to the crowd of men as they threw their helmets into the air and cheered. For the time being, he forgot he was an old man and let the men tote him about till past his mealtime and the hour of his afternoon nap.

I watched them from the edge of the dusty arena and asked myself if I was the only one in the station who understood how hopeless our situation was. A little learning, I understand all these years later, makes everyone more than a little vain; others, probably Father himself, knew our fate as well as I did. Everyone there marched and sang and was happy anyway.

VI.

AD 2284–2285

The emperor left Father waiting in Garden City for more than a year. The general's health improved during this long interval of doing nothing beyond lying about his house and worshiping his precious Sophia. He became positive again in regards to his future and spoke to me of returning to the East as soon as Luke Anthony gave him approval to leave.

This long stay was my first time in the capital city. Helen and I moved into a tenement building well to the north of Father's house and there slept nights among the city's numerous poor. I was disappointed on this my first visit to find so few of what the history texts would have called the true Pan-Polarians dwelling in the capital of the Pan-Polarian Empire. The bustling city of then over forty million souls seemed to me to match the multinational society of the army, except that the capital was constructed upon a much larger scale, as creating citizens is a simpler matter than making soldiers. One could walk up the fifteen stories of our building and pass through fifteen different nations, none of which were North American, for Garden City, the mother of the northern world, had drawn all her children to the shadows of her mile-high slopes. In the narrow alleyways of our neighborhood I could see no one who might have been a descendant of Darko or even Pius Anthony. There were few thereabouts who could have even spoken to Darko in words the emperor of long ago would have comprehended.

I actually understate the situation: in our tenement there were a total of 1,020 people who came from twenty-nine different lands. We might as well have been in Baghdad or Calcutta, because Garden City looked and sounded the same as any other large city in the world, including those outside the Empire. In the bazaars on our street there were thousands of small-time merchants dressed in the bright orange-and-red synthetic cloth the poor wear everywhere, and they were selling every useless article a person from anywhere could possibly want. I could buy translucent plastic jewelry from the Far East or contraband handheld message machines from Ethiopia or leaves from South America men chewed like cud to make themselves happy for a few hours or strange North African fetishes made to resemble human babies which were sacrificed in lieu of real infants to the savage god Minit.

Everything in the noisy open-air markets was for sale, including the people. Hawkers barking to the passing crowds sold prostitutes of both sexes and of any size, color, or age the client might desire. The whores of all nations crowding the narrow street wore the blond wigs that mark their profession even if the wearer's skin is jet black. (This, I think, is the street's sarcastic comment upon the original Pan-Polarians from North America.) Most of the foreign children of mother Garden City could only look at the various goods for sale and pray for the day they could purchase them, for they were on the dole, and their meager allowances bought them no more than some highly processed food in a tube and a place to sleep. The lucky ones among the poor found a niche in the street economy, the very lucky found something legal to do in that same marketplace, and the rest lived for the gory spectacles the emperor staged for them in the city's sports arenas now that television rarely broadcast anything other than snow, even when the electrical generators were working. I should confess that Helen and I had an easier life during our stay than did our neighbors in the tenement; we had a little of Father's money and the time to walk to the public baths near the city's central plaza and the cash to pay for the luxury of cleaning ourselves and using the toilets there while our neighbors had to dump their waste in the open sewers that lined the streets, a fact of life in Garden City that made the city smell worse than it looked or sounded.

One morning during our stay in the city, shouts of anger and the clattering racket of rocks ricocheting off stone walls awakened us in our upper-story quarters. Upon looking out, we saw the street rabble had gathered before a fishmonger's shop and were tearing the cobblestones from the roadway and heaving them upon a shapeless heap of dirty rags lying before that shabby place of business, which was merely a stall with a curtain drawn across its open front. Helen and I dressed and ran down the stairwell to see what was taking place. The crowd parted for us, for I always wore the whitest linen outfits and had embroidered hems on my skirts, which made the common folk think I was some manner of nobility, given the soiled and lice-ridden garments everyone else in the neighborhood had to wear. When they had given way to us, I found at my feet a body—rather the bloody fragments of a body—that had once belonged to a small dark woman with elaborately braided hair.

"She's an enchantress!" someone in the crowd informed me.

"She cursed the fish!" an Arab woman told me.

I explained to them, in my overly rational manner and in my unfamiliar version of Syntalk, there was no such thing as an enchantress and they had stoned to death a young woman for no reason.

"She has the idols upon her!" exclaimed the Arab woman. She reached into the gory mess lying before us and produced a calf's ear that had hung about the dead woman's neck.

"See?!" she said as she held the pitiful object before me.

The crowd nodded in agreement, and at once they began overturning the baskets of fish the late witch had supposedly cast a spell upon. They stomped upon the slippery haddock and bonito, some of which were yet alive and flopped about under their feet. When the mob had reduced the fishmonger's wares to sticky and disgusting bits of bone and fins, they tried to set fire to the heap of offal they had created. They found it was all too wet to take the flame, so they pushed the crushed fish and the poor dead woman into a single heap they shoved into the open sewer, where they left it all for the city's overworked policemen to sort out.

Never, not in the most remote places Father had taken me, had I seen behavior that was more barbarous than this completely unnecessary carnage that took place in the heart of the capital. The rough-and-tumble life I knew in the army camps seemed genteel by comparison. In the army there was purpose and order. Men therein at least respected the power of violence, as they knew it could destroy them as well. Among the capital city's citizens violence was something that interrupted the tedium of mere survival; it was neither contemplated beforehand nor afterward remembered. The Arab woman told me with a shrug that other witches and wizards had been killed in the neighborhood and more would die in the future. She advised me I should not give the incident any thought.

I heard it told many times during my time in the capital that food came from the north country, gold and other precious metals from Siberia, culture from Britain, manufactured goods from Japan, soldiers from the Boers, servants from Central America, the new gods from the Middle East, but leaders came exclusively from the prominent families of Garden City. Two months after arriving in the city with Father I learned I had not yet beheld any of these leaders because these "real" Pan-Polarians—the ones owning long, ancient names and even longer lineages that reached back to republican times—lived in the airy suburbs above the city or in the more remote estates on the slopes of the surrounding hills. One saw these leaders of half the world only when the Senate was in session or when they came down to the city in the midst of their flocks of servants to attend an athletic exhibition in the Field of Diversions. The first time

I saw them coming down to one of Luke Anthony's grand shows I knew I was looking at the very characters I had read of in Overton's plays and Catman's lyric poems: pampered women wearing their hair piled high atop their heads in turrets of gold and brown and dressed in nearly transparent cloth that was programmed to change colors every ten seconds and who had nothing better to do than gossip and flirt while they hung on the arms of patrician gentlemen wearing big golden rings and leading scores of bodyguards. Never had I seen flesh so white or beheld human skin accented by so much red lipstick and rouge as I saw upon these real Pan-Polarians on their way to watch men fight to the death for their entertainment. On their necks glistened much of the gold of five continents. Most of the rest of the world's treasure was hidden in secret provincial bank accounts under their celebrated names.

"They have never dug a trench nor fought in the field," was Father's judgment upon the real Pan-Polarians as we watched them line up beside us outside the Field of Diversions. He told me they were not worth gawking at.

Later in my life I can appreciate that the real Pan-Polarians were not as worthless or as idle as Father judged them to be. These elegant people were busy in their beautiful homes writing thousands of screenplays that were so lovely they could never find a producer or director, let alone an audience. They composed millions of poems so fine no one has ever read them. They created mountains of learned treatises upon science and the management of business and government, but their efforts in nonfiction were no more appreciated than was the imaginative literature they had made. The real Pan-Polarians were particularly talented when expounding upon the law, which was an interesting subject to treat during an era of tyranny when there was no law other than the will of the emperor. Yet they filled entire libraries with the mountains of learned treatises they composed upon the subject. Whenever they were not writing or debating, the real Pan-Polarians were conspiring: the women at love, the men at making money, and both sexes were wildly successful in their secretive ventures. The wealth and promiscuity of the Empire's upper classes were the twin wonders of the contemporary world—wonders matched in their magnitude only by the cowardice the same people displayed each time they ran up against the capricious whims of the absolute ruler.

At my first combat show in the Field of Diversions my Father and his legitimate family sat on cushioned seats close to the action with the other real Pan-Polarians while Helen and I had to go high into the crowded plebeian section. From our high ground we could look across the enclosed space of artificial turf on the arena's floor and down onto the emperor's box, which was girded by City Guardsmen and was in the center of the seats on the other side of the stadium. Despite some new girth he had added in the three years since I had seen him last, Luke Anthony remained the handsomest man I had ever seen. Most of the well-born young women seated around him were of the same opinion and were trying (in vain) to catch his eye; they were furiously adjusting their dresses so he might catch glimpses of their bodies and ordering their servants to fetch cold goblets of ersatz wine they rubbed against their bosoms to demonstrate how their delicate persons were suffering in the heat of the Mexican sun. The emperor did not turn his head toward any of them. Sitting next to him was his wife—yes, he had a legal wife—one Barbara Crisp Anthony; she was a smallish, nut-brown woman the emperor would exile and execute four years later for committing adultery in the palace, though there was never any proof she had committed any such crime or had ever done anything during their marriage other than meekly obey Luke's often insane demands. Immediately above the emperor and watching tiny Barbara as an owl watches a rabbit was the striking beauty Marcie Angelica, the emperor's favorite concubine. Well known among the common people because she was as tall as most men and had an athlete's square shoulders, Marcie had a cascade of black hair that fell to her waist and had yet blacker eyes, the two of which would have set the back of poor Barbara's head ablaze had they the power to shoot flames.

"They say she has killed men fighting hand to hand," Helen whispered to me of Marcie.

"They have something to say about everything," I answered her.

Despite knowing what he was, I felt a flutter inside me when I looked upon the emperor's ruddy, perfect face and the inverted triangle of his powerful frame. I was nearly eighteen. Like every other young woman present I fantasized for a moment I was the doomed Barbara sitting next to him. Were I in her place, I told myself, my love would be enough to make him change. I knew in my heart I could make him become a decent man. Tens of millions of other women must have felt similar emotions in regard to Luke Anthony during the course of his reign.

The first fighters out of the gates and onto the ankle-deep fake turf that day were a series of seven criminals condemned to die for the entertainment of the 180,000 watching them from the stands. Two of them appeared to have had some athletic training and knew how to handle their anachronistic edged weapons; the other five could only wildly flail the air around them when it came their turns to fight, turns which consequently passed very swiftly, for they quickly took the fatal blow while the crowd ate roasted sunflower seeds and mocked the combatants' inadequacies. The worst performer in the lot was a portly man the master of the games had armed with a section of lead pipe and brass knuckles; he had no notion of how he should defend himself with these implements of street warfare so popular with Garden City's nighttime gangs. He did know some of the wellborn faces in the stands above him. The instant he was released from the gate he ran to the balustrade and called to a man among the spectators. His former friend turned away rather than acknowledge the condemned man. The doomed combatant recognized a dowager in a cluster of elegant ladies; she pretended not to hear when he called her name; she looked to her companions and, a smile fixed upon her face, pretended to have a conversation with the nearest one of them.

"Lucy! Lucy!" the fat man cried. "David!" he called to the man, as his opponent ran toward him.

The other contestant soon cornered the fat man in the curve of the arena wall. The feeble combatant collapsed upon his haunches and screamed aloud for mercy. I closed my eyes while the crowd booed the fat man's cowardly death.

The last two contestants left standing were the two experienced men, both of them carrying a knife and a metal bat. They fought hand to hand for the better part of an hour, wounding each other several times and boring the crowd that had come to see men die, not to hear the clanging of metal on metal. When at last one of them succeeded in battering the other to the ground, the mob called for both of them to die because the men had wearied the gigantic crowd. The emperor obliged the mob and promptly ordered his City Guardsmen to shower the two men with bullets.

Spectacles had always been horrific; even when they had been computer-generated productions they had been frighteningly bloody. Luke Anthony made them real and fatuous at the same time. After the bodies had been dragged away, there appeared two midgets who battled each other with oversized clubs. When they were both dead, a dozen blinded horses were set upon by hungry mountain lions and jaguars. For the finale the emperor had his men push a high carbon filament walkway into the arena from the top of which he shot the wild cats with a hunting rifle. He had a good vantage point atop this artificial hill, and his soldiers drove the beasts toward him with the noise they made from the edge of the arena. As I had learned at Progress, Luke Anthony never had to fire more than once at each animal after he had it within his sights. After the big cats were dead, the game master released tall flightless ostriches from Africa into the arena. Luke Anthony shot them with smart sabots that expanded into crescent-shaped heads that would swiftly slice through the animals' long, narrow necks with horrific effect. The crowd went insane with approval at this grotesque beheading of the confused creatures. Several women yet attempting to impress the emperor clapped with such enthusiasm they knocked their neighbors from their seats.

From where I sat I could see Father complaining to his wife and knew without hearing his words he was declaring it was a disgrace for an emperor to perform in the arena, a place normally reserved for criminals and paid thugs.

"His father, Mathias, would never have done this!" Father would be saying.

My legitimate brothers were situated near Father, their new wives next to them, and they grudgingly nodded to whatever the general was saying. Their hearts were not in their actions or in the gruesome events unfolding before them. The two of them never showed much enthusiasm about anything while Mr. Golden's very wide daughters were nearby. Like most of the real Pan-Polarian men in the Field of Diversions, my half brothers were pleased when the performance was concluded and they and none of the people they knew had perished with the other victims of the afternoon. They would wait to celebrate those happy results until they were in the company of their mistresses, women whom I suspect were much prettier than the daughters of Mr. Golden. But then, nearly any women would be.

A year and a half after Father's terrible day in the palace antechamber, the emperor remembered (or someone reminded him) that the general was in the city. Luke Anthony summoned Father to his presence in one of the gardens on the palace grounds that had been converted to an exercise space. The emperor put aside the epée sword he was fencing with long enough to say to Father, "We need you to go to Britain for us. There is some unpleasantness there."

Having made such an enormous effort to address an affair of state, Luke had a servant wipe the perspiration from his face, and he returned to his training.

The unpleasantness in that distant northern land was a massive rebellion that had begun among the people and had spread to a brigade stationed in the far north of that island province. Another uprising had occurred on the island during the previous year because of a famine, and Jerome Perlman, who ran both the City Guardsmen and the day-to-day operations of the imperial administration, had sent Britain bombers full of napalm to appease her hunger. Rebellious citizens and the land's brutal winters in a time of failing electricity sufficed to make any soldier posted there unhappy in the best of times; in the fourth year of Luke Anthony's rule, someone in government—perhaps the emperor or some of his friends, but must likely Jerome Perlman himself—had helped himself to the army payroll, leaving the soldiers unpaid for five long months and unable to feed their families or to buy charcoal to warm their homes after their generators had ceased to run. As Father oft said in his characteristically understated way: "Even good troops get out of sorts when they see their children starve." The soldiers in Britain positioned immediately south of Edinburgh had now gotten so out of sorts they had killed most of their officers and were pillaging the nearby farms to support themselves.

To suppress this revolt, the emperor went so far as to equip Father with a bundle of letters bearing the imperial seal. "We are promising them they'll get paid," explained Mr. Perlman, to whom had fallen the task of explaining the details to Father before he set out across the North Atlantic. No additional forces or money could be spared for the mission. There was trouble in the Far East, as there was always in that portion of the Empire, Mr. Perlman related to us to explain the paltry resources he could give us.

"You may have to read the letters to them, General Black. I doubt any of them can read proper English anymore, though, ironically, that is where the language originated, don't you know?" were Mr. Perlman's last words of advice to Father before showing the general the palace door.

Father, Medus, Helen, and I—our entire expedition force—traveled across Mexico to Tampico, where we took a diesel-powered ship across the ocean to Cornwall, and from there rode a truck north to Scotland, the homeland of the northern rebellion. To a woman like myself, who had spent most of her life in the sunny Middle East, England was a wet, cold land of bogs and fogs, the most inhospitable land I had ever seen, or so it was until I saw Scotland. Some cleared farmland exists on the southern part of that second nation. There some hardy grain flourishes and the natives raise some excellent livestock. Immediately north of that same region one finds the smoke-filled provincial capital Edinburgh, the most aromatic city for its size I have ever visited. The rest of the nation is a fen of green thickets in the summer and a block of ice in winter, and the farther north we traveled, the worse the cold weather became. What exactly the mutinous soldiers were pillaging from this frozen countryside that was of any use to them was a mystery to us. A second mystery was why the Empire was defending this wasteland when the only people who wanted it already dwelt there.

By the time we arrived at Edinburgh the mutineers had abandoned their siege of the city and were too sick with hunger to travel farther south or to continue fighting. Two well-paid and loyal brigades remained on the island, one stationed at York and the other at London. Upon arriving in Britain, Father had ordered the provincial governor to use these loyal troops to seal the rebellious legion in the northern wastes without engaging them in battle, thereby assuring that the mutineers would either surrender or starve to death in the cold. A final brutal snowstorm struck before we arrived in Scotland and had prodded the famished men into making the obvious choice. They meekly gave themselves up to Father the day he rode into their camp at the head of a dozen cavalrymen he had collected in the south.

Before his terrifying experience inside the antechamber in Garden City my father would have immediately arrested the leaders of the revolt and put them to death; next the old General Black would have had the men in the ranks draw lots, and he would have executed one in every ten of them. Nearly dying had changed Father. He walked unannounced and unescorted into the heart of the rebels' camp, climbed the crest of an earthen wall, and holding up the letters from Luke Anthony he spoke to the men in the thunderous orator's voice gentlemen soldiers learn as schoolboys.

"Citizens of Pan-Polaria," he said to them in a pidgin Syntalk they would understand, "I am General Peter Black. I have come from the emperor, the father of the nations. Like any good father, our emperor is saddened to learn that some of his children have strayed from his family. So great is his love for you who have disappointed him he has sent me across the world to tell you this: come back into the army, return to your posts, and no one will be punished. I swear by all the good things that remain in the universe that his word—"

A soldier holding an assault rifle in his hands ran from the crowd that had gathered around Father. The general stopped in midsentence to heed him.

"We killed the other toffs, and now I'm going—," began the soldier, but his comrades tackled him from behind and disarmed him.

"Let him up! Let him up!" Father commanded. "Do not harm him!"

Father hurried to the astonished soldier and put a hand on the rebel's shoulders so he could look directly into the man's eyes.

"My friend, you whom the goddess Sophia loves," said Father, "I am only a man, as you are. Yes, you could kill me. Any one of you could strike me down any time you wish," he proclaimed to the others. "Should you do so, the emperor will send more men in my stead, men who will bring armed divisions marching behind them. The emperor will send as many men as many times as it will take to destroy you. A far better course for you would be to negotiate a settlement with me. Do this and you will not bring a dire fate upon yourselves and your families."

To a man, the mutineers thought Father had fallen to them from heaven. They selected a delegation from among their three thousand members to confer with the general while Father sent a messenger to London with orders to bring food from the imperial warehouses. A handful of surviving officers crept from their hiding places in the besieged city of Edinburgh after they learned of Father's arrival. They would be of no utility to us, as the rebellious men refused to take orders from them. The rebels told Father their former leaders had stolen what little money had arrived in their district, and that they, the rebels, would rather die than follow such thieves again. After three long weeks of talking and waiting, the brigade commander to our south in York sent us some money and twenty-three truckloads of food. With full stomachs, the mutineers became more open to Father's demands; they agreed to elect a delegation to return with us to Garden City and there make their complaints directly to Luke Anthony. To our regret, Father assented to this plan before he knew what shape this delegation would take. The rebellion's leaders returned to Father's tent the morning after their final conference and announced they had chosen a group of no less than five hundred men to make the long journey to North America in our company.

"Why not send the whole bloody brigade?!" Father asked, showing the rebels a little of the old Peter Black's anger.

The men replied it was all five hundred or nobody. The various groups within their ranks did not trust each other—the Boers did not feel secure about the Turks, those with Latin blood hated the local Celtic soldiers, and so on—and so they had chosen someone from every ethnic group and every religion to give fair representation to everyone concerned. Seeing no other solution, Father reluctantly promised them they could travel with us.

"This cannot end well," he told me in confidence. "The emperor is likely to see them as an invading force of assassins rather than a delegation. He is apt to slaughter them for rebelling and me for not punishing them. We will have to send messages ahead to make our way smoother, Justa," he said, and ran his hand across his bald head. "Perhaps Mr. Golden can bribe someone again."

"He will want something in return, sir," I said. "Your army in Turkey buys coal oil, like every other military unit does. In the event of a shortage, the commander can make an auxiliary contract with the fuel factors. You are the commander, Mr. Golden is a factor, and we could have a shortage. . . ."

For the first time since he had been stricken in the palace, Father laughed aloud.

"Justa," he said, "you have been too long in Garden City. You now think as they do. Whom will Mr. Golden contact on our behalf?"

"He will know without our telling him," I said. "I expect it will be this Mr. Perlman; he seems to have his finger in whatever business the emperor is doing his best to neglect."

We dispatched an encrypted message to Garden City and began our long trip south with the five hundred soldiers at the first sign of the spring thaw. Because the men's transports were no longer operable, they were afoot, and as some of the roads in Britain had not been maintained for many years and were that spring rivers of mud, our return journey took much longer than the trip north, which had been on the frozen ground of winter. We could not obtain a ship to carry us directly to Mexico and had to sail across the Atlantic to North Carolina. By a lucky stroke of fortune Father heard from a merchant we met on the highway in northern Alabama that a farmer in the vicinity of Gadsden had captured an enormous boar in a pit. Out of curiosity, we made a detour to the hill country and inspected the peculiar animal, which was being kept inside a cage the farmer and several of his neighbors had fashioned out of cables and steel bars. The bristly creature was as large as a cow, and had enormous tusks growing in curls that reached above its eyes. It was a creature from myth, I commented to Father, though in fact it was a product of the vast wilderness that decades of neglect had created in southern Appalachia. While we examined it, the wild pig's great size and fearsome looks combined with my mention of mythology to inspire a plan in my mind.

"What are you going to do with it, sir?" I asked the farmer claiming ownership of the boar.

He was a simple man whose pride was greatly swollen by the attention he was getting. Hundreds of travelers, he boasted, had stopped in the past fortnight to have a look at his prize.

"I shall sell it to the fellow what runs the spectacles in Birmingham," he said. "He pays top price for big pigs."

"In Birmingham?!" I said. "You should sell it to the emperor. He will put it in the Field of Diversions in Garden City. He'll pay more than any small-timer here in Alabama. Stay put, please."

I ran to our lorry and got one of the letters Father had carried to Britain. I stuck a bit of the red sealing wax over the mouth of its envelope and presented this note to the illiterate farmer as a commission from the emperor giving General Black the right to collect any interesting animal specimens he might find. The farmer and his comrades gasped when they saw the seal on the creamy white paper.

"The emperor will dispatch a messenger with money to pay you as soon as we reach Garden City," I told him. "He is a wonderful man—and one day he will be named a god. He will be very pleased with you."

The bumpkin insisted we take the giant boar with us that very day. Some of the soldiers from Britain loaded the beast's cage onto a railroad car. The load was so heavy we needed twenty-eight men to heft the creature onto the flatcar it would ride all the way to Mexico.

"Whatever did you want that thing for?" Father wanted to know after we too had boarded the railway train. "The farmers hereabouts say it has eaten men. Right down to the marrow, they say. We can't use it as food. Even our mutineers won't touch meat that's been fed on human flesh."

"Luke Anthony will love it," I said. "We'll feed it apples and corn cakes five times a day; it cannot get too big."

"Why would the emperor want it?" asked Father. "The thing's a damned pig! It's nearly as ugly as that damned crocodile I killed in Egypt."

"Honestly, sir," I said as we rode along, "don't you see? Luke is going to slay it in the arena. The rumor mill says he is wild about ancient myths. Do you remember how Hercules slew the Erymanthian boar?"

"You are running ahead of me," said my father. "What do this Hercules chap and that strange-sounding pig have to do with young Luke?"

The word humming about Garden City at the time of our departure to Britain was Luke Anthony had developed a fascination with the supposed son of Zeus and Alcmene. Insiders in his court whispered about the capital that when the emperor exercised among the athletes he kept on the palace grounds, he sometimes carried a club as Hercules had. Since this particular aspect of Luke's behavior was at this juncture of his life a private vice and not one of the public outrages he would later practice, it was a subject that caused much laughter in the better houses of the city's suburbs. I am discomforted to think I may have, in a small way, nudged the emperor in the direction of his later excesses when I directed Father to give him the huge boar. At the time, I thought the pig ruse was the cleverest thing I had ever done, especially when I urged Father to send another message ahead to inform Luke Anthony of our magnificent find.

A company of City Guardsmen met us at the railway station the day we entered the capital. They loaded the creature onto an enormous truck that conveyed the boar to the Field of Diversions a full three days before all five hundred of our party reached the city. The emperor immediately received Father in one of the dining chambers in the heart of the palace and allowed the vast delegation from Britain to camp in one of the city parks, where he provided them with food and drink. At the reception he gave Father, the one occasion I was allowed to accompany the general into the emperor's presence, Luke Anthony could speak of nothing other than the gigantic pig.

"He is as big as a room!" he exclaimed to Father. "Are there more in Britain like him?"

"To tell the whole story, my lord," said Father, "the beast comes from Alabama. However, speaking of Britain, my lord, these men I brought with me come from the unit that, as you know, I was sent . . . How should I put this? They are, so to speak, from Britain. That is to say, they are from the relevant portion of the island of Britain, that part you sent me to, you know, see about, my lord."

"Yes, yes, yes," said the emperor, waving away the topic. "Let's get to the point: where in Alabama did it come from?"

"In Alabama, my emperor?" asked Father, who had presumed the emperor might want to discuss the British rebellion.

"Where exactly did you get this wonderful boar?" demanded Luke Anthony.

"North of Gadsden, my lord," said Father. "A farmer caught it in a pit up in the mountains."

"A thousand men to the woods north of Gadsden," Luke commanded his chamberlain. "The beast may have a mate!"

"The situation in Britain, my lord—," began Father.

"I will deal with that, Black," said the emperor. "You can go. Those people you brought with you can go too," he added, referring to Medus and myself. "Aren't you supposed to be in Asia somewhere?"

"In Turkey, at Van City, my lord," said Father. "I command the Scythia Divisions and—"

"Boring, boring, boring," said Luke Anthony, and covered his ears. "Go back there. Well done, however. Well done indeed. I'll have to give you a title or something. Now, please clear the room. I have an exhibition to plan."

His chief concubine, Marcie Angelica, acted as a sort of household manager in the palace. It was she who held out her palms to show us she was pushing us from the opulent room that had seascape holograms projected on its walls and the interior of a saltwater aquarium on its ceiling. This was the one time in my life I was able to see her at close range. I could discern at that distance she was not as beautiful as I had thought she was in the arena. She did have ivory white teeth and hair that glowed as if it were somehow polished. I was put off to find Marcie's face was all sharp angles; there was nothing round or soft in her features, despite the layer of powder she put upon herself each morning. She hissed at us in Syntalk to move. That and her peculiar masculine build sufficed to hasten us from Luke Anthony's vicinity.

After six months of deep thought the emperor did finally get around to dealing with the five hundred mutineers from Britain camped on his doorstep. He told the group he would see they were paid, eventually. Then he told them to start walking back, and perhaps they should think of getting a ship when they came to the ocean. Since someone had to be blamed for what had happened or else people would blame him, Luke Anthony decided the onus should fall upon Mr. Perlman, the City Guardsmen's commander. I do not know enough of this Mr. Perlman to judge his soul. My rule is that in Garden City one should always believe the worst one hears about others. Jerome Perlman stole money and murdered innocent people, much as everyone else in government did. Had he not murdered and stolen he would have perished long before he did. History, that perennial liar, states that the delegation from Britain demanded the unfortunate man's death. I was in the city at the time; I can tell they were in no position to demand anything of Luke Anthony. The emperor alone decided his former friend's unhappy fate. He had heard through his informers that in a drunken moment Mr. Perlman had once spoken of overthrowing the emperor and installing his own son on the throne. The fool should never have been in his cups among other City Guardsmen;

being their leader, he should have known the ranks of his men were full of secret agents who traded loose words for gold. The emperor gave Mr. Perlman to the Guardsmen he had led for nearly five years, and the men bade farewell to their former commander by taking him into the streets and tearing him to pieces the way hunting dogs tear apart a hare. The hour after that task was completed, the emperor sent another group of soldiers to call upon Mr. Perlman's son, whom they found hiding beneath a bush in the family garden before they sent him to that place wherein each of us may rightfully dream of greater glories.

The emperor declared a triumphal parade for himself in the city and would have added the title "the Conqueror of Britain" to his list of honorary names, as he credited himself for defeating the rebellion. Someone in the palace reminded him he had already taken that name the year before when the late Mr. Perlman crushed the previous mutiny. (He would add "Conqueror of Germany" and "Slayer of the Spaniards" for similar slaughters of his own unpaid soldiers before he was through.) To atone for the lack of a new title, he held some games in honor of himself. In the grand finale of the same he killed the giant boar we had brought him. Luke Anthony set the proper scene inside the Field of Diversions for the final denouement: a forest of pine trees was imported from the Rocky Mountains to be posted around the legendary beast, and he engaged a famous actor to recite a poem upon Hercules and the Erymanthian boar while Luke himself stole on tiptoes through the artificial forest armed with an elephant gun on his way to slay the creature. To add some drama to the already overheated scene, a maiden (actually, she was an actress and like all actresses was far from being a maiden) stood before the boar and screamed for some hero to rescue her. No one in the stands seemed to mind that she was not in the original story; this was art, and art cannot lie as long as it remains true to its intentions. Besides, almost none in the crowd had read the original story. Many present could not hear the poet's words recited over the actress's yelps, and most of them were thankful for her strong lungs. The theoretically ferocious boar was staked to the ground and was calmly chewing on some turnips from its trough while the epic story unfolded around it. When the actor exclaimed, "Then the haughty earthbound son of Zeus did let his death bolt cut through the hushed air," Luke Anthony shot the pig in the heart. The beast gave a surprised grunt, rolled over on its hairy side, and expired with a final turnip protruding from its mouth. The famous actor could not complete the recitation of his poem for the thunderous and sustained applause that followed the animal's demise.

After the performance the emperor named a new man to perform the necessary administrative chores Mr. Perlman had once done. He chose for this position a former chicken farmer of unknown descent who bore a Greek last name, a small dark man almost as handsome as the emperor himself, but one possessing a slight build and a sharply defined nose and chin, in contrast to the emperor's features, which were as wide as the muscles on his arms. This new chamberlain was the soon-to-be famous Otto Cleander, who soon proved himself to be more cunning than Sao Trentex and more vicious than Mr. Perlman, and who would one day rival the emperor in power. The people did not perceive any danger in Mr. Cleander on the bright day of his appointment; they saw in him only a reserved, cautious public servant, one favoring the shadow mechanisms of imperial government over the sunlight of public acclaim, for from the beginning Cleander moved upon his victims as unobtrusively as a viper does upon mice, and few realized how deadly he was before the moment he had his fangs in them.

Father and his household were on a steamship bound for Istanbul when the boar fell and Cleander rose. On that day we were overjoyed to think that every passing minute put more of the placid, blue-green sea between us and Garden City. Our home in eastern Turkey lay ahead of us. There we would again find Van City's square walls and Father's little garden behind the military station's only three-story house, and we had no intention of ever sailing back into the capital's troubled waters.

VII.

AD 2293

By May it was clear we had to leave Mars for our old home base in Turkey, where the soldiers of Father's former command had also declared for him. Mr. Golden's couriers had brought the nanomachines we call the new metal plague with them from Earth, and already the mining station's computers were failing to produce naught but display screens of scrolling numbers. The last two members of Father's command who had implants within their systems had likewise perished. We had to evacuate soon, or else we would be trapped on an alien planet while we waited for our atmospheric systems to fail.

We loaded the entire 1,628 members of the mining station onto the gigantic ore ferry that normally carried rock from Mars orbit to orbit about the Earth. By using the barge's shuttle, we filled up its empty hold,

150 passengers at a time. Despite the cramped quarters we had, our veteran pilot, Captain Mbasa, expertly pulled the vessel from its path around the Red Planet and went directly into the solar wind, wherein the barge's expanding wings and nose scope could collect radiated energy to power our nuclear generators and bring us home. In only fifteen days' time, Mbasa hit the retro-rockets to slow us down enough to flip us around the Earth and put us into orbit. In reverse of the process we had used on Mars, the shuttle craft carried 150 of us at a time to Van City, or so it did for almost ten round-trips.

We soon discovered the surface of the Earth was rife with the nanomachines. The shuttle carried millions of them onto the ore barge, and within two days they caused our oxygen system to fail. Those of us left in the hold had to put on the individual respiratory tanks the miners had used and hope that the ninety minutes of breathing the tanks allowed would give us enough time to reach solid ground. The shuttle craft exploded on its tenth return trip back to the barge, leaving Father, myself, our four servants, and one hundred and twenty-two others stranded 630 miles above ground.

We would have perished like live sardines packed inside a large can if brave Captain Mbasa had not hit the retro-rockets one last time and sent the barge into the Earth's atmosphere, where the ungainly ship was not designed to fly and naturally began falling like a stone. While the captain manually held the craft on a nearly steady course, the rest of us rushed to the escape pods and ejected into free fall in the upper stratosphere. When the parachutes on the eight pods opened, we softly landed in a scattered pattern across eastern Turkey, and the soldiers from Van City had to spend the next week gathering everyone who had escaped the ore barge. We were safe, though Father had been shaken by the experience after already having been weakened by our time in Mars's reduced gravity. Ours, however, was a better fate than that of courageous Captain Mbasa, who rode the ore barge until it exploded like a supernova in the cloudless sky and was strewn across the mountains of southwestern Asia. To my knowledge, ours was the last flight to escape the other planets. For a month afterward the two radios we had at Van City that still functioned received desperate messages from those left behind on the mining stations and scientific posts in the Asteroid Belt and on the moons of Saturn and Jupiter where the nanomachines had also reached; soon the messages ceased, and there was again only icy silence in the expanses of the solar system above us.

By early summer we had learned from travelers that what Mr. Golden had foretold had come to pass: Abdul Selin and his Army of the Heartland had reached Garden City, and in a single day had disposed of the pretender John Chrysalis. A letter from Mr. Golden informed us that as Selin's advance guard approached the city, Chrysalis had made numerous desperate appeals to the Senate. He had proposed restoring the ancient rights the senatorial class had enjoyed in republican times, provided the current senators supported him against Selin. Chrysalis had requested that representatives of all the city's religions go to meet Selin's troops on the march and tell them John Chrysalis was willing to share his rule with their commander. When the army reached the capital's suburbs, the Senate and the City Guardsmen, both of whom had served the pretender when Selin was far away on the Great Plains and Chrysalis's money was nearby, at once turned on their master. John Chrysalis's last day on Earth found him running through the hundreds of rooms within the palace, calling out to servants who had disappeared and peering out the high arched windows for Guardsmen who had taken off their uniforms and blended into the civilian population. The last soldier on watch intercepted the frantic man in a hallway and stabbed him to death, so that his body might be presented as a welcoming gift to Selin when that terrible little man at last entered the capital city proper.

The death of one rival did not appease the general of the Army of the Heartland. He did not pause a few days to hold a parade for himself. He went right to the business of establishing total rule. Selin at once dismissed the Senate and mixed the present City Guardsmen into the regular army and made new Guardsmen from the ranks of his own force. Many noble families—including those who had the surnames of Chrysalis, Whiteman, and Black—disappeared or went into exile. Father's wife and his two legitimate sons became prisoners in their homes. The other members of father's extended family were put to death. As Mr. Golden had predicted, Selin quickly seized the fleets stationed at San Diego and Tampico. From the latter of those two ports he sent troops to North Africa to take control of the solitary division stationed in Egypt. Thus his two remaining rivals were left isolated in distant parts of the world: Whiteman was walled inside Britain and Scandinavia, and Father was trapped in Turkey.

Mr. Golden's letter assured Father we still had support among the common folk in Garden City.

"Every day they call out your name to Selin and his thugs when they march through the streets," he wrote. "The African turns a darker shade of black when he hears their taunts. He has murdered thousands for your sake; still he cannot stop the people from loving you."

"Golden is betting on every spot on the dice," commented Father as I read the letter to him. "He fears there may yet be a popular uprising on my behalf. I wonder what he is saying to Selin."

As I read on, we learned that Selin had sent a large army across the Mediterranean in the direction of Istanbul.

"We will have to meet him there," said Father. "He'll be most vulnerable while he's making the crossing. Once he gets into Asia, his larger army will overwhelm ours. We have to defeat him at the Bosporus . . . or we won't."

My father was weak that summer day. None of us in his household dared to say aloud that knowing what Selin had done to his cousins, nephews, and nieces was the affliction that was bringing him low. We did not wish to distress him further. Father's pulse beat too fast when he awoke. He had to remain in his bed until it slowed and his head did not spin when he stood upright. When he finally got his feet under himself, he could not move quickly. All of us—including nonbelievers like myself—prayed to Sophia to aid him in the long struggle he had before him. In the evening, I, the skeptic, took his place in the cult's ritual processions while Father watched from his couch, as the exertion of the long, slow shuffles the deity requires would have undone him. He promised the officers who came to visit our house he would feel stronger soon. He assured everyone that when that time came we would start marching to the west to defend Istanbul.

VIII

AD 2286

Any discussion of a possible marriage in my future ended after our first trip to Garden City. I became confidante and chief advisor to Father—not that he ever would have given me any title—and I would remain so for the rest of his days. Father wanted me always at his side, to read him his correspondence, to manage what money we had, to give my opinions on his plans, or simply to rub his tired legs when there was no one else to do so. I knew he wanted me near him more than he wanted to see me wed. There were so few others to whom Father could reveal his thoughts, and after that horrible day in the emperor's antechamber, Father believed Luke Anthony's agents were constantly watching him, and they undoubtedly were.

For my part, I was wary of becoming anyone's wife. The soldiers my father led dwelt in constant want, received little pay, and knew the ever-present threat of sudden death. In our time of diminishing expectations their wives suffered the same existence and did not have any of the honors soldiers can win in battle. In Garden City I had seen the privileged wives of the upper classes; those women knew no hardships, and they cared for their husbands less than the poor soldiers' wives in Turkey did for theirs. Marriage in Garden City provided entrance into the highest tiers of society and gave license to a noblewoman to sleep with whomever she pleased. Joy, companionship, and love were not parts of the institution the noblewomen knew. My old teacher Mathias the Glistening had the romantic notion that marriage was the reunion of two incomplete souls that had been split in twain at birth into one perfect spirit. There had been, according to Mathias, some manner of perfect union in the mind of God before the parted souls were dispatched into the world. I wanted with my entire heart to believe as he did. Mathias, like my father, was a good man in spite of the horrible things both men did, and above all else I wanted to imitate the good. It was my misfortune to be born into a world wherein the divine powers Mathias had spoken of had sent forth men and women possessing less than half a soul or no soul at all. Most Pan-Polaric citizens living away from the frontiers tried union after union and found each one they formed to be incomplete, regardless of how many times they attempted to put things together. Wise Mathias himself had married Gloriana, the evil woman responsible for shaping young Luke Anthony. My father never said so, but I knew he had become increasingly distant from his legitimate wife and did not regret his separation from her, as she was a woman of patrician birth and had patrician tastes and had come to look upon my father as a rustic buffoon armed with a rifle rather than the usual tractor. I additionally knew his affair with my mother had meant nothing to either him or her beyond the physical pleasure it had given them.

Despite knowing the romantic dangers of my times, I too had once been in love. When I was nineteen I had secretly given my heart to a young merchant working in Van City. My darling had gentle eyes and sold scrap metal to the army, which our engineers used to reload spent ammunition cartridges; his was a humble calling but an honest one and therefore a superior one to most I had seen being followed in the capital. Twice a week he came to the base and set up a stall at the main gate alongside the other local traders. I found an excuse to walk past his place of business several times a day whenever he was there, and took care to turn this way and that so he might look fully upon me in my long, linen dresses that only the female members of a superior officer's family can wear. I spoke to him only of the quality of his goods and of the weather and of how the crops were prospering in that part of the Empire thanks to genetically altered fungus that had replenished Anatolia's soil after 2192. When I pretended to look away from him, I saw his eyes always followed me for as long as I was visible to him.

One day when I was with Father in the markets outside the encampment walls I saw my beloved and five of his mates progressing through the crowded streets. My dear one was dressed in women's clothing and was leading a donkey on which rode a statue of the lewd goddess Marilyn, a deity whose adherents worship by performing unnatural sexual acts rather than by merely praying as those in most other religions do. Father and I stepped around a corner and watched my dear one's friends playfully strike him with flails as they sang "Happy Birthday" to him. From our hiding post we listened to his friends proclaim what they were going to do to him when they reached Marilyn's temple and performed their sordid rituals. I realized as I looked upon his painted eyes and the red layers of heavy paste upon his grinning lips that he and I were not going to make a perfect union, not even if our joining together included whatever fractions of a soul his five friends and the donkey might have, and I drove him from my heart.

I confess I also once had tender feelings for Harriman, my father's second-in-command, despite knowing he was already married to the daughter of an important family in Garden City. That feeling also passed. The more I knew of him, the more I realized Father kept the handsome young man on his staff because Father saw in him a younger version of himself. Harriman was as recklessly brave as he was loyal. He knew how to make men march from one point to another, and nothing of why they should be marching anywhere, nor did he think to ask why. I expect his marriage to the titled lady in Garden City was no more successful than Father's nuptial arrangement was, and any connection I formed with him would be much akin to that which had once existed between my father and my late mother.

As I have already admitted, I, like many thousands of young women of the age, had entertained feelings for Luke Anthony when I first saw him—feelings I quickly came to regard with disgust. I was so repulsed by the creature behind his pleasing face I came to doubt the sentiments of my own heart, and I decided it was for the best I remain Father's maiden assistant for many years to come. I told myself I would either become wiser over time or else time would lessen the passions within me.

My maid Helen alone refused to give up the hunt for my future husband. She had told me more than I wanted to know about men; some of what she told me was actually true, and that made the subject even more disgusting. She said if I wanted a man I should pray to one of the clay idols she brought along whenever the household traveled. She knew spells I could use to enchant an unsuspecting fellow; I only had to repeat his name over and over, dropping the first and last letters of his name each time I said it until there were no more letters to say. Then the object of my love would be mine forever more.

"Didn't you once tell me that was the formula used to make one disappear?" I asked her.

"This is completely different," she said. "I would use my own name to make myself disappear."

Helen advised me to wear cosmetics to lighten my dark face, a feature she thought made me look like a savage.

"A little mercury powder on your cheeks, child," she told me, "or men will think you're a native girl."

"I am a native girl," I said.

"Lineage is traced through the father," she said as she tried to dust my face. "Your mother could be from India, and you would still be a general's daughter. Now, pay attention to me: when you walk behind the master your father, and the men in the camp can see you, you must keep your back straight and your breasts out."

"Helen!" I exclaimed, though my protests never discouraged her.

"Men are perverse," she said, and tried to adjust my dress into a more suggestive mode. "They like that sort of thing. Things used to be better for us in our great-great-grandmothers' times, but in times of constant war, men naturally have mastery of the world. We have to endure them."

"As you endure Medus?" I asked.

My father's servant Medus was terrified of his domineering wife. If he ever disobeyed her, Helen would threaten to put a curse on him, and the superstitious fellow never did anything but what she demanded of him, and no man in the world had ever been so thoroughly ruled by a woman than he was.

"Heaven gives me the strength to suffer that man's tyranny," she said.

My dear Helen was able to say absurd things of that sort and sound as if she meant them. Luke Anthony himself did not have a greater talent for dissimulation.

I thought for several years after our trip to Britain my father might not mention a possible husband for me ever again. Then, as so many of our other periods of misfortune began, there came a letter from Mr. Golden, Father's financial patron, and trouble arrived in Van City close behind it.

"What a beautiful woman you have become, Justa," Father said to me one evening after dinner.

Father was resting on his couch while his food digested, as he had grown accustomed to doing when we still had television to watch after dinner. I was mending a tunic he had torn on the thornbushes that grow everywhere on that edge of the frontier. Father never complimented anyone other than soldiers who had fought well. I knew something was afoot.

"Thank you, sir," I said.

"Everyone tells me how beautiful you are," continued Father.

"Who is everyone, sir?" I asked.

"Everyone," he said. "Everyone . . . you see, Justa. Simply everyone."

"Then I thank everyone for the compliment, sir," I said.

"Any man would be proud to have you as his wife," said Father, revealing more of his mind as he went on. "How old are you, my dear?"

He never made the effort to call me "my dear" any more than he ever complimented me. I was now certain the something that was afoot was going to be something enormous.

"I am twenty, sir," I said.

"Long past the time you should be married," noted Father, straining to sound offhanded, as though telling me I should be wed were something he mentioned every day. "When I was younger, we married later. Now, young people don't know what tomorrow will bring. Getting married young makes sense."

"You know I have decided to stay with you, sir," I told him. "I am of use to you here. When I can be of no more use to you, I will go to the Scholars' Library in North Dakota and write a book upon how random possibilities influence evolutionary patterns."

"Women do not become natural philosophers! Or any other sort of philosopher!" said Father. "No one should become one, if you ask me! What good do they do? Stir up a lot of trouble! Have philosophers ever held the center of a line? Have they ever supported an assault? Eh? You tell me!"

"Mathias the Glistening was a philosopher and a scientist, sir," I said.

"Mathias was a good sort," conceded Father. "Different, but good enough, in his way. What's that worth? He's dead now. What's a good dead man worth these days? How is it important a person knows anything anymore? Other than knowing how to fight, I mean?"

As he spoke Father made a sweeping gesture with his right hand and knocked over the small portable table the servants had placed beside his couch. Both Medus and the ever-grinning Mica rushed forward to clean up the mess he had made.

"What I am saying," said Father after the table and the several plates
he had broken had been taken away, "is that . . . you see, Justa . . . I have
become, over these many years, very fond of you."

"I have always loved you, sir," I said.

"Don't talk like that!" Father boomed.

His outburst frightened poor Medus, and the man jumped straight off
the ground upon hearing the master roar. Though he knew Father was all
bluff and never beat his people, Father could certainly still sound like the
warrior he had once been.

"Poets talk like that," said Father. "And look at what a sorry lot they
are! All that lovey-dovey nonsense! You have better blood in you, Justa!"

"Perhaps, sir," I said, not looking up from my sewing, "it was my
Syrian blood making we say such lovey-dovey nonsense. Perhaps, given
our situation, I also think it is best I at least love whom I can."

"Our friend Mr. Golden has a young associate," blurted out Father,
unable to keep the secret inside him any longer. "His name is Titian."

"Titian what?" I asked, curious to learn if the man in question came
from a decent family and why he had such an absurd name.

"He is a new citizen of the Empire," explained Father. "He doesn't
need another name. Or I wouldn't think he would. I understand he uses
'Golden' when he has to sign any legal documents."

"What does this Titian Golden have to do with us?" I queried,
knowing full well where Father was headed.

"If Mr. Golden, the young man's patron, ceases paying money to the
emperor's friends, I will be killed," said Father.

Father arose and went outside. The tension he had created when he
made his revelation had been more than he could endure while inside our
house's rough stone walls. He returned to me about an hour later, but discussed Titian no more that day. He instead asked if I had made an inventory of the army's food supplies.

Four weeks later, the aforementioned Titian arrived in Van City on a
private jet plane, one of the last few to remain flying outside the military.
Given the example of Luke Anthony, I should have learned I should not

judge anyone by his or her outward appearance. My late instructor Mathias would have expected me to do no less. I will therefore only remark that Titian was so fat he had a hump like a bear at the top of his neck and his neck disappeared into his jowls, and I will not tell the judgment I made of him. Because he had contracted the Swedish disease when he was younger, Titian had grown a heavy beard to cover the rash on the lower half of his face. As was the fashion for bearded men in Garden City, he had used a hot iron to curl his facial hair into ringlets every bit as elaborate as those the patrician women wore atop their heads. Like his patron, he was a fuel factor, a man who buys coal oil and propane and diesel fuel at low prices and sells them at higher rates, and a man willing to consider that sort of skullduggery a true profession.

"The Empire depends upon us," were the first words I heard him say.

I had looked out the upper-story window of Father's house and overheard him discussing his calling with the two officers escorting him into the secure confines of the military camp. The short stroll from the front gate had left him winded, and Titian's enormous body wheezed like a gasoline engine in the grip of the new metal plague when he spoke to his companions.

"We are as necessary to the general well-being of the Empire as you chaps are," he said. "Perhaps more, if I may say so. Mind you, we are well compensated for what we do. That is because of the risk we take."

No one had told Titian that the two men walking with him were Tajik and understood nothing he said to them in proper English.

Helen poked her head out the window beside mine and got a good look at him. The first impression of him that she related to me was he resembled a sow standing on its hinders.

"You must refuse him," she advised me. "He is only recently a full citizen. You are a general's daughter."

"My father may die if I say no," I said.

Helen, being Helen, had many ready schemes for rescuing me from a marriage to this disciple of Mr. Golden's. She had a vial of synthetic blood and a type of paste that would leave a line on human flesh that would resemble a cut.

"You put a bit on your wrists," she told me. "Scatter the blood about, and your papa will think you attempted suicide. The general will be heartbroken, and he will send the fat pig away."

"I cannot betray my father," I said.

"I can get a narcotic designed in India," said Helen. "We all know how clever they are down there. One pinch and you will sleep like the dead for two days. Even your heart will go into hibernation. This toad from Garden City will leave us, and you will awake safe and sound."

"No," I said. "Father would never be safe. Turkey has spies, as does everywhere else; they would tell Mr. Golden I am still alive."

Medus came upstairs and informed us Father wished me to come below. In the lower chamber the general introduced us to the fuel factor. The servants and I bowed to him, for Titian was a man of property and needed to be shown some measure of respect. Upon beholding me on the stairs in my tailored white gown, Titian flexed and unflexed his pudgy hands several times.

"My special friend Mr. Golden said you were beautiful, Justa," said Titian as he bowed to me. "He did not tell me half the truth."

(He did not speak as plainly as I report it here, for in the fashion of all smart young men in the capital Titian put a North American aspirate in front of every exposed vowel, a habit that gave his English a repetitious, hissing sound.)

"I am pleased to meet you, sir," I said, taking care to lower my eyes for him.

"She has good manners," said Titian to my father. "My special friend Mr. Golden said she would. Everyone knows he seldom lies."

"No, he lies frequently," I thought, and I again bobbed my head to Titian in response to his sweet words.

"Enough chatter," snarled Father, who I could sense had formed an unfavorable opinion of our guest.

We ate some dried fruit and fried corn cakes for our midday lunch, a not-uncommon meal on the Eastern frontier. The rotund Titian was very hungry from his long trip from Garden City, yet he deigned to eat nothing we served him. He fingered at the small repast Medus sat before him like a stray dog pawing a dead cat, and made dreadful expressions of disapproval.

"Is this everything there is?" he asked Father.

"You are in an army camp, sir," huffed the general. "We eat what we have."

Titian then promised us he would soon show us what a real meal could be. He would rent a house in Van City and bring the necessary supplies from the imperial capital.

"Justa will need to learn how things are done in Garden City," he said, and smiled at me. "Seeing as how she will soon be living there."

My bowels felt ice cold in response to his glance. I again bowed my head to him and left my thoughts unspoken.

For the next two weeks Titian threw himself into the preparation of this grand dinner, at which I dreaded we would be wed by one of the cult chaplains on the base. Each day, at my father's behest, I went to Titian's rented house and sat on a couch opposite the fuel factor while he ordered about his enormous household of more than fifty servants. I nodded my agreement when Titian spoke, as my father would have wanted me to do. My husband-to-be meanwhile spoke of his estate outside the capital and of the vast wealth he had acquired by manipulating fuel prices after problems in the electrical grid made it impossible to create hydrogen and the Empire had to again use fossil energy. As he spoke, he slyly—or in what he thought was a sly way—touched my legs as he gesticulated and leaned his ample frame into my breasts.

"The secret to my success is my special friend Mr. Golden," he told me. "He has many important contacts within the emperor's court. Everything in business was tied up when Mathias ruled and we had to act so proper. His son has opened up so many new opportunities for those willing to cultivate the right sort of relationships."

I quickly learned his special friend was Titian's favorite subject. Mr. Golden had stolen more money from citizens of the Empire than a freight train could safely carry, making him in Titian's eyes the most admirable man in the capital and the very model of what the younger man wanted to become.

"My special friend has dined in the palace with the Concerned One himself," he said. "That, by the way, is what the emperor wants everyone to call him these days: the Concerned One. Luke Anthony sounded too much like his late father's name. My special friend addresses him as such: the Concerned One Who Rules. Oh, the meals they have! Our little dinner will be fine, for here in Turkey; it will hardly be as they have in the palace! There they have runners on the remaining hovercraft going back and forth from the Sierra Madre Oriental, bringing them snow they mix with crushed fruit to make a delightful dish to cool the stomach after eating spiced meats. They could just eat ice cream, but ice cream had been done to death, don't you think?"

An entire caravan of overladen trucks were needed to transport the food and utensils for Titian's feast from the airport into Van City. He ordered his men to show me each of the items they brought through his front door. He said since I would be presiding over the banquet with him I should know the food in order to participate in the event as I should. From local merchants he purchased sundry types of fish from the Black Sea and five butchered lambs. From his personal collection he brought forth two complete dinner servings, enough to provide for a hundred diners; one set consisted of golden plates on the edges of which were depictions of General Halifax's expedition to China in 2078, and another set of plates were of silver and on them were scenes of Captain Marcels's landing upon the planet Mercury in 2114. The Garden City goldsmith who had fashioned the tableware had made General Halifax and Captain Marcels both resemble Titian, a device that would keep the guests mindful of their host throughout the feast. The wine we were to drink came from California. The markets in Van City supplied Titian with live birds kept in cages and dead ones stored in gelatin. From the seaport at Trabzon he brought twenty barrels of shellfish so foul after they had ridden in trucks that no longer had refrigeration compartments they made the dogs along his street bark when Titian's men brought them to his house.

"This will be a treat for you," Titian told me. "You have never lived like a human being before."

Each day I visited his rented house Helen insisted I wear a lovely lapis lazuli necklace she had borrowed from the household of another officer. The dress she made me wear during my visits was pure white and had light green silk woven into the long skirt so that it appeared there were blades of grass gently rustling about my legs as I walked. But the blue stones she had me put on must have cost as much as the gown and my father's entire estate back in Garden City put together.

"I thought you did not like Titian," I said to Helen as she dressed me. "Why do you want to make me look pretty for him?"

"I know more of the world than you do," she told me, and smoothed out the folds in the fabric. "He will not think of you. He won't see past the jewelry."

Each day I came to him, Titus would inquire about the lapis lazuli. I could only tell him my maid gave it to me.

"Your maid can give you lapis lazuli from the Black Mountain in Afghanistan?" he said, and his tiny eyes became twice their normal size.

I was unaware that Titian spoke privately to Helen about the jewelry or that she told him she got the baubles from Arab traders who had crossed the great desert to our south. I certainly did not know she told him the Arabs had heaps of the blue stone for sale at only twice the price of gold. The matter was of great interest to Titian. Without my knowing of his actions, he visited Helen as often as I visited him in his rented home. She also introduced him to a third party who connected him to a band of Arab traders encamped in the desert outside Van City. I would later learn through Helen that these men were going to arrange a business transaction with the avaricious young fuel factor.

The food at Titian's' grand banquet was inedible. The meat and poultry were prepared in the high Pan-Polarian style, which is to say they were aged unto putrefaction. To heighten the effect, the food was served to the guests in disgusting presentations, such as putting the smaller fish inside the mouths of larger fish and boiling an entire sheep without removing its skin or wool. The cooks put the sausages and other loose meats inside the abdomen of a cow, and when the servers cut open the animal's belly, the links fell onto the floor as real intestines would had the animal been gutted in front of us. A flock of live birds, feathers and all, were sewed inside a pig; they were supposed to fly about the dining hall when the pig's belly was cut, but the heat inside the cooked animal had killed them, so after they fell limply onto the floor they were each laid at the guests' tables as macabre party favors. The original plan had been to project holograms of cartoon swordfish dueling amid the piles of rotten food, but we were spared that because the projectors had the new metal plague in them and no longer worked.

Titian alone enjoyed the food. He ate and drank for four consecutive hours and three times went outside to vomit, as diners in Garden City are wont to do. The whole time I sat at his feet like a pet dog awaiting scraps from its master. From his vantage point above me Titian could look down the front of my gown and could fondle my breasts with his greasy hands whenever he desired. He leaned forward and whispered to me in what he considered a tender voice, "What a fine wife you will make for me." I closed my eyes and thought of my father's safety whenever he touched me. Father could see from his sofa what was happening to me, or he could have had he not chosen to look away. He said nothing to anyone nor touched any of the food during the long, stomach-turning feast.

Titian again commented upon the blue stones I was wearing. It was a second necklace Helen had borrowed from yet another officer's house. My maid had also arranged for a third set of lapis lazuli jewelry she was wearing herself as she sat behind us.

"Did you get both of these from the barbarian traders?" Titian asked her.

"They are nothing, sir," Helen told him. "You must see the really expensive ones they sell."

At the dinner's climax a giant silver tub containing red Mediterranean crabs, some of them boiled in their shells and some still alive, was rolled into the room. Titian's cooks tossed the crabs into the diners' laps, eliciting screams of agony when a steaming shell met bare flesh or a crab's talon bit into a diner's fingers. It was at this serene moment Titian proposed to me.

"Listen up, my dearest Justa Black," he announced in a strong voice the entire hall could hear. (Father grimaced when Titian used his name in connection with me.) "You are the loveliest lady in creation," he said, and teetered backward. "You have made me the happiest—"

He fell off the couch before he could finish. Being the game fellow he was, Titian laughed and climbed back up on his perch.

"Will you marry me?" he asked.

Fate (or, perhaps, simple dumb luck) intervened before I could answer. Titian became sick to his stomach again and had to be taken outside to vomit for a fourth time. Upon his return to the sofa he was disconcerted by the wine and the decaying food he had consumed and forgot what he had asked me only moments earlier. He soon thereafter passed into sleep. The rest of us set aside his appalling food and left while a half dozen of his larger male servants carried Titian to his bed.

When I visited his house on the day after the feast, the fuel factor was not there to welcome me. On the day after that I found his rented house remained empty. I asked Helen if Titian's servants had said anything to her about where their master might be, and my old nurse winked at me in reply.

"He has gone to buy Afghan lapis lazuli from the Arab traders," she laughed. "They say it is more precious than natural diamonds."

"Where are the traders staying?" I asked her. "Are they nearby?"

"They and the gentleman have left for the desert south of the Tigris River Valley, my darling," said Helen, clapping her hands with glee as she spoke. "That is where they told him the precious jewelry comes from."

"That is beyond the frontiers of the Empire. The Pan-Polarian Army has not set foot there for decades. Is it even safe there?"

"For us it is," cackled Helen. "Not so safe for the gentleman."

As Helen well knew, the Arab traders had no valuable jewelry for sale. My nurse had tricked Titian into venturing across the frontier in the company of one of the many bands of desperate men who forever hovered about the edges of the Empire and whose numbers had grown exponentially as the Empire weakened. Six weeks after he disappeared into the wastelands, another group of nomads brought a message to the base: Titian had been taken prisoner; the Arabs had seized the little money he had been carrying and wanted a ransom to guarantee his safe return to us; specifically, they wanted Titian's considerable weight in gold. Father had no money of his own and had to relate the kidnappers' message to Mr. Golden in Garden City. That wealthy man wrote us in the spring of the seventh year of the Concerned One's rule that he had decided Titian was not worth as much as the Arabs were demanding. By then the matter was moot anyway. Two months before Mr. Golden's letter arrived in Van City the kidnappers had grown tired of waiting for us to pay up; they left Titian's head, wrapped in a brown cotton sheet, in the sand outside our southern gate.

"Looks as though the wedding has been called off," said Helen the morning soldiers brought the last of the fuel factor to Father's house.

Father saw to the burial of Titian's remains, such as those we had of him. We gave the dead man the proper rituals of Father's religion and planted the head facing toward the East, whence Father believed the Lady of Flowers would one day come to resurrect the fallen. As small a recompense for Titian as the ceremony was, it was more than his special friend in Garden City had chosen to do for him in his time of need.

IX.

AD 2293

All of July Father lay prostrate on his campaign bed. Unable to direct his troops in the field, he dispatched Brigadier Harriman across the Bosporus to block the passage of Selin's army into Asia. Healthy or bedridden, Father could not have selected a worse man for the mission. Brigadier Harriman was ordered to fight a series of delaying actions in the passes Selin would have to take to reach the channel crossing. Rather than do as he was told, the hothead swept through Thrace and Greece, smashing any military outposts that happened to be in his way and putting to death some of Selin's supporters he captured in the larger towns. Thus he succeeded in turning the entire region against our cause while he exposed Father's brigades to the advance of Selin's much larger force.

Father had to order Harriman to make a forced march back to

Istanbul or Selin would have cut off Harriman's line of retreat on the European side of the Bosporus. Father then lifted himself from his sickbed and went to take command in person. He gathered his entire army in Istanbul, and in so doing blocked Selin's advance outside the walls of that heavily fortified city. We were to some degree aided at that moment by a rebellion in North Africa, in which the Empire lost that entire region to the indigenous Muslim Arabs, and Selin had to rush to Tunis and evacuate the twenty thousand members of his extended clan to safety in Italy. This bought us several weeks of delay before we had to clash with Selin's army another time. With every ember of fury he could flag into life, Father berated—in front of the other senior officers—his protégé Brigadier Harriman for failing to follow his directives.

"You were to sit in the mountains and wait for him to come to you!" Father shouted at the headstrong young man. "Now we have to stop Selin right at the coastline or we are lost!"

Never one to retreat to a more humble position when he could create a scene, Harriman put his hand on his sidearm and announced to the entire staff, "I will kill myself for displeasing my emperor!"

"You will do nothing of the sort," said Father. (In spite of our dangerous condition, Father pitied the young general more than he was angry at him.) "I will still have need of you," he told Harriman.

Father had to lie down after he had spoken to his officers. He called the disgraced brigadier into his residence to confer with him at his bedside while Medus rubbed Father's aching legs.

"I want you to take a third of the army back into Asia," Father told him. "March south to the Hellespont and block any forces Selin tries to land there. This will be your chance at redemption, my friend."

Harriman went to one knee and took Father's hand.

"You will not regret this, sir," said Harriman, shedding tears over my embarrassed father. "I will avenge my failures in Greece a thousand times over. I will drive Selin's men into the sea for your sake. I will—"

"Yes, very well said," said Father, who never could endure histrionics. "Mind this, my young friend: you are to meet the enemy at the coastline, take on Selin's men as they struggle through the surf. You will have the advantage there. He no longer has any aircraft or armored vehicles. He has more men, but they are not as well protected as we are. Should there be too many of them, and they drive you back, retreat farther south into the Cilician Gates. Do not, for any reason, attempt to fight Selin in a set-piece battle on open ground. Take up a defensive position at the Gates, and I will sweep down from the east and into their rear. Do you follow me? The radios don't work, but my Boer scouts will tell me where you are."

Brigadier Harriman swore on everything he held sacred he would obey Father's every dictate.

As soon as the young general ran off to do his duty Father told me he knew he had made the wrong decision.

"He will make a new disaster," he sighed from his bed. "His misadventures in Greece will weigh upon him. He will rush into a massacre to prove everyone was wrong about him. Poor brave fool."

"Why then did you send him, sir?" I asked.

"We have already lost," said Father, not letting a note of self-pity sound in his words. "We lost when the armies in the North American heartland declared for Selin. We could have never reached the capital or the naval bases before he did. Never could we have as many troops or as much money as he does. We now have to die well. Harriman deserves to die a brave man's death in battle. The living will forever after speak well of him. Selin is an old soldier, whatever else he is. He has kept something of a soldier's ways. Even he will admit afterward that young Harriman was courageous."

"Will we die well also, sir?" I asked.

"Not you, my beautiful Justa," he said, and sat upright long enough to touch my face. "I have plans to save you."

To delay the inevitable, Father had made other plans also. He wished to foray from Istanbul and by so doing to cut Selin's supply lines across Greece. Fate had it that the men he sent through the city gates to make the long strike into enemy territory chanced to see an owl perch atop one of their standards the moment they reached open ground on the European side; a swarm of bees attacked the bird and drove it out of sight. Among the men in the vanguard of Father's army was a Swedish mystic claiming to have the gift of augury; he announced to everyone about him the owl represented General Black and the bees were the countless forces of Selin that were going to attack him. The omen terrified the entire army. In those years of the Empire's decline most of the soldiers carried on their persons some such nonsense as a talisman or a hare's foot stuck under their body armor to ward off death in battle, and they were afraid of birds calling in the night and of dogs that had a bad eye and of every other harbinger of bad luck the superstitious can fear. To a man they retreated into the city and refused to move out again.

Father had to fortify the walls of Istanbul against a siege that was sure to follow. Thereafter he crossed the majority of his men once more into Asia. Many families in the city he was abandoning had declared for Father's cause and had already been condemned to death by Selin. Fear can be as effective as bravery in a hopeless situation, and in the later stages of the war the frightened city of Istanbul would hold out against Selin's mighty army until the issue of who would become emperor had been decided elsewhere.

Soon after reaching Asia we learned that Brigadier Harriman had lost his life and his men in one headlong attack against the enemy. He had waited while the bulk of Selin's army crossed the Hellespont, then had engaged the entire hostile force in a senseless battle near the lake we still call by the ancient name Cyzicus. A third of Father's men had perished with him.

Selin was now racing to get between us and our home base in Van City. Since we could not proceed south, Father placed his remaining troops in the narrow pass between Nicea and Eribulus and there awaited his fate. The few horsemen left in Father's command were Turks, as Selin was. Some of these soldiers were even members of Selin's sun-worshiping mystery cult. In the dead of night these same horsemen slipped away to join their countrymen in the other army. The infantry force Father was left with could now have reached the relative safety of the Cilician Gates only if they had grown wings to fly to that destination.

X.

AD 2287

Six years earlier, Father had saved Selin's military career as well as his future rival's life. Abdul Selin was then military governor of the Great Plains, the vast province composed of fourteen former American states that had Kansas City as its capital. Like every other general or administrator serving under the Concerned One, Selin's survival depended upon keeping the erratic emperor's favor. When the emperor had a change of heart, men in Selin's position often came to a sudden and very bad end for no particular reason.

Cleander, the new chamberlain in Garden City and the unacknowledged leader of the City Guardsmen, was at this time helping himself to the treasury while the Concerned One spent the remainder of the Empire's fortune on his houses, his harem, his spectacles, and on his throng of hanger-ons who clung to the emperor's court as other lowlifes cling to famous athletes and celebrated actors. In this era of good stealings, army payrolls set aside for forces far removed from the capital often magically shrank before they arrived at the offices of the various military paymasters. In a repeat of what had happened in Britain two years earlier, some soldiers served for months with no pay at all. Selin's men in the Great Plains were among the most neglected. To air their grievances to their temperamental commander, these soldiers formed a committee and presented him a petition an educated man among them had rendered into good English. The little African of Turkish descent met with the committee one morning right after breakfast, and that same afternoon put them to death in the so-called old style, which is to say he stripped the men naked and had them clubbed to death with iron bars before the entire mustered army. He ordered the entire army in his province to draw lots and intended to kill every hundredth man among them in a similar fashion. His impudent troopers had the gall to revolt before he could execute his plan.

A common soldier named DeVries, a man possessing the mind and leadership abilities rarely found in men of any station, took control of Selin's rebellious troops and led them west from Kansas City into the lightly populated center of the Great Plains, where many farmers and villagers were sympathetic to the rebels' cause. From hidden bases within that sea of grass and grains, DeVries waged a guerrilla war upon the unprotected towns and villas of the neighboring provinces. He freed thousands of local citizens from the rule of the tax farmers, and many of the rural folk joined the rebels' ranks and let them have the livestock and grain DeVries's men needed to feed themselves. In Garden City the Senate spoke of this rebel leader as a second Robert E. Lee; they and the emperor feared DeVries would cross into Mexico and lay hold of the capital, defended as it was by only a single division of Guardsmen. For months it seemed as if the center stone of the Empire were giving way. Everyone feared the rebellion would bring down with it the entire weakening imperial structure.

The Concerned One—or whoever was doing his thinking for him at the time—knew enough of his generals to know he did not dare send any of his more brilliant commanders into the Great Plains to put down the rebellion; the brighter stars in the military firmament might well use the occasion to join DeVries and mount a still greater revolt, one that was sure to overthrow the emperor. The one general the emperor could rely upon was Peter Black, for only he could be trusted both to do his duty and, for the sake of the emperor's late father, to remain loyal to the line of Anthonys. The Concerned One recalled Father from Turkey and put him in charge of three divisions of heavy infantry, ten thousand auxiliary troops, and a thousand pieces of mechanized artillery that still could be guided by satellites and two observation planes, although there were no longer any assault aircraft that would fly. The frightened emperor told Father to destroy the rebels by any means he could. We were marching north at the head of this considerable army when we met Selin as he fled toward the capital with two thousand soldiers—most of them relatives from his personal guard—who had remained true to him when the rest of his force bolted. I remarked the house of Selin was now wearing a new type of sun-shaped decal on their uniforms, a symbol that was an onyx disk with golden rays sprouting from it. I was told the cult had adopted this new style of sun fetish after a particularly large meteorite (or "sun rock" as the devotees of the sun religion called it) had fallen to Earth somewhere in the Siberian wilderness; the members of the cult said it was a sign from heaven. Selin took Father off the roadway and held a conference with him in the middle of a grain field. The little Turk from North Africa looked on his outside to be the same man we had seen in Progress; he still had a slight, muscular build and a bushy head that was too large for his body. We could not tell from how he appeared that the interior part of the man was in agony. He paced the rows of barley like a caged wolf and ran his hands through the forest of hair on his skull as he built up the nerve to reveal himself to his fellow general. He told Father he feared for his life; not because of what DeVries's soldiers might do, should they catch up with him, but because of how the emperor might react to his failure to suppress the revolt.

"You have to give me your legions, Peter," were the first words out of his mouth when he had Father out of earshot from us. "I will give you anything you want in return. Look, you and I are both outsiders. I'm a Turk from Tunis, my father was a construction worker, and you have no money. Those fancy boys in Garden City eat our kinds by the handful. If we don't help each other, who will? One old warrior helps another, and so on, don't you see?"

"The emperor was specific," said Father. "I alone am to proceed north with this strike force. My servant is carrying the papers the emperor signed in his own hand."

"Orders, orders," said Selin as pleasantly as he could. "We make up our own orders out here, away from the pretty boys. Who cares about the emperor's hand? How about letting one hand wash the other, as the old saying goes?"

"My hands are tied, sir," said Father, for once almost creating a witticism. "I have no other options."

"Did Cleander send you after me?" demanded Selin, and bounded away from Father. (Father said Selin might have been said to have become hysterical at this point. The little Turk forever went about in such a constant fury it was hard to tell his one mood from the other.) "He sent you to kill me, didn't he?! Don't mention the Concerned One to me! He doesn't do anything anymore besides amuse himself with his whores!"

"The emperor alone sends me," said Father. "I am to tell you to use the men you have left to defend the Rio Grande to prevent the deserters from going farther south."

Selin calmed momentarily and took Father deeper into the field. He paced about and fingered his beard as he fought to regain control over his emotions. When he spoke again to Father, his words sounded as soft as a beggar's.

"They will blame me for this disaster," he told Father. "You must see how it is: I have to redeem myself. These are my divisions, and you know how those people in Garden City jump to judgment just because of little facts like that."

"Were I to give you these men, the emperor would kill me," said Father. "I sympathize with you in your position, sir, but I have a family as you do. However, I do have a friend in the capital who might help—"

"You think Golden the speculator could save me?" sneered Selin, once more letting his true, pugnacious personality come forth. "Did you really think I don't already know of him? I know everything!" he said, drawing close to Father's chest. "The Concerned One isn't the only one with agents! I watch everyone, including you! I'm not an idiot the pretty boys can order about like a trained dog! I am not you! You know what the pretty boys in the capital call you? The Black Zero, because that's a number that never comes up on the roulette tables in the new casinos. Do you know why they call you that? Because you are an imbecile! A man of your position would be frightening, General Black, were you not so very, very stupid! Don't tell me about your friend Mr. Golden! I could pick both of you off the Earth like ticks off the emperor's athlete friends!"

"I think we have spoken as much as we should, sir," said Father, and walked away from him.

Completely given over to rage, Selin threw a dirt clod at him and nicked Father on the flank.

"Go on to glory, you moron!" Selin shouted. "Abdul Selin and the Selin Clan don't need your help! We won't beg to you! Selin has lived through worse than this! You wait and see if he doesn't make it through this crisis, you sand ape!"

We in Father's household expected that noisy conference might be the last time we would see the Turk from Tunis above ground. To our misfortune (and the Empire's), he was not exaggerating his ability to weather the worst situations. An adage from India tells us gluttony is a virtue in a time of famine. Selin had a gluttony for power that would serve him well in an era when there was little power to be had outside the emperor's throne room. The ferocious little general would feed his great virtue until he devoured every morsel of power in the Empire, including that invested in the throne, in the purple stripe, and in everyone wearing the purple stripe, and still he would be hungry for more. We should have known when we parted company with him in the barley field the question was never whether Selin would survive; the question was who or what could possibly survive Selin and his ravenous kinsmen.

DeVries's deserters quickly learned of Father's advance. Our Boer scout planes told us the rebels had broken camp on the South Platte River and were on the march toward the central Rockies. Should they reach the mountains before we did, they could either cross over to the Great Basin and seal the passes behind them with a few thousand men, or the entire mutinous army might find refuge in the highlands of the northern mountain basins, from where we would need dozens of divisions and years of effort to dislodge them. Father abruptly turned west on the remnants of the empty Highway 70 and made a dash to head off the rebels before they could leave the Great Plains. Since we no longer had any usable transport trucks and only two observation planes, Father made his men go triple time, running them for twenty steps then marching them for twenty more before he made them run again. They marched for seventeen hours a day, resting for ten minutes of every hour. At night Father did not let his troops make camp: he bade them sleep on the bare ground, as we in his household did, and he made them eat their meals cold and right from their knapsacks. Father loved the excitement of riding up and down the moving lines in our last four-wheel-drive vehicle and shouting to his men, "Step lively, boys! Look at me: I'm an old man, and I can still outmarch any of you!" The years rolled away from him during the excruciating journey. He would dismount from his vehicle ten times a day to get beside the soldiers and show them how a real trooper marched heel to toe, heel to toe. As he stomped along next to them, he told his troops the story of the Egyptian crocodile, and the beast in his story became larger and more fierce each time he got off his vehicle to tell the tale. In nine days of flat-out exertion we beat DeVries to the mountain pass beyond Denver and were drawn into battle array when the rebel force appeared in the east.

The deserters' army was less than half the size of Father's, and it lacked any heavy artillery units to soften us up or any cavalry to protect its flanks. Had they turned tail and run back into the plains, Father's Mexican horsemen could have easily gotten behind the enemy infantry and slowed their flight until our troopers overtook them. Since the rebels had been trained to be soldiers of the Empire, they spread themselves out and dug parallel lines of trenches, which was the only defensive formation they knew and is a devastating tactic against irregular opponents fighting in haphazard order but is much less effective against other soldiers trained in the Pan-Polarian way, for we positioned ourselves in exactly the same formations and had the added advantage of picking at them with our heavy artillery. DeVries's one chance was to smash the center of Father's lines with one quick charge. To counter this possibility, Father had decided to enfold the mutineers; he would give ground slowly at the middle of his line as his men retreated from their first two trenches while his cavalry and his lightly armed auxiliary troops swept around the enemy on the left and right, and in that way trap the whole of them in a circle of steel. The deserters could pierce our soldiers' body armor with their conventional gunpowder rifles only if they drew within twenty feet of our positions, which of course exposed them to the murderous fuselage of our mortars and cannon. Some of the deserters saw what was happening as they advanced, and they retreated from the snare Father had set for them before it closed completely. The men in the front lines of the rebel army stopped a thousand meters away, just out of killing range of our rifles, before they made their final charge. Their advance revealed the complete disadvantage the smaller force bore, because at close quarters everyone could see that Father's infantry reached far beyond the ends of the deserters' lines. Pan-Polarian officers train their men to hold their fire until they can hear the other side's footsteps, but in this situation the deserters were reluctant to venture farther, as it was obvious they could not win. Father's troopers called out in their vulgar soldiers' patois for their opponents to surrender and avoid further bloodshed in this pointless battle.

"Come over to us!" they called. "Our General Black is a soft old man! He hasn't executed a deserter in years!"

"Does he pay you?!" the mutineers called back.

"He gets our payroll direct from the emperor's hand!" our men replied.

For several minutes the men stood apart and shot over one another's heads while they discussed the surrender. Once terms were agreed to, the battle ended more quickly than it had began: the rebels laid down their arms and submitted to their former rivals. Less than a thousand men had been lost on both sides added together, and nearly all of the fallen were from the ranks of the deserters.

Father's one demand of the rebels was they give the leaders of the insurrection to him. DeVries and the other principals had slipped through the gap in the closing circle moments before the battle was joined, leaving behind a mere seven leaders of the uprising, all of whom were dispatched to a swift death by a flying tribunal that needed only a couple hours to hold its trials and to carry out the verdicts. Father then blended the rest of the mutineers back into the army. After the deserters had taken the oath of allegiance a second time and each had been given a few coins of the money the Concerned One had sent with us, Father marched them back to their old bases on the Great Plains. When they filed out of Father's column three weeks later in the green heart of the Missouri Valley, the former rebels cheered the old man they had been trying to kill at the foot of the Rockies a fortnight and a half earlier.

General Abdul Selin did not cheer Father when we met him on the road near San Antonio as he was going north to resume control of his men. That angry, ungrateful man did not so much as dismount from his horse when he confronted Father. He explained that since we were all on foot or mounted on horses he did not wish to make our exit from his province longer than it already would be. Selin might have contained his natural inclinations had Father simply saluted him at the spot where chance had put them together. Father regrettably attempted to give the little Turk an account of the swift victory he had won.

"I have sometimes wondered," said Selin, interrupting Father's account, "if you were conspiring against me with the pretty boys in Garden City, with that bloodless reptile Cleander, maybe with the self-styled the Concerned One himself. I have come to think no one would want you in on their plots. I called you a moron, Peter, when last we met. Never have

I spoken truer words. I cannot imagine why anyone, not even that diseased simpleton we call our emperor, would trust you with any authority."

"I am one who does his duty, sir," said Father.

"You may think I am destroyed," said Selin, and grinned. (Seemingly hundreds of white teeth showed through his beard.) "You may go to the capital and tell them how you saved my skin. They will give you a triumphal parade. In their conferences, the pretty boys in the Senate and in the palace will talk of punishing Abdul Selin for his incompetence. 'He lost control of his men,' they will say, 'and look: old General Black got them back for him.' I have foreseen these possibilities, old man. Be warned, Black Zero; I am prepared for whatever may happen."

He hit his horse with his lash and spun the animal about in a circle, a nervous gesture that accomplished nothing and was typical of the man, and typical of one still unfamiliar with riding a horse.

"Selin will live through this crisis," said Selin after his horse had come about and he faced Father again. "He will live a long, long time. He will live for the day he can thank you properly for saving his army and making him look a fool. You may trust in that."

Tiny bits of saliva gathered on his beard about his mouth as he spoke. He was smiling as he threatened Father and was simultaneously trembling with rage.

Father was too weary to argue and too old to fight with Selin any longer. He saluted to the furious little man and walked back to his carriage without another word passing between them. At Garden City the emperor and his court welcomed Father as a hero, exactly as Selin had predicted they would. The Concerned One gave Father a triumphal parade in the emperor's golden chariot (which had replaced the golden hovercraft after the latter ceased to function) and named Father not only governor of Turkey but general of all the armies on the Eastern frontier, though by then that meant only the forces in Turkey and what remained in western Siberia. The emperor had sculptors make a black onyx bust of Father that showed Father turning his eyes to heaven, and it was placed inside a recess of the palace's central hallway. Other artists constructed a second portrait of Father, this one a mosaic depicting the general in his long white robe as he performed a processional ritual for Sophia, the Lady of the Flowers. This second portrait was placed on a wall near one of the palace's interior gardens in which the emperor and his friends exercised. The Concerned One, however, was not so generous as to give Father any money.

The honors the emperor rained upon General Black made my father scores of new enemies in the capital, the most dangerous of them being Cleander, the imperial chamberlain. This sly, scheming man jealously guarded access to the interior compartments of the palace where the emperor lived and diverted himself. The chamberlain was most upset that the Concerned One not only had spoken to Father in the throne room but had as well put up Father's likeness in places the young emperor and his entourage were certain to pass every day. The former chicken farmer disliked anyone of any importance communicating with the emperor in person, for then the Concerned One could give orders that might contradict other edicts Cleander had given in the emperor's stead. Besides the scores of athletes the emperor trained among in his garden courtyards and the harem that entertained him in his bedrooms, the two people Cleander regularly allowed into the emperor's presence were the chief mistress, Marcie Angelica, and a strange lumbering giant, a former professional wrestler named Norman Alzedo. Cleander could daily change the cast of prostitutes and aging fighters who visited the imperial living quarters, except for Marcie and the giant, both of whom the Concerned One demanded always be near him. The emperor claimed Norman Alzedo was teaching him how to fight hand to hand. As for Marcie, it was widely rumored that only she could devise methods of satisfying the Concerned One's unusual desires. She was, however, far more than his concubine. "The Amazon," as she was called outside the palace, was creating a power base second only to Cleander's, and when the emperor did get the chance to speak to important men, the words he spoke were often more hers than his. She was another reason why the chamberlain did not want Father speaking to the emperor, for such conversations gave her an opportunity to project her will into the world lying beyond the palace's marble walls.

Cleander visited Father one evening at the general's house in the Field of Heroes two days after Father had been given his parade. To protect him on the dangerous city streets, the second-most-powerful man in the northern world brought along two inconspicuous bodyguards he left in a weedy lot outside Father's residence. Wearing a simple gray suit as a government aide might adorn himself with to demonstrate his humility and carrying no rings on his hands to proclaim his rank, Cleander slipped into the garden at the rear of the house where Father was sitting alone, looking up at the stars. He nearly frightened Father out of his chair when he announced his presence in the darkness. He had to introduce himself to the general, for Father had never before seen Cleander up close.

"I think, sir," the chamberlain said, getting right to the purpose of his visit, "you should be returning to the East."

He would not sit when Father offered him a place on one of the garden's wicker chairs. Cleander remained standing in the garden shadows, half hidden behind a column.

"I haven't been given any orders to leave," said Father.

"You have them now," said Cleander. "A ship is ready in Tampico. A sailing ship, but swift, and blessed with an experienced crew. You can be on board tomorrow."

"Why should I be, sir?" asked Father, leaning his ear toward his guest to catch the man's soft, nearly whispered words.

"Because we do not need heroes in Garden City," said Cleander. "The senators say you are a sergeant with a general's rank. I think they mean that as a compliment. Every sergeant I have known did not argue when given an order. You shouldn't either. Good night, sir, and have a safe and swift journey."

While Father could be slow at times, he had enough good sense to have himself, me, and his two principal servants on a ship leaving Tampico the next day. There was something cold, almost unliving in the slight chamberlain that terrified the veteran of a hundred pitched battles into acting without asking further questions.

We were not yet back in Turkey when Abdul Selin made good on his vow to redeem himself in the emperor's estimation. The chief rebel DeVries, still alive and still hungry for vengeance, had journeyed from the Great Plains with a small group of his confederates across the Rio Grande and into Mexico. Dressed in wide straw hats and carrying bouquets of flowers, they infiltrated the capital posing as religious pilgrims attending the Festival of the Great Goddess, and intended to assassinate the emperor when he made an appearance at the footraces held in the Field of Diversions. Unbeknownst to them, Selin had a paid informer within DeVries's group, and the little Turk already knew every part of the conspiracy. On the very day when the former soldiers were massing in the stands and were preparing to rush onto the field and hack the Concerned One to death at the moment he made his formal salute to the runners, Selin and fifty of his relatives charged into the arena and revealed everything to the City Guardsmen. In an hour the emperor's soldiers had swept the grandstands, killing everything in their path, including DeVries, his comrades, and a hundred thousand innocent spectators who happened to be in an unlucky place at an evil time. Everyone left alive in Garden City proclaimed Selin a hero. Later that same year Selin's army helped repulse a foray some starving French Canadians made south of the Great Lakes. The emperor gave him a triumphal parade in Garden City equal to that he had given Father, and he granted Selin the honorific title 'The Canadian,' one of the names he had already granted to himself. All talk of punishing Selin for the rebellion in the Great Plains quickly died within the imperial court. The ferocious man from Tunis had survived to make certain others did not do the same for very long.

XI.

AD 2293

Father carefully prepared the ground inside the narrow canyon pass between Nicea and Eribulus, the place he intended to fight either his or Selin's final battle. The open fields of Bithynia to the south had 2,600 years earlier given Alexander the Great the room to outmaneuver Darius's Persian hordes. Father had no intention of facing Selin's relatively enormous army of fifty thousand on that fabled battleground and turning the Turkish bantam into a second Alexander, as Selin's superior numbers and his swift-moving cavalry would make short work of our soldiers in open country. Our only advantage lay in the fact that Selin no longer had any way to contact the Empire's observation satellites, nor did he have any aircraft; he was thus as blind as we were. In the rocky cliff above the pass and to our left Father's scouts had located a small pathway that was inaccessible to horsemen and heavy infantry. There a single file of lightly armed troops could advance unseen from the canyon floor. Father sent five thousand Boers onto the high pathway and set the remainder of his men in the narrow defile at the bottom of the pass where only ten men could stand shoulder to shoulder. Father's plan was to draw Selin into the constricted pass and check his advance while the Boers moved along the high path; from their vantage point the light infantry would rain down grenades and incendiaries upon the enemy below them as our men advanced to cut off the one possible line of retreat. In their rush to escape the trap in which their overly aggressive general had placed them, Selin's men would panic; those not trampled in the headlong retreat would be cut down from above or overtaken by the organized advance of Father's heavy infantry. To improve their position, the men at the front of Father's army dug four shallow trenches before their lines so that Selin's men would have difficult footing as they drew near and would in effect be fighting upslope and down while our men would shower them with bullets from the sure footing of a section we had leveled off to give our troopers a firm place to stand. Our men had removed the heavy armor plates from several disabled vehicles from our old base at Van City; these plates they buried upright in front of the leveled ground, which gave them some additional protection from enemy fire. Kneeling behind the upright shields, our men could kill their foes at twenty feet, while their opponents would have to close to point-blank range to do us any damage.

While they waited, our soldiers made themselves as ready as they had made the patch of earth where Father had chosen to make his stand. They rubbed greasy fire retardant over their faces and forearms to protect them when the flames started. Those few with long hair—mostly men from the East—tied their tresses atop their heads as part of a strange ritual they had learned from their warrior fathers, who had in turn learned it from their fathers. Each made his final prayers to his particular gods; they kissed their amulets and their hens' feet, and some made the sign of the cross, for although Christianity was no longer prescribed in the army, the men were allowed to consider every possibility in those anxious moments when they could hear Selin's troops approaching. While everyone could still hear, the men shouted encouragement to each other and said good-bye to those they had served with for many years.

In the last hour of the morning, our men saw the drab breastplates of Selin's troopers moving toward them. I was far to the rear of Father's army, yet I could hear the enemy soldiers banging their mail fists off their body armor and making thunder echo off the canyon walls. They called out to Father's men to surrender as Father's soldiers had called out to the deserters in the Rockies.

"We have the real emperor on our side!" they shouted. "Don't fight! Come over to us!"

Father had set his best, most experienced Boer soldiers at the front. They held their fire until the men opposite them had reached the shallow trenches and had to drop their eyes to direct their feet; then Father's select men pressed close to the carbon armor plates and fired into Selin's ranks. Their sabots had been powered with extra packs of methane boosters, and they sped their shaped loads through the first three enemy rows, impaling man against man. The Boers overhead simultaneously hurled thousands of incendiaries onto the close-packed enemy, and those who looked up could only watch the lethal spheres descend upon them. Father's men in the very front did not give an inch to the crush of Selin's superior numbers; those behind them passed forward loaded clips of ammunition and allowed their comrades to fire volley upon volley into the stunned enemy. Within seconds of the battle's start the four trenches at our front were filled with the dead and dying, creating a barrier over which Selin's men could not advance. The larger army could not charge over the piles of their fallen comrades without exposing themselves to more volleys of supercharged sabots. At the same time they could not engage the light infantry creating the hailstorm striking them from above. The thousands of foot soldiers and mounted cavalry at the rear of the enemy army pushed farther into the narrow pass and jammed the troops before them into even tighter ranks and rendered them yet more helpless before our weapons.

As these events were unfolding inside the heart of the canyon, Selin sent thousands of his lightly armed auxiliaries up the same high pathway the Boers were using. I had anticipated this move before the battle began and had advised Father as to what he should do. The Boers' advance guard had lain in hiding on higher ground and caught Selin's auxiliaries by complete surprise when the latter men tried to clamber up the far end of the trail. Our troops had taken the crest of the mountain first; the enemy had the steep uphill slope before them and were nearly as helpless as the heavy infantry trapped on the canyon floor. Selin's auxiliaries fell off the cliff walls in fiery clusters of hundreds when they blundered into the Boers' barrage of incendiaries. From the rear of our positions I could see them cascading down the sheer gray wall and onto their compressed allies. The confusion among the enemy was total. Unable to strike at Father's soldiers, Selin's men attempted to fight their way through their own ranks while their enraged general screamed at the personal guard around him to press on. The cavalry at the enemy's rear literally rode down the infantry before them and fired their sidearms into the backs of their comrades until the heavy infantrymen turned and killed them. The little Turk's personal mounted guards, composed entirely of several thousand members of his sun-worshiping clan, rallied about their beaten general to protect him from their army's breakneck retreat.

At this moment of absolute triumph, when Father's army had emerged as if from the grave to win a complete victory, an officer on Father's staff ran back to him and caught him by the forearm.

"You have done it, my emperor!" the man exclaimed. "Your victory this day will live for a thousand years!"

"We're not through yet, sir," said Father. "You see that green flare from way down the pass? That is the signal I've been waiting for! It means that hothead Selin has sent his entire force past my Boers! Push the men on! We have them all!"

Father drew his pistol and charged into the ranks. His men cheered him as he surged toward the front lines. He gaily waved back to them as if he were strolling through a parade review. The soldiers lifted up their rifles in celebration of the victory that was apparent to them as well as to the enemy.

"On, boys!" Father shouted. "We'll show this rabble what real Pan-Polarians can do!" he told his army, which was composed mostly of alien mercenaries and most of whom could not hear him above the tumult anyway.

The rows of men pushed onward for Father's sake. Father ignored the pleas of his officers to fall back. Bullets and shrapnel pellets were flying about him as he drove onward over the heaps of enemy dead at the trench line, over the last organized lines of Selin's infantry, into the roiling mob the beaten enemy army had become. Hundreds of enemy soldiers, who only minutes before had beckoned Father's men to surrender, threw down their arms and let themselves be captured. Father took off his helmet so the men in both armies could see how he had contempt for danger. His bald white forehead and his sunburnt face had the leathery look of every veteran serving long years in the sunny eastern provinces. He was one of his men, and his men were such magnificent warriors they were destroying an opponent who outnumbered them by nearly three to one.

In those happy minutes, when he knew he had beaten Selin, Father was the undisputed emperor of the northern world. Everything that had happened to him and his family and the powers gathered against him no longer existed. He had endured the likely prospect of his death and the scorn of the powerful and their scheming, and he could still say to himself, "I will arise tomorrow in spite of everything I faced today! Defeat was a dream, a dream for others now, not for General Black! What are these frightened men retreating before me? Are these the same ones who last night sat at their campfires and boasted of bringing me to Selin in chains? They are shadows! Let them melt into the other shadows in the Earth's dark crevices! They will plague me no more!" He knew then why in every statue of an emperor the ruler's gaze is elevated above the vision of other men, for in those happy moments Father, the former sergeant, could look down the narrow pass, beyond the present carnage, and glimpse the same glittering prize only a very few had seen before him.

Whatever he saw, fate did not allow him to gaze upon it for long. Strong winds arising from the sea and rushing across the land are common in that portion of the world. Within the constricted mountain passes of northern Anatolia these winds are severely compressed and can be made as strong as a wall of water rushing from a broken dike. Such winds can knock a strong man flat on his back if they take him by surprise. During those sweet moments when Father had won the battle and made himself emperor, one such wind charged into the pass between Nicea and Eribulus. The Boers on the high ground were nearing the end of the pathway and about to cut off the whole of Selin's army when the unlucky wind hit them straight in their faces. The unexpected blast knocked several of the light infantrymen off the cliff altogether, sending them to their deaths in the canyon below. Others among them were knocked back onto the high pathway, even as the flames were pushed forward onto more of Selin's trapped men. In the ensuing confusion, Selin and several hundred of his personal guards turned and sped toward the open end of the canyon. The Boers were able to recover their footing in a few seconds and to surge forward once more. Our men still cut off the line of retreat for the vast majority of the enemy in the narrow defile, yet Selin and some of his relatives escaped into the open country to the west ahead of our advance. The Boers fired their rifles at the fleeing little Turk and his cohorts, and they did kill several of the horses, although at that range the bullets bounced harmlessly off the enemy's body armor.

Word of Selin's disgraceful retreat quickly spread through the trapped mass of the enemy. Within minutes those in the front of the broken mob were attempting to surrender to us and pleading for favorable terms, promising to commit to Father's cause. At first Father's men continued to slaughter Selin's defeated army. Father had to demand his senior officers run forward and order the men to cease firing. Even then the command had to be relayed to the Boers on the high pathway before the firing ended several minutes later. Then we made the enemy march single file from the canyon and made each man give up his armor and weapons as he passed through our ranks. For eight long hours the surviving forty-one thousand enemy soldiers made their way to our rear, and only then did Father have any horses with which he could mount a pursuit of Selin. By then, as could have been expected, the other emperor was far away, and we had no hopes of catching him. The thousand mounted infantry we sent after Selin returned to our camp during the night with only a handful of the little Turk's relatives to show for their effort, and none of them had any notion of where Selin might be.

"I cannot trust any of you," was Father's judgment upon the forty-one thousand prisoners, some of whom had earlier been members of Father's army.

"But I will spare you," he told them. "The Lady Sophia instructs us to forgive even those who have sinned against us."

Father was not doing the defeated men any favors by letting them wander into the hills of Anatolia. Unarmed former soldiers of the Empire set free in a rebellious province were marked men. The indigenous peoples of Turkey, like those in North Africa and western Asia, were rising against Pan-Polaric rule and could be expected to kill any soldiers they got their hands on. Our own force of seventeen thousand marched west toward the Bosporus and the relative safety of Europe, wherein most of the people were not Muslim and had not rejected rule by a Pan-Polarian emperor—not yet anyway.

Father had by then lost sight of whatever it was that he had glimpsed down the canyon when the battle was being won, and we traveled in a much gloomier frame of mind in spite of the victory we had won.

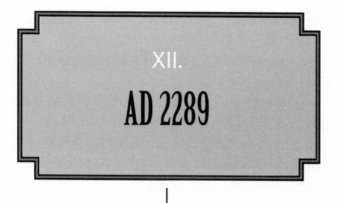

XII.

AD 2289

Four years before the battle in the pass a messenger had flown to Father in Turkey inside a coughing, sputtering, propeller-driven airplane and had told us Father had been named cospeaker of the Senate.

"You are to remain here," the messenger informed him.

That was such a curious order even my unworldly father thought it was odd.

"Shouldn't a speaker of the Senate serve his term in Garden City?" he asked, as the Senate normally elected two such officers to preside over their affairs every two years.

"The chamberlain Cleander bids you remain where you are," said the messenger.

"Cleander bids me?" said Father. "Shouldn't the emperor be the one giving the orders?"

"The emperor is preoccupied," said the messenger, and explained no more.

Father was a gentleman and did not ask with what the emperor was occupied.

"Am I a speaker for foreign or domestic affairs?" asked Father, for such were the separate obligations of the two offices.

"Does it matter, sir?" asked the courier with a shrug.

Seven months later another messenger visited Father on the Eastern frontier.

"Congratulations, Peter Justice Black," said this second man. "You are speaker again." (As befitted a man in jeweled armor, this courier was more formal than the previous one and he kept his hand over his heart while he addressed Father.)

"Again? I thought I still was," said Father.

"There have been six others since you were last in, sir," said the messenger in the fancy armor. "There could be some more by the time I get back home."

"Why has Cleander given me this honor?" asked Father.

"He said you did well the last time you were in office, sir," replied the messenger.

There would be twenty-five cospeakers that year. Most of the other officeholders would purchase the great honor from Cleander for a few days at a time. Father's first consulship had been a gift from the fuel factor Mr. Golden; his second term in office occurred because Cleander had, by a fortunate turn of circumstance, murdered the gentleman who was speaker at the moment, and the chamberlain needed someone to hold the position for as long as it took to seek new bidders. Rich men remained eager to have the title (particularly when Cleander intimated they should purchase the position from him or perhaps die an early death), and within a couple weeks' time someone with ready cash took Father's place.

We heard nothing more from Garden City until November, when we received notice that Father was to return to the capital; the emperor needed him. The tenor of this summons, brought to us by a man on a fast-sailing yacht, was not threatening, it was in fact slightly pleading, and for once we returned to Garden City without the usual anxieties that destination inspires in travelers, albeit we had to make the journey on the same sailboat that had brought the messenger to us in Turkey.

At Tampico we heard that Father had been not only speaker but a prefect of the City Guardsmen for six hours nearly two years earlier. A merchant on the ship with us revealed the incident to us for the first time as we pulled into the harbor.

"Cleander says to the Concerned One," the man narrated, "'General Black's got the guards this morning till I get the old prefect buried and a new one elected.' He always gives you these positions, sir, while he's waiting for another offer. Around the first hour of the afternoon some bigshot buys the post for a couple days, and you're out without knowing you was in, don't you know?"

"I was in the East at the time, sir," said Father.

"What's that got to do with the price of cheese?" asked the cheeky fellow. "I tell you this, my lord, that Cleander could sell water to the fish. He's the cleverest man in the city, which makes him the cleverest man in the world, doesn't it?"

After the emperor, Cleander had certainly made himself the richest man in the Empire. The former chicken farmer of dubious heritage had done well in the three years since his conversation with Father in the garden. He had continued to live as humbly as a Hindu holy man as his wealth and the number of his crimes grew; for a residence, he maintained a small house built onto a wing of the palace much as a toadstool is fastened onto the roots of a mighty tree. He still never wore garments more extravagant than his plain gray suit. A stranger from a distant land would not suspect, unless he were told, that this slender reed of a man controlled the administration of the entire faltering Empire or that all the leading men in Garden City feared the serene, unimposing Cleander might any day decide to kill them and sell their positions to someone else. It was he, and not the emperor, whom Father first called upon when we entered the central section of the capital and noted for the first time that millions of wood fires inside the millions of homes had created a smoke cloud to replace the carbon monoxide haze that once had lingered over the city.

Cleander kept a dozen scribes in his small home—double the number Emperor Mathias had kept ten years before, as Cleander reasoned the Empire had become twice as complicated and at least twice as difficult to rule since the time of instantaneous communications. To these twelve Cleander dictated letters to every legal and military official across what was left of his realm. In doing so he exerted his rule over four billion subjects, or at least he said he did, though in fact many of our fellow citizens had either died from want or had tossed off the Empire's yoke during the past decade. Cleander was busy with his dozen chosen men when Father was admitted to his residence. Cleander lifted his head to Father but did not salute the general and continued to stroll around the long table at which his scribes (who had not one computer among them) were seated while he read from a document he held before him. He pointed with his free hand to a place on a bench he wanted Father to sit.

"You have arrived, General Black," he said. "Good. I told the emperor he should send for you in this time of crisis. You soothe him. It is very odd. I think you remind him of his father, the divine Mathias. Not that you are the learned scholar Mathias was." (He condescended to glance at Father a second time.) "I mean to say: you are a career soldier . . . and a brave one . . . and apparently honest. The emperor meets so few honest men here in Garden City." The chamberlain permitted himself to make a small laugh. Father told me later that these fleeting seconds of amusement were the only time he saw Cleander become almost jolly in a normal, human manner.

"There is a crisis, sir?" Father asked.

"Two of them, if you count the viral plague," sighed Cleander. "I do not. Biological plagues decimate the lowest, most dependent sorts of people more than anyone else; that translates into less crime, fewer bellies to fill, fewer spectacles to put on for their entertainment, and many more affordable flats to let. The price of bread and housing goes down. One can almost walk the streets in safety, provided one has a few armed guards with him. No, I do not at all see the viral plagues as necessarily bad things. Looked at from an administrative perspective, a plague among humans can be a blessing, really it can. The metal plagues are, of course, always with us. We have electricity only in a few isolated places. But then, there has to be more to our civilization than electricity, doesn't there? The other crisis, the real one, is a conspiracy. You might not have heard of it in the East, isolated as you are there. It would seem certain persons in the city wish to have me removed."

"Imagine that," said Father, who did not take the precaution of speaking under his breath.

"As the city rat in the famous anecdote said to the country rabbit: 'There goes a man who runs the risk of being witty,'" said Cleander, not in the least outwardly perturbed at Father's remark. "Don't try to be clever or whatever you were trying to do. Wit doesn't suit you, sir. Anyway, I believe your friend Mr. Golden is a principal in this plot against me. Has he ever written to you concerning one Patrick Dion? Don't bother lying. I will know if you do."

"Mr. Dion is somehow mixed up in the fuel business with Mr. Golden, isn't he?" said Father.

"He was a fuel factor," said Cleander, ever moving in a circle around the room of busily scribbling men. "The emperor, in his divine wisdom, has made him commissioner of commodities, a very important post, given our present constant wants. Coming as he does from that cadre of speculators who call themselves merchants, this Patrick Dion is on very good terms with those he should be controlling. He is the wolf appointed to watch over the farmer's sheep . . . or so my people tell me. My people tell me much, General Black." (Cleander had, thanks to the emperor's immersion in his private diversions, taken control of the Empire's network of internal informers, and could hear the grass grow anywhere the Pan-Polarian flag still flew.) "That is how I know what a stiff-necked Spartan boy you are. You, Peter Justice Black, may be the last grown man alive to believe the tripe you gentlemen types were taught in school. Washington crossing the Delaware and Pius Anthony living on bread and water and

for the moment armed City Guardsmen came charging out of the side halls.

The Concerned One had been maintaining his strenuous system of exercise and diet during the four years we had been away. He fenced every day with Japanese long swords, jogged five miles around the gardens, and wrestled for two hours with his athlete friends. Father told me the emperor's body rippled with hypertrophied muscles anyone possessing eyes could behold, as the Concerned One went about the palace as bare-chested as a cabana boy and wore only a silken loincloth about his waist. His skin was golden brown from many hours spent in the sun. His blond hair and beard were fuller and curlier than Father remembered them to be in years past. A servant followed the lovely new-look emperor about the vast palace carrying an open bottle of perfume from the Canary Islands and a cluster of ostrich feathers, the latter of which the young servant dipped into the powerful fragrance every few seconds and whisked onto the emperor's broad back. ("If I were a woman or a freethinker from the West Coast," Father told me later, "I would certainly be attracted to him. As I am and have to be, I felt damned uncomfortable having him sitting across from me in that little bitty getup of his.") The chief mistress, Marcie Angelica, and the giant wrestler Norman were also present to greet Father. The woman had been following the same routine the emperor had been partaking of, and Father said she was as muscular as most soldiers. ("Let me say again," Father told me, "if I were a woman, I might have found her attractive, too.")

"It's an odd world, isn't it?" said the Concerned One, sitting himself on a footstool directly across from Father and striking up a conversation as though he were Father's oldest friend and they were going to have a casual chat.

Father agreed with him on the point of it being an odd world.

"One never knows who we can trust," said the Concerned One. "I thought I could trust that fellow Cleander once, years ago." (He bent over the small table containing Father's food and whispered his next sentence.) "You know, General Black," he said, "I don't think he has been entirely forthright with me."

Father allowed he had heard certain rumors.

The Concerned One told Father there had been two more attempts on his life while we were in Turkey. One plot had involved poisoning the emperor's dinner. The plotters had succeed in killing the imperial taster, who, said the Concerned One, was easily replaced; given the abundance of starving people in the city during these times of constant shortages, it had been a simple task to find a man willing to eat a bite from each of the emperor's dishes in spite of the obvious risks. On the second occasion someone tried to assassinate him, one of the athletes training with the emperor had somehow substituted a sharpened steel sword for the dull lead one he usually had during sparring sessions.

"I have a scar on my forearm from that," said the Concerned One, and showed the same to Father. "The rogue backed me into a corner. He would have got me if Norman here hadn't broken the rascal's spine."

The giant standing behind the emperor grunted at the mention of his name.

Before this time in his life the motto the emperor had lived by was "I can, therefore I will." He daily committed such atrocities as raping young virgins and running at night with an armed gang and associating publicly with actors, and he had taken pleasure both in the sordid acts themselves and in knowing he was offending his late father's standards of conduct. During this interview Father recognized something different in the emperor's speech and mannerisms. The Concerned One no longer calculated how he would affect others. When he spoke he sounded as sincere as a child—an impossibly naive child who happened to be the titular head of a gigantic and collapsing empire. Other than his obsessive regard for his personal appearance and the stolen objects of art in the hallways, much of the extravagance was gone from Luke Anthony's court, and the new drabness signaled more than the lack of electronic equipment. Marcie was the sole courtesan Father could see in the emperor's living chambers. The palace no longer hosted thirty-course banquets, for, as I said above, the Concerned One had adopted an athlete's diet. The guards standing watch about the palace grounds—and there were remarkably few of them compared to the small army that had attended the emperor earlier in his reign—were Mexican policemen instead of the ermine-robed Canadian mercenaries and City Guardsmen dandies in their gold-embossed body armor the emperor had once favored. Time makes sense of nearly everything, and the something different Father sensed in the emperor, this new austerity in his home and habits, which Father vainly hoped marked the onset of the emperor's long-delayed maturity, was actually the first signs of the madness that would dominate the later portion of the Concerned One's life. The excesses of his youth, the murders he had committed upon gaining sole rule, the sudden and violent deaths of his former associates, and the attempts to assassinate him had worn on the son of Mathias the Glistening like running water wears on stone, and in his later twenties the Concerned One was beginning to change from being the most evil of men into the most insane.

The emperor confessed to Father he was worried about his legacy. He said he had been reading Drummond's book about the first twelve emperors and he had realized he had not accomplished as much as they had.

"Darko built most of the city we see today," explained the emperor. "I have left my name on only one important building, and Cleander built that for me."

"Pardon me for saying this, my lord," said Father. "I have a faulty memory of Drummond. My daughter, I think, read him to me once. Isn't his section on Darko, well, isn't it rather unflattering?"

"Yes, indeed. Drummond was on the side of the Senate. The Senate and the Republic and all that. Most of those moralists were. Except for my father," said the Concerned One, and he stole a piece of cheese off Father's platter and had raised it to his lips, but put it back when he saw the formidable Marcie frowning at him. "Drummond was tough on most of the really interesting rulers: on Cepphus the Stealthy, on Tyler the Ostentatious, especially on Darko. The people didn't share his opinion. To this day, General, the people put fresh flowers on Darko's grave every month. They loved him. Still do. A man doesn't cut that big a swath through the world and not win the love of a lot of people. I mean to say, he killed so many, he had to have killed quite a few the people hated."

"Wasn't Darko, my lord, supposed to have burned the original capital in the north so he could build the new one here in Mexico?" asked Father.

"Rubbish," said the Concerned One. "Drummond himself doesn't claim that. He accuses Darko of flying a kite in Maryland while the city burned. That is an idea though, isn't it?" (The Concerned One paused and fingered his chin.) "What were we discussing when I first came in here?" he asked Father when he spoke again.

"My lord," said Father, "you were saying how difficult it is to find someone you can trust. Next, you reflected upon Cleander—"

"Don't mention that snake to me!" roared the Concerned One and became agitated. "He's the one plotting against me! I know it's him! You're not a friend of his, are you?"

"My lord," said Father, who had dropped a small scone when the emperor exploded, "I hardly know the man."

"Good, very good," said the Concerned One, regaining his composure. (He slapped himself on the thighs and frowned.) "He is a very, very bad man, General. Always scheming." (Again he leaned forward to whisper to Father.) "We are going to steal a march on him this time. Our side . . . you have a friend among the fuel factors, don't you?"

"Yes, my lord, the famous speculator Mr. Golden is a friend of mine," said Father. "We are related through marriage."

"There you go then," said the Concerned One, and sat upright on his footstool. "You are already in on it then."

The emperor made meaningful gestures to Marcie and the giant Norman.

"In on what, my lord?" asked Father.

"Oh, that is good, Black," chuckled the Concerned One. "Play dumb. That will throw them off the trail, eh?"

"In fact, my lord," said Father, "no one has told—"

"No need to speak of it," said the Concerned One, and held up a hand. "You never know who is listening." (He glanced about the vast, utterly empty room.)

"Cleander's men are everywhere. Remember that, General Black. You'll need to be careful of everything you say if you're going to live in the palace with us."

"Here in the palace with you, my lord?" said Father, putting little joy into his words.

"To keep an eye on things," said the Concerned One. "I don't know what we'll call you. Everybody here has a title of some sort. I have some fool already whom I call the Chief Guardsman. . . . Would you like Marcie to think of a title for you? She's very good at that sort of thing. She thought of whole new names for the months of the year I'm going to use someday. I'm sure she can come up with something for you."

"I would rather not distress the lady, my lord," said Father. "I am content to remain the governor of Turkey."

"Of course you can still be governor of Turkey," said the Concerned One, and clapped his hands. "I'll make you governor of Arabia and Armenia too, should you want that. Do we still rule any part of Armenia and Arabia?" (He looked to Marcie, and she explained that Pan-Polaria influenced the governments in those lands, but they both had their own rulers.) "Well, how about Lithuania?" said the Concerned One. "I've never been there. They tell me it's a terrible cold place; however, I do enjoy saying the word. Lithuania. Lithuania. Lith-u-a-nia. You say it, Black."

"Lithuania, my lord," said Father.

"What were we talking about?" asked the Concerned One.

"About Cleander and his plots, my lord," said Father.

"Cleander, yes," agreed the Concerned One. "He's out to take my place, you know. I need you to protect me. Take charge of these Mexican police chaps I have around here. I need time. A counterplot is under way against Cleander. I already said that, didn't I? Well, you know all about that anyway. I have to run, General Black. Can't lollygag the whole day away talking to you."

Father rose when the emperor did, and he bowed until the Concerned One and his two companions had exited the room.

"Splendid fellow," he heard the emperor tell his two friends before the door was closed behind them. "I always had a place in my heart for the old boy."

Father threw himself into the new assignment that very afternoon and did his usual efficient job. He dismissed the guards on duty who had families or were under thirty years of age. Father reasoned—with some assistance from me—that family men could be compromised by Cleander and young men could get themselves involved with the chamberlain's female agents during their off-duty hours. Father recruited two thousand additional men for palace duty from the naval station at Tampico. These sailors were grateful for what they considered soft duty on the palace grounds, and the emperor's half-naked regal person awed them as it no longer did the jaded soldiers already stationed in the capital. Better yet, these old sea dogs were ignorant of matters of state, making them the complete opposites of the all-too-knowledgeable City Guardsmen they replaced.

By an odd bit of good luck, it happened that most of the emperor's secret informers in Mexico at this time were either policemen or state bureaucrats working for the chamberlain. Unless Cleander wanted to spy upon himself, the men working beneath him availed him no use as secret agents, and the policemen were all locked up in the sprawling palace hallways with the emperor. As aging veterans of the rural *federales* or of the quartermaster corps, the spies among the policemen were too old to join the elite City Guardsmen. Years of eavesdropping and betraying others had made nearly everyone in the area despise them, save for the emperor, whose vices were already common knowledge and to whom the policemen had taken an oath of loyalty. If the Concerned One were to die and Cleander to seize the purple robe, any informers within the palace would be put to death as soon as the change came, and therefore the usually most devious men in the city could be counted upon to be the most loyal to the emperor's cause.

Father kept his man Medus with him in the palace, where the Concerned One had given him a suite of rooms. Father sent Helen and myself to a villa belonging to Mr. Golden deep in the countryside north of the city. Other families able to afford the refuge joined the two of us in that remote locale while Garden City suffered the visitation of new diseases that, like the new metal plague, were no doubt created in Asia. I felt enormous guilt in being so far from my father while he was endangered both by Cleander's wiles and by the natural calamity that was befalling the city. The beauty of the estate we had as our temporary home made my guilty feelings that much stronger. Each day I awoke amid the green vineyards and horse pastures and I contrasted them in my mind with the scenes of horror that would be besetting Father at the same moment. In the twisting streets beyond the public spaces lying in the center of Garden City, corpses wrapped in coarse cloth sheets were left each night before the facades of every house and tenement hall; horse-drawn carts carried them away like cordwood before the morning. In our villa we watched the farmhands gather the grapes as they ripened and listened to them sing an old song in Spanish about the Weeping Woman.

Those who have seen the results of the diseases the enemies of the Empire send to punish us know the cursed microbial visitors can take many forms. There is first a kind of new influenza that makes its victims cough and spit green bile until they reduce themselves to shells of the people they once were. In the lower elevations of the Empire's tropical zones there is a new strain of malaria that can strike when the mosquitoes swarm in the summer; the stricken there will perspire and become progressively weaker until they swoon into a sleep from which they never awaken. The third and more common type of new viral plague, the variety that was ravishing the capital during the tenth year of the Concerned One's rule, was a new type of smallpox that was as devastating to everyone it struck as the new metal plague had been to anyone with mechanical implants; anyone this affliction came upon developed telltale swellings upon his skin and either recovered or lost hope within a week's time. Because we had no medical understanding of this type of smallpox and because superstition flourishes wherever there is ignorance, the citizens of Garden City fancied they could protect themselves by burning incense at the front doors of their homes throughout the day and night, for there was an ancient folk belief revived among the people which proclaimed that incense purified bad air. Those able to afford unlimited supplies of incense wore smoldering burners around their necks or put lit sticks of it in their hair to protect themselves while they were on the street. Some in the city said the affliction in fact came from eating food grown in the organic way; they recalled that in the old days the Empire's citizens never caught the pox when they ate only the fruits of fields that had been enhanced by chemical fertilizers. Many others, including many at the villa in which Helen and I were staying, believed the old Christian God had sent the plague because the people were accepting new religions from the southern world. The devotees of this theory held the followers of El Bis to be the worst offenders, as members of that sect worship only one new god, the supreme Singer of Songs, and reject all the old ones, while followers of other new deities, such as Invictus or Sophia, often continue to adore the gods of their ancestors in addition to the new ones. The followers of El Bis themselves claimed the plague marked the end of the world. They gathered in torchlit congregations in the dead of night in secret places far beyond Garden City's suburbs and listened to their priests explain that more than three hundred years had passed since the Singer of Songs had come to mankind, and now he was about to return to the world and to lead his beloved into the land of grace. They painted images of the Singer's guitar on walls everywhere in the city, and revealed themselves to their neighbors and families because they proclaimed now was the time for those they loved to convert to their faith, seeing as how judgment day was at hand. To appease the people—and the old gods—the Concerned One and Cleander together ordered the execution of thousands of the El Bis sect. Rather than kill them for sport in the Field of Diversions or tie them to poles and make living torches of them, as previous emperors had done to other troublemakers on previous occasions, the Concerned One and his chamberlain impaled ten thousand of the followers of El Bis along the roadways leading into the city. For miles in every direction from Garden City, the City Guardsmen planted a victim every twenty paces. Crowds of jeering civilians journeyed out to watch the hated believers in the Singer of Songs slowly bleed to death and to mock them with taunts such as "Listen, the Singer is gone, but the song remains the same!" and "There will be no more dancing for you in hell!" Vendors brought carts filled with casks of beer and strips of barbequed meat so the crowds could purchase snacks while they watched their former neighbors perish. People said the ancient gods must have looked down approvingly upon this grotesque scene. As winter came on and cold weather returned to the high country around the capital, the diseases waned. By the beginning of the Concerned One's eleventh year in office they had disappeared altogether, though they had taken at least a third of Garden City's population with them into oblivion.

Father traveled to our villa hideaway every fortnight accompanied by two score of his sailors from Tampico. He was on each occasion happy to be away from what he called "the emperor's morgue." Being my father, he was equally anxious to return to Garden City and perform his duty. He told me during these visits that life in the palace had changed completely since we had been there in the aftermath of the rebellion in the Great Plains.

"The palace has become the most luxurious athletic training camp in the world," he said. "The emperor rises before sunrise, boxes for an hour with that great oaf Norman, and bathes with that terrifying whore of his in a little tub of ice-cold water. For breakfast he has a bagel and half an apple—that's everything he eats before noon. The rest of the morning he does calisthenics among his muscle-headed chums, then he has a midday meal with them a pack of wild dogs wouldn't touch, and after he has a nap he practices his combat skills. I must say, the boy is handy with a fencer's sword, for an emperor, anyway. In the army he'd be a terror to every one of his comrades stationed around him. He doesn't have a clue of how a real soldier fires and defends in actual combat. You've seen him use a hunting rifle. Now, with that, he's as good as any man I've ever had under me, except he doesn't know when to stop shooting."

"The empire would be better off if Luke Anthony were a soldier serving under you, sir," I said.

"I couldn't afford to feed him in the army," said Father. "Not when he and his mates get down to a real meal; that's when they eat up more meat than a brigade of regulars in the field. They don't waste a lot of wood cooking it, either. Just cook it a little. Luke Anthony—excuse me, the Concerned One—he has these quacks from California around him giving out health advice; they tell him overcooking destroys the vital juices. He won't eat ordinary pork or mutton, no indeed. He and his chums eat predators: lions, leopards, jaguars, wild boar. The quacks told them the animals' strength goes straight into their bodies. There are a couple thousand merchants getting rich bringing the poor beasts to the palace right from South America and Africa. They bring each creature in to his kitchens, kill it, butcher it, and boil it up right on the spot. Blood and guts and everything. Then the emperor and his fellow idiots wolf it down, each of them holding a big chunk in his hands and gnawing on it like a bloody bunch of cavemen. It's the vilest thing I've ever seen, Justa."

"What are they doing about Cleander?" I asked him.

"Nothing I can see," said Father. "The emperor and his crowd keep to the interior gardens; they run, they spar, they take turns lifting big barbells over their heads. They gallivant about showing their bare chests and bare legs like they're woodland nymphs in some silly poem you might read. That nasty woman Marcie Angelica struts around wearing no more clothes than the men. She lifts and fights right alongside of them. Her arms have gotten so big they stick out from her sides like she's a heron forever spreading her wings. She's disgusting. You'll never lift barbells or walk around naked and such like that after I'm gone, will you, Justa?"

"Sir, I promise I will never lift great weights or parade about naked," I laughed. "Now, what about Cleander?"

"Strange to say," said Father, "he still has an official office in the palace, and comes in every day, though he does all his work inside that little adjoining place he keeps next door. The emperor is frightened out of his wits when he catches sight of him. Cleander strolls around the hallways, hands behind his back, most of the time moving without an escort. He wears these funny little driving slippers like the European swells used to have, so he doesn't make hardly a sound when he takes a step; he goes about piddy-pat, piddy-pat, like a cat sneaking through an alley, not a care in his heart. The emperor and his thick-necked friends scurry away like mice when they see him. An ambassador for another land would look at them and guess Cleander is the emperor and Luke Anthony and his bunch are some sort of entertainers rehearsing for a big show. A very odd place the palace is these days, Justa."

During his visits to our safe haven in the country Father enjoyed walking through the wide vineyards and seeing the grape clusters dangling from their weathered trellises. So many years had passed since he had left the family farm far to the north Father remembered next to nothing of horticulture. He could merely pretend to understand what the farmhands were doing as they busied themselves in the fields. "Well done, lad!" he would call out to some startled worker tending the crops. "He certainly can wield that farming whatyoucallit," commented Father in regards to the farming implement true sons of the soil call a hoe. I would tell him what I had read during the previous two weeks while he and I strolled arm in arm through the verdant furrows. He was content to listen and nod his head, though both he and I knew he understood less about science and philosophy than he did of farming.

Each time before he left the villa we would perform one of his fatuous Sophia rituals in a grove of sycamore and oak trees at the far end of the estate's fields. We put wildflowers and twigs from young saplings in our hair and were as lighthearted as the children of nature the goddess supposedly wants the whole of humanity to be. Father did not scold me if I softly laughed while he performed his singular skipping dance and twirled the rattle in his hand. Sophia—if she ever existed—seemed to smile upon our humble ceremonies, for she let Father be a happy man while he was with us in the cool, green hills and far from the cursed city.

Sometime during each visit Father would repeat to me the awful details of the wild animals the Concerned One ate. He told me in confidence there was nothing he had done in his career that distressed him more than to see the Mexican policemen carry into the palace one of those magnificent creatures in a tiny steel cage. He said when one of his men dispatched the trapped animal with a bullet to its head one could sometimes hear the beast's dying screams echoing off every wall in the emperor's maze of corridors.

"They slice them up, boil the pieces, and the emperor and his companions gobble them up like a bunch of noisy hogs at a slop trough," said Father, forgetting he had told me the same thing during a previous visit to the villa.

Father explained to me he purchased the more common fare the palace staff ate from a different dealer in the city's markets every week. Cleander's spies watched him from the streets as Father went shopping accompanied by two hundred men from the Imperial Navy. Because Father was careful never to frequent the same stalls on two consecutive occasions, Cleander's men never knew which food they should poison. It was during these expeditions to the various open-air markets, the places the common people of Garden City go to gossip, that Father gleaned from sundry merchants what the secret plan of Cleander's enemies was. As the cold weather began and the pox vanished from the city, the price of food should have fallen after the harvest from the Mexican countryside and the one from Texas arrived in the capital; instead the cost doubled during the first half of December. Father, as I have said before, was never the most cunning of men, yet he clearly perceived that the speculators were hoarding grain in their rural granaries to create an artificial shortage. The new commodities commissioner, Mr. Dion, put it about Garden City that Cleander had diverted a large portion of the grain shipments to his native southwestern Europe to combat a famine there. In the markets Father contacted several travelers who had recently been to Greece, and they informed him they had seen no evidence of famine in that portion of the continent.

Since Cleander had warned Father not to make contact with any of the speculators, I convinced Father to let me go in his place to speak to his financial patron Mr. Golden in the produce market next to the city's central plaza in order to sound him out on this matter. I found the unpleasant man, one of the wealthiest individuals in the entire Empire, seated in a tiny stall where he was cheating some poor soul out of a few dollars for a basket of rotten onions.

"You will eat and be strong," he was telling the wretch as I approached from the street side, and the fuel factor put a hand on his fat arm to show the truth of his promise.

The wretch paid at least four times what the onions were worth. Mr. Golden snickered as the fool walked away carrying a load so decayed the basket's underside was leaking. This fat patron of Father's, a man worth millions, glanced upward to thank the heavens for this opportunity to steal a few pennies from a dole recipient.

He and I had not met before that day. I had previously only seen him from afar at the spectacles in the Field of Diversions. Until I stepped before his place of business and pulled the light hood off my head he had never beheld me.

"Well, hello, beautiful," he said, and pursed his lips to make what he meant to be a complimentary expression. "One could quickly make a sizable fortune selling you. Exotic girls are very big this year among the smart set."

"That may be your business, sir," I said; "it isn't mine. I come to you to speak on behalf of my father, General Peter Black."

"Oh, so you're Black's Syrian bastard," he said, and clicked his tongue. "No wonder your old man keeps you under wraps. You have already made me a fortune, by the by. That dolt Titian paid me well to arrange a marriage with you. Could you stand sideways, girl?" he asked, and craned his neck beyond the edge of the stall so he could ogle my figure from the side. "No wonder you were fatal to him. I must say: you would be a lovely way to die. Worth every cent. My goodness, child; nature has lavished her gifts upon you! Were I younger, I would buy you for myself. Sad to say, only a little bit of you would kill me these days."

"I'm not for sale, sir," I told him.

"Everybody is for sale, sweetheart," said Mr. Golden. "Some just demand a higher price. Come around and into the back and tell me what your old warhorse of a daddy wants this time."

I was reluctant to enter an enclosed space with him. He had risen from his bench and started toward the rear of the stall while I remained upon the street.

"Oh, come, missy," he said to me over his shoulder. "You are safe here. See that man over there?" he asked, and pointed to an individual in a heavy long coat he wore buttoned tightly around his body on that warm winter day. "He has a couple assault rifles under there. So does that one, and that one, and him over there," he added, indicating three similarly dressed men. "I have eight men around the place to protect me from Cleander's thugs. We are hardly alone."

I went around the shop's front and into the house behind the shop; Mr. Golden had rented this space to several barefoot families who gaped at me as I hurried through their crowded front room. I had to exit the home to access the back of the produce shop, and there found Mr. Golden lowering his enormous frame onto a tiny stool. Beside him was a burning lamp shaped like a phallus. Looking about the semidarkened space he divided from the street with a sliding glass door I could see the shelves and ground around me were full of similar devices.

"My, my, my," he exclaimed, again clicking his tongue. "Let me have a look at you. My dear, I'll give you a thousand dollars cash, if you will just take off your gown for a few seconds. I won't even try to touch to you. Your skin, my precious fawn, is the same color as clover honey."

"Quit that, sir," I said. "I am not a whore you can talk to like that! I am here as my father's representative. He would come to you himself, but Cleander is watching him."

"Women in politics offends heaven," laughed the fat man. "What would please the gods, both old and new and those beyond our imagining, is you naked and bent over my sofa. Oh, yes." (He ran his tongue over his upper lip as he pondered the image he had created in his mind.) "You have one of those pretty heads spoiled by higher notions, don't you, honey? I expect your by-the-book father is to blame for that. Rules and standards and such. So tell me, darling, what is bothering the old soldier these days?"

"He has heard the phony story you and your comrades are spreading concerning the famine in Greece," I said. "He wonders why you think anyone would believe the chamberlain would take the risk of transferring food to his homeland. Merchants arrive in Garden City from that part of Europe every week. You can't keep saying there is a famine there when those who have been there will say there isn't."

"The people already think the worst about Cleander," said the fuel factor. "They want to think he's sending food to his homeland and starving Garden City. As for the merchants, the ones telling stories, we in the city's business world can hire other merchants to say there is a famine over there. We will cause one if we have to. We only need time. The day is coming when the people will demand Cleander's head. Wait till they get really hungry.

"Why don't you have a chair, pretty one?"

"I won't be staying long," I said, although I did not see where one could have sat among his hundreds of little suggestive sculptures. "What if the chamberlain arrests you and your friends before the people revolt?"

"As long as the emperor lives," said Mr. Golden, "Cleander cannot strike at us. Not openly, anyway. He cannot send his division of City Guardsmen into the palace after the emperor for fear of causing a civil war. The armies up north in the Pan-Polarian heartland would march on the capital in that instance. Your father's job, his only job, is to keep the young emperor alive until the spring comes. The fate of the Empire rests upon those old shoulders of his."

He bent the upper half of his body toward me and sniffed at my person like a nosy dog checking out a female of its species.

"You smell good, too," he said, and closed his eyes and inhaled deeply, smiling at the same time as if he were transported to new places of delight. "Like a flower, or better. Some women use—I don't know how you little cuties say it—they use these little deceits under their outer clothing to give themselves that delightful liquid movement. I can tell from how your dress clings to you, my love, you are entirely true. Are you wearing any underclothes, darling?"

"I am a general's daughter, sir!" I told the fat man. "Your remarks are extremely disrespectful!"

He thought my objection to his crude behavior was beyond amusing. He sat on his tiny stool like a fat frog on an undersized lily pad and laughed at me. He laughed until his flabby sides hurt, and he had to pat his ribs with his short, pudgy arms to assuage the pain.

"We in the market know you are a family of honor," he chuckled. "That is why we wanted old Black for this job. He is the one man we know of who still cares about the old formalities, the old codes of behavior. You are much like him, pretty one."

"I am?" I said, momentarily startled because I never thought of myself and Father as being in any way alike. "What would you and your kind know of honor, sir?" I said upon recovering my wits.

"Nothing," he allowed. "But we know where General Black's gorgeous bastard daughter and the rest of his family are. That is everything we need to know."

"And if Cleander gets to the emperor in a roundabout fashion?" I asked. "What if he kills the Concerned One?"

"Then he wins the game," conceded Mr. Golden, and very nearly frowned. "When one plays, there is always the chance one can run up against a better player. We in the market are doing everything we can. Your father has to do his part. We ask no more of him than that."

I bowed to him, though he did not deserve the gesture, and turned to go.

"Oh, my," I heard him call after me. "I had not yet seen this side of you, love. You have been literally sitting on a treasure all your life, pretty one. Would five thousand dollars change your mind? Just lift your skirts a little so I can see!"

I turned and backed into the private home as he laughed at my modesty.

Among the few visitors the emperor allowed into his gardens was an acting troupe who daily entertained the Concerned One and his friends now that there were no more electronic devices to divert them. For those who have never been to the capital I should explain that except for the lavish inner gardens, the throne room, and the banquet chambers, the grand palace built by Darko a century and a half earlier and slightly enlarged by each of his successors is a patchwork of hundreds of smaller rooms the long hallways bind together into a two-mile-long structure. Some of these rooms are kitchens or storage spaces, and others are the living quarters of the palace staff. In each room, no matter how small, there is a recess in one of the four walls and therein is placed a stone bust of someone of great import to Pan-Polarian history. In the Concerned One's time most of these small statues were of the Concerned One himself. Several factories of artisans employing a couple thousand workers existed for the sole purpose of creating new works of art that featured the Concerned One as military hero, athlete, or hunter. One could guess the importance of a palace resident by gauging the splendor of the statue of the emperor in his room. The actors had in their rehearsal suite a magnificent onyx statue of the Concerned One in the guise of Mercury, the ancient winged messenger, which they proudly carried before them when they paraded through the long hallways on their way to a performance. When Father's policemen saw the statue coming toward them, they stepped aside and let the actors pass into the Concerned One's presence. Father was not as lenient as his men were. He always counted each actor and never let any of them come within ten paces of the emperor's person.

During the Concerned One's rest period, when the emperor and his friends ceased training for an hour or so, the actors re-created scenes from the life of Tom Sawyer, the emperor's favorite character in classical literature. The troupe re-created the whitewashing of the fence, the day Tom met Huckleberry Finn on the lower Mississippi, the pair's travels in the Wild West, et cetera. Father recounted to me that the presentation of the time young Becky kissed Tom on the cheek was entertaining but the troupe had made the scene indecent. The actress playing the part of the young girl was, he confessed to me one day at the villa, quite comely.

"She was, as you say, pretty in an actress's way," he told me, and blushed.

"You have long had a keen eye for the ladies, sir," I teased him. "What exactly was she wearing that was so indecent when she kissed Tom?"

"She wore little before and less afterward," said Father. "I had to close my eyes and think of Sophia till she had left the area."

On the afternoon the actors performed the story of Tom joining Huck on the river, Father espied the actor cast as Jim drifting to the rear of the garden after he had delivered his lines. While the emperor and his entourage were watching the two young actors left on the stage discussing their return to Missouri, Father observed that "Jim" had disappeared among the columns of the garden's peristyle. Father took two sailors and quickly circled the perimeter of the garden and ran into the hallway the actor would have had to have entered. The man had made some excuse to the guards standing watch there and had walked a hundred paces into the corridor by the time Father and his two men overtook him.

"You there, come back here!" Father called to the actor. "This place is off limits to you!"

"I'm sorry, my lord," the man said, and strolled toward Father and the two sailors turned security guards. "I have to relieve myself. I did not know—"

"The kitchens are back this way," said Father. "One of the lads here will take you to the bathroom. You will not be harmed, sir, but procedure demands we search you."

The actor had swallowed hard at Father's pronouncement.

"My lord, I am an actor," he said, and forced a laugh. "I have to return to the play."

"We will work quickly," said Father. "Only take a moment of your time."

The actor stepped back from Father. The two Guardsmen slipped behind him, cutting off a possible escape route.

"My kind lord," pled the actor, and backed against the wall, "I am a poor man. I have children. You can ask the others about me. I have never once before been in trouble."

"I'm sorry," said Father. "We have to take care. You were straying too close to the emperor's food."

The guards in unison took a step toward the man. Father told me later the actor breathed out heavily and slumped his shoulders. The life force, said Father, seemed to pass out of him into the confined air of the hallway.

"They said they would murder my kids if I talked," he said.

Father pitied the trapped man in spite of the loathsome profession he followed on the stage. Were they in his camp in Turkey, Father told himself, he would let the man go home to his family.

"Who is—?" Father began.

He was about to ask who was the "they" the man referred to, but the actor had taken a packet from the folds of his tattered stage costume and had tossed some white powder into his mouth.

"Stop him!" Father ordered the sailors.

They moved too slowly. By the time they seized him the actor had already consumed the powder. The guards attempted to force open his mouth as the actor slipped to the tiled floor and went into convulsions.

"Back away!" Father told his men. "Give him room!"

The dying man bounced about the marble floor like an eel on a fisherman's boat. The powder he had taken worked quickly; in a few heartbeats he was still. Father knelt beside the body and closed the man's eyes. The priests of Sophia had taught the general the dead want to look from this world to paradise as quickly as possible.

"What was it, sir?" asked one of the guards.

"Something Cleander's men gave him to put in the emperor's meal," said Father. "Round up the other actors. Find out this one's name and where he lived. Cleander might not yet know he is dead. If we hurry, we might get to his home before they do."

The other actors said the failed assassin dwelt in a tenement in the rancid slums lying beyond the produce markets. Father led twenty men posthaste into that portion of the city. They knew they had not moved as quickly as they should have when they arrived at the late actor's flat and found the door smashed to splinters: the ever watchful Cleander had sent someone there already, perhaps before the actor had fallen dead in the emperor's hallway. The few bits of furniture inside the apartment had been pushed to the walls, leaving an open area in the middle of the flat in which Cleander's thugs had left the actor's wife and her four children lying in a tidy row, the woman at the left end of the line and the smallest child on the right. After they had shot them, their killers had pushed the stiffening muscles of their faces into gruesome smiles. With the family's blood, one of the murderers had written on the apartment's wall: "Next time, Black Zero."

When he became an old man, Father's heart became too tender to suit an emperor or to do an emperor's work. He regretted the actor's suicide; the murdered children made him grieve for the whole decaying world for weeks afterward. He took the dead family to the wasteland beyond the city and buried them in a spot beside the only bush he could find in that place Garden City dumps her garbage and lets the wild dogs and the mentally defective scavenge for scraps. He prayed to his goddess that these, the least of the city's residents, be received as kings in the next world. As soon as the ground had accepted the dead, Father sent word to his legitimate family members that they should leave the city and go to the estate of a relative far to the north. He also dispatched twelve sailors to carry a message to Helen and me, ordering us to take the money the men were carrying with them and buy our passage back to Turkey by way of Guatemala. His letter read:

"Cleander's men are swarming over the road to Tampico. You and your maid must leave via the south.

"Should I not see you again, Justa, you must go to a moneylender named Samuel Van Coons in the port of Amsterdam. He is keeping some money I set aside for you when I made my first agreement with Mr. Golden. Show him your silver ring to let him know who you are. The money will suffice to provide you with a comfortable life, or it will make a handsome dowry, should you heed my wishes for once in the course of your lifetime and choose to marry.

"You go with my love,

"Your father."

I defied his orders. Helen and I returned with the twelve sailors to the palace. Father was furious with me—or so he pretended to be—upon beholding us in the eerily blank white hallways in the company of his men. I knew he was embarrassed to meet me so soon after he had used the taboo words "father" and "love" in his letter to me. In his aged heart I knew he also feared being alone in the enormous palace, surrounded by scoundrels and lunatics. While he would never admit to it, he was pleased to have me there. Good form demanded he give me a dressing down in front of his men; he told me I was a disobedient child, that women had no business butting into men's business, and told me how abashed he was to have these, the men in his command, know what a rebellious child he had raised. Then he gave Helen and me the servant's room next door to the quarters he and Medus were using. In that small space we set up a modest but sane home for him, an island on which Father could find refuge on the expansive palace grounds that elsewhere contained almost no modesty or sanity. Within five days of our arrival Father had forgotten he meant to be angry at me. He let himself slip back into the habit of letting me prepare meals for him in our private quarters and allowing me to read to him as I always did while we were in the East.

"Justa," he told me one day while I was reading his correspondence to him, "you are not my ideal of a daughter, but you are a very good soldier. You have put yourself in grave danger here. I expect you know that. You can't carry a rifle, so I'll make you my chief of personal logistics, something like that."

I bent over his bald pate and kissed the crown of his head.

"Don't confuse the issue with your womanly kisses," he warned me.

"Daughters may vex their parents; soldiers must follow a commander's orders. You are not to leave these two rooms during the daylight hours unless you are certain the emperor is exercising in his gardens, which he will be doing nearly all the waking hours. Stay away from the inner chambers, always. You can't let the Concerned One or any of his crazy friends see you. Never, not ever, can you leave these two rooms during the night. That's when the young emperor goes about wandering. There will be these corrupt policeman chaps everywhere to protect him. Everyone, even you, will have to stay out of their way."

I said I would endeavor to do as he wished. It was a solid testimony to my love for him that during my stay in that madhouse I usually did. My sense of duty to Father was assisted by the constricted circumstances in what was in fact a besieged fortress; heavily armed men of both the Concerned One's and Cleander's factions were everywhere on the palace grounds, and my rebel spirit had scant opportunity to do as it would in such a strange situation.

From my servant's room in the east wing I could see the grand Christian church the Conquistadors had built in what they called the capital of New Spain; it was a surprisingly conventional building—when compared to the palace—in spite of the church's soaring spires and exotic stained-glass windows, for it had a single roof over a single large chamber. The Concerned One shunned everything that bore the memory of far grander times, and he had let the former cathedral become a barracks for a company of City Guardsmen. As Cleander and the emperor had both intimated to Father, these men had taken the chamberlain's coin and were on his side during this long wait for the standoff between Cleander and the speculators to break. Unlike the catch-as-catch-can soldiers my father commanded on the frontier, where men dressed in rusted body armor and khaki uniforms that were made locally, the City Guardsmen loitering around the palace's perimeter and the policemen within the walls were resplendent in their molded breastplates, bright red topcoats, and shining gilded helmets. The fighting ability of both groups of armed men was questionable. What they were undoubtedly good at was presenting themselves; indeed, they were the best troops in the Empire when it came to making a display on a parade ground. During the long standoff we were to endure that winter both sides expended their energies tramping double-time in tight formation through the hallways or around the exterior walls. The City Guardsmen—the more numerous of the two armed camps—were the first to start these daily exhibitions, which they no doubt thought would frighten our men. Our men responded with similar demonstrations, using the multicolored banners the emperor had given them to show how serious we were. As days passed and both sides became accustomed to seeing their potential opponents on the march, the daily parades became a competition to put on the better show. If the City Guardsmen went double-time around the palace, the policemen ran triple-time through the hallways and gardens. When I looked down on the procession from my high window, the men resembled a giant centipede as they rambled past the open-air ponds and colonnades. After the policemen put the brightly dressed athlete friends of the emperor in their vanguard, the City Guardsmen hired acrobats to tumble before them as they advanced. To top this the policemen hired a marching band to lead their daily parades and drew after them the emperor's golden carriage. The City Guardsmen then dressed Ethiopian immigrants in chains as they would dress captured enemy soldiers and disguised exotic dancers as hundreds of Miss Liberties, and while they pulled the former along behind their formations, the latter skipped ahead of the City Guardsmen, tossing rose petals onto their pathway.

Only God can tell what excesses both sides would have committed had Father not put a stop to these spectacles on the eighth day of my arrival at the palace. Father mustered the Mexican policemen and the borrowed sailors into the largest of the central gardens in the morning while the emperor still slept and addressed them in his gruffest provincial manner.

"I think it unseemly that the men in the same army that once ruled half the world should stomp upon the capital's soil as if it were theirs to abuse," he told them. "You are marching in triumphs before you have won anything. Let the damned City Guardsmen put on shows if they like; they have the men to spare for such folderol, and they were never real soldiers anyhow. Real soldiers would know they need not make a show of themselves; their actions in the field will speak louder than any vain display."

Had he stopped there, I would have said Father had spoken well enough to his men. The city policemen were afraid of the battle-scarred veteran, and were duly ashamed that they had put him out of sorts. Father then chose to relate his story of the crocodile, a tale the city policemen had never heard before that moment. As Father told how he had raised his gun to the menacing beast and warned it that it should think better of showing that many teeth to a soldier of Pan-Polaria, I could see the men in the garden were wondering where the old boy was going with this strange tale. I slipped behind him and whispered in his ear, "Tell them you will increase their rations if they behave themselves and do as you wish them to. Wave and walk away before the cheering stops."

As much as Father hated to quit in the middle of his favorite anecdote, he wisely did as I bade him. The men were still chanting his name as I took his hand and led him away.

"I have no confidence in these city fellows we have tending to the emperor," he told me as he accompanied me back to my room. "They are a sharp bunch. Much sharper than the sort I'm used to. They're not smart, mind you. None of them have a snippet of real brains like you have, Justa. Just clever. Clever enough to be actors, or attorneys even. And they're better at their schemes than that poor fellow who killed himself. They are pretending to be soldiers, and pretending to protect the young emperor. We can thank Sophia of the Flowers the City Guardsmen outside are bigger frauds than the fellows on our side are, and thank her again we have the two thousand honest sailors."

"You must let only them come near the emperor, sir," I presumed to advise him.

"I will spare a few of them to stand guard on you," he said. "If that meets with your approval."

The City Guardsmen I could see from my window soon tired of making parades after the policemen stopped competing with them. Since they and their patron Cleander could not storm the palace lest they cause the frontier armies to march upon Garden City, they idled in the winter sun and played lawn darts with their pocketknives. Whenever there was a fight in the Field of Diversions there was no one on the palace grounds besides Father's men, for the City Guardsmen would leave their posts to watch the combatants and gamble on who would win. Despite the money the chamberlain was giving them, they had no interest in who would win the ongoing struggle for supreme power. Either the rising price of bread would bring a rebellion among the starving population or Cleander would assassinate the emperor before that happened, and they left the contest for others to play.

I many times saw their master Cleander stealing about the palace. He often walked past the gardens while the emperor was exercising with his friends. From my observation spot behind a column I could see the chamberlain smiling to himself as he watched the Concerned One hopping across the tiles on his flat feet, sword in hand, his fencing partners retreating before his advance. Whenever Cleander's gaze shifted to Father or the incorruptible sailors, Cleander's good spirits would fade from his narrow face. His gray person would soon likewise fade into the shadows as he padded away on his driver's slippers.

He surprised Father one afternoon by coming up on his shoulder and announcing in soft, spectral words he had seen a man stabbed to death in the market square that morning. Father nearly jumped out of his boots when the slender man spoke to him. Like everyone else, the general seldom heeded the chamberlain's nearly silent movements.

"Do you know the second-most amazing fact in the world, General Black?" asked Cleander. "Before he died, this unlucky speculator I mentioned—after a bit of torture—told us you came to Garden City knowing nothing of this scheme Dion and his associates have devised. I wouldn't have guessed until I heard the fellow say it. You came here and are protecting the idiot we have for an emperor because . . . why? I would think you must hate him more than I do."

Father kept his eyes diverted from Cleander's person. He watched the emperor in a distant garden lift a set of barbells over his head and give forth a grunt worthy of a bull in rut.

"Force of habit, perhaps," Father said. "I served his father, sir; now I serve him. I am obligated."

Cleander was for once baffled by something someone else had said. Father would not have added to his confusion if he spoke in Mandarin Chinese. The chamberlain shook his head and twice shaped the word "obligated" with his mouth to check how it would fit with the other words he was accustomed to using.

"What does obligation have to do with governing the world?" he asked Father. "We aren't living in the dear, dead republic your great-grandfather rhapsodized about. This is an imperial state. We have a ruler. Everyone else is ruled. The point of all politics is to become the emperor, and failing that, to influence him. I expect even you understand that."

"I understand Mathias lifted me from the ranks," said Father. "He made me a man my family could be proud to claim. He would want me to serve his son."

"Mathias the Glistening is very dead," said Cleander.

"We owe the dead as much as the living," said Father. "Perhaps more. We are everything they have left."

Cleander examined Father's person as a prospective buyer might look over a side of bacon he was considering purchasing.

"You know what the most amazing fact in the world is?" he asked Father. "You are not the beribboned buffoon I thought you were. You are a competent commander, formidable even. . . . I let you come to the emperor because I thought you would make a muck of the assignment. You are actually making this difficult for me. Bringing in those sailors was inspired. That's why you have to go away. Leave us, Black; go back to Turkey while you still can. Take my advice as you did before."

"I take only the emperor's commands," retorted Father. "He remains his father's son."

"Why are you here among the Pan-Polarians?" asked Cleander. "What strange accident has brought you among us at this time? Look, old man, do you see the open sky above the garden? Remove the guards at the south wall for an hour, and I could have a sniper up there like that. Look away for a second, and the Concerned One will have a poisoned bullet through his throat. No one will know what you did. You can say he was accidentally killed by one of his sporting mates. Everyone knows they're idiots, and the emperor does let them handle weapons. I'd thereafter kill them all before they could tell any outsiders what really happened. The world would say you kept your obligation, whatever that entails. I will make you cospeaker of the Senate for life. Comrade of the—"

"I would know what I had done," said Father.

They watched the emperor press another enormous set of barbells and afterward prance about the tiled floor as proud as if he had conquered India.

"Do you want women?" asked Cleander. "You must have been lonely out there in Turkey all these years. I know some men can't live without females. They have that weakness. I can give you the thousand prettiest women in the city. You can live with them in your own palace. You can lie about on satin pillows for the rest of your life and make love to a different one each morning and afternoon."

"Sir, I think we have spoken long enough today," said Father.

"You want money then, don't you?" said Cleander. "A man your age needs to set something aside for his children. Five and a half decades of service, and what do they pay you? I have been to your house. Remember? The emperor's gamekeepers have better quarters. I could fill a stadium with gold for you. I could. Just say yes to me. Or don't, if you wish. You only have to look away. Luke Anthony, the Concerned One, is a disaster. You know that. Look at the clown carrying on: he thinks he's some sort of modern gladiator! Mathias may have smiled on you rough-and-tumble soldiers out there on the frontiers; at the same time he despised us sophisticates in Garden City. He gave us his idiot son because he knew what a calamity he would be. He thought the Empire was finished, and Luke Anthony would administer the final blow. You would throw away your life, your children's lives, everything, for the obligation you have to this creature we see before us?"

"I suppose so," said Father. "We have to throw our lives away on something."

Cleander walked around Father, trying to catch his eye as he moved. Father kept his gaze upon the athletes in the garden.

"After I have killed the emperor," said Cleander, "I will cut you open so we can find the obligation in you. Once we have it, I promise you, old man, I will put it atop the broadcast tower in the Field of Diversions so the curious may come from across the Empire to see what Pan-Polarian obligation used to look like."

Father told me that for the second time in his acquaintance with Cleander the chamberlain presented Father with something very like a smile. This expression of bloodthirsty delight was far more horrible than the slender man's normally dour expression.

After that conversation those palace guards we could trust were put on full alert. Father stationed men on rooftops, in the doorways, behind the curtains that covered many of the interior walls in the emperor's living quarters, and in the hallways leading to whatever portion of the building the Concerned One happened to be occupying. Father ordered the servants not to leave the palace grounds unless they had armed men with them. He next made an inventory of the entire staff and discovered two gardeners listed on the rolls were missing from the palace grounds.

"They went over the wall a week ago, your generalship," a maid told Father when the general questioned the domestic staff on the matter.

Upon hearing this report I cautioned Father that the next attempt on the emperor would come when the absent gardeners returned.

Two men resembling the missing servants did appear at the palace three days after Father's inventory was completed. The two men wore the dark blue clothing of the emperor's staff, and several other servants Father brought to observe them from a distance said the two men looked familiar.

"One was an old man like that," one of the servants told Father as they watched the truant gardeners work, "and the other was a black man, a Nubian from East Africa, like that. But . . . I don't know, sir. The old man, I think, looks bigger than he was. You know, sir, those two had been here only a couple days when they came up missing."

Father asked the Concerned One to remove the two men from the palace until they were properly identified. The emperor was in a mood to show off in front of his athlete friends that day and told the general he worried too much.

"You are an old woman," said the Concerned One. "Are you afraid of gardeners now? Come, let's have a look at them."

The emperor and his comrades started for the garden in which the two servants in question were digging the soil. Only because Father ordered his men to run ahead did Father manage to get a dozen guards in front of the Concerned One as he strode through the blazing white marble hallway and into the open air above the garden's central space. A boxer at the emperor's right was the first to recognize the black man for what he really was.

"Nicholas Street!" said the boxer. "What a man for a servant!" To the Concerned One he said, "You remember Nick Street from the Summer Games, my lord; he is the best—"

The blockhead had not finished telling the emperor of this Mr. Street's prowess as a fighter when the two "gardeners" broke open the handles of their spades and withdrew two long, narrow swords. From their first agile strides across the garden soil and toward the guards it was clear they were well trained for their assignment. The supposed old man caught the exposed thigh of a policeman who had rushed forward to meet him, and his partner slit the wounded man's throat as he pitched forward. The old man drew a knife from the side of his belt and threw it at the emperor's head. A guard deflected the missile with his body armor. The sailors turned palace guards let fly a barrage of bullets, two of which hit the old man full in his unprotected head and brought him down. The black man took everything fired at him on the protective armor he wore beneath his clothing. One bullet did strike him on the cheek; the deep gash it made there caused him no more apparent discomfort than would a splinter in his thumb. An instant later he had dashed into the rows of pillars at the far end of the garden, trailing blood behind him as he ran.

"Get him!" Father ordered his men.

They chased the killer through the pillars and into a hallway where two policemen had been stationed. The Nubian had wounded both of them in a flash and sped toward a window that opened into a courtyard before Father and the sailor guards could charge halfway down the long passage. They saw him leap through the window, breaking the bulletproof glass before him with the carbon filament blade of his weapon. Upon reaching the opening Father and his men looked down upon a group of idle City Guardsmen standing outside and looking upward. The blood trail went through the cluster of men and thence around a corner of the palace's exterior.

"Why didn't you stop him?" Father demanded of the City Guardsmen.

"Stop whom, General?" one of their number called up to Father.

Father realized he was addressing some of Cleander's paid henchmen; still he dared to question them further.

"What is your name, trooper?" Father called to the City Guardsman responding to him.

"Go to hell with the heathens, that's my name, sir," said the man, and he and his comrades turned their backs on the window. They would not respond when Father ordered them to pursue the fleeing black man. Father did send a force of thirty men from his palace force to chase after the assassin, though everyone knew the black man would be long gone by the time our men reached the street.

Upon returning to the garden, Father found the Concerned One's athletes examining the body of the older assassin. They had smeared the makeup on his face, revealing a long, distinguishing scar on his right cheek.

"He's old Sampson from Colorado," said one of emperor's friends.

"Who's that?" asked Father.

The athletes arched their eyebrows and muttered in soft voices about Father's unbelievable ignorance. The assault had frightened the emperor into a state of uncontrollable fidgeting. He had been helped to a nearby bench when he became unable to stand.

"Sampson was the master of the club and knife," said one of the athletes.

"He's killed a hundred men. Been retired for years, General. I heard he teaches at a school for new fighters someplace in Texas."

"Did he train this—what did you call him?—Nick Something?" asked Father.

"Nick Street?" gasped the man, who was shocked by how little Father knew of the world. "You've surely heard of him, sir? He's the best, sir. The absolute best. No one in the fighters' guild would face him, so they let him fix his fights so nobody got hurt. Fifty regular soldiers at once couldn't fight him."

"Before my men in Turkey," snapped Father, "this Nick Something would go down like every other enemy of the Empire has gone down before them. Now you gents can help the emperor get to someplace safer."

The Concerned One had seen much blood in his twenty-eight years, most of it shed by his own hands. This attack, like the previous attempts on his life, was different from most of the slaughter he had witnessed; this time someone was trying to kill him. Seeing as how he was the emperor and was going to be declared a god one day by the Senate, the threat of sudden death was terribly offensive to him and his delicate, almost divine nerves. His muscular companions had to carry him to his sleeping room. There Marcie and the giant Norman stood watch over his quivering body until the imperial physicians gave him a double dose of something that put him asleep until the following morning. When he awoke and regained his senses, the Concerned One at once summoned Father into his bedroom.

"We have to leave the city," he told Father from his bed.

"Where would you care to go, my lord?" asked Father.

"To the hacienda of the Anthonys," said the Concerned One. "We'll be a good four miles from the city. You can garrison the place like a fortress. I'll eat food grown right on the estate, nothing else. Here Cleander's killers can sneak in like rats. The streets, the filthy streets here are built right up to the palace walls."

Father dreaded the idea of conducting the emperor through the crowded city. Cleander's men were certain to infiltrate the emperor's procession when the Concerned One and his guards left the palace on foot and were exposed to the more numerous City Guardsmen. The emperor did not see any danger; while huddling in his bedclothes he had devised a plan that removed all the risks.

"We will have Mr. Dion's people stage a disturbance in the northern slums," said the emperor. "Cleander will think it is a food riot. It will be, in the sense that the people who import the food will be starting the riot.

While the City Guardsmen are putting out the fire, so to speak, we will slip out of town."

"My lord," said Father, "when the City Guardsmen put down riots, they kill everyone they can and let heaven judge the guilty."

The Concerned One had to muse on this possibility for a moment.

"Your point is . . . ?" he asked.

"My lord," said Father, "are not the people in the north of the city citizens as we are?"

"They are citizens," ceded the Concerned One. "We, on the other hand, are leaders of citizens, aren't we?"

"Yes, my lord," said Father.

"Do you not believe," continued the Concerned One, "they will go to a better place after they are dead and will live forever among the clouds and all of those angels and things?"

"I think there is a world after this one, my lord," said Father.

"There you are then," said the Concerned One, and slapped his bare thighs, as he was wont to do when he thought he had made a point. "Eternity in the afterlife has to be a whole lot better than a lifetime in the slums of here and now. We're doing them a favor, really we are. The things you worry about, Black. If you don't want to sully your hands with this, I will take care of the arrangements myself. I know someone specializing in these sorts of things."

The following day there was a confused uprising beyond the produce markets. Teams of armed men threw incendiary grenades through the basement windows of a thousand tenements, causing a massive conflagration that forced millions into the smoke-filled streets. There were of course no fire engines left in the city. The City Guardsmen raced to the stricken area in long lines that were four abreast. To restore order and a sense of safety in the neighborhood, they fired away at everyone they could reach until the blood in the streets ran ankle deep. Back on the palace grounds, the emperor and the muscular Marcie were at the same time crawling into a carriage that transported them to the hacienda of the Anthonys south of the city. Eighteen hundred loyal members of the city's policemen marched alongside the emperor, and were joined at the ranch by fifteen hundred of the sailors from Tampico. Father would not allow me to join the progress. Five hundred more of the sailors remained inside the palace, and some of them were posted outside the door of my room to keep Helen and myself in the city.

Cleander stood at the doorway of his little office and watched the emperor and Father's men march out of town. Before the sun had set, thousands of mounted City Guardsmen had ridden down the highway and had taken up postings around the emperor's new home like kites hovering above a dying horse. In the open countryside the men trapped inside the ranch could behold how much more numerous the full division of City Guardsmen and their auxiliaries were than their numbers. Father would later tell me Cleander's men had such confidence in the new situation they allowed the escaped assassin Nick Street to ride among them when they swarmed upon the hills beyond the edges of the estate. The guards under Father's command mended the stone walls that—along with the rows of gnarled oak trees—marked the hacienda's boundaries. They kept a constant watch on the scores of snipers they could see stalking through the high brown grass, looking for an opportunity to shoot at the emperor, who cowered inside the main house and never went outside for any reason. On the day after their arrival at the country estate, Father's men captured two civilians attempting to smear poison on the garden vegetables the Concerned One would eat. Without knowing the import of their actions, these loyal men had foiled the last attempt on the emperor's life Cleander would ever launch.

The Concerned One might have lingered at his new home for years, doing his exercises in the safety of the ranch house's front rooms and doing whatever else he did at night in Marcie's company, had not the small riot he and the fuel factors had staged three days earlier sown the seeds of a general rebellion among the city's populace. The City Guardsmen had repressed the disturbance with the brutality that was as natural to them as eating and sleeping are to others. They had mown down anyone they suspected, including any they came upon, and had captured a thousand additional victims they had impaled on stakes along the access highways as a warning to other unhappy civilians who might be considering revolution. Similar actions had quieted the people in times past. Now, due to the high food prices, the city was starving. Dying from a bullet wound did not at the time seem nearly as terrifying to the populace as slowly wasting into skeletons. A great rally of a quarter million people was held in the Field of Diversions, where an unknown but brilliant orator (I expect he was an actor in the pay of the fuel factors) incited the massive crowd into such a frenzy they forgot the immediate danger and began marching south toward the emperor's new residence in hopes of gaining an audience with the Concerned One. Cleander misinterpreted the crowd surging down the roadway as a threat to him. In a moment of thoughtless panic he ordered the City Guardsmen to attack. As soon as the mob moved beyond the city limits the cavalry and infantry smashed into the swarm of unarmed people, and swelled over them like a wave breaking over a defenseless beach. In the first minutes of the dreadful clash thousands perished before the Guardsmen's guns or were crushed in the mob's wild retreat back to Garden City. As the huge crowd reentered the city, the City Guardsmen, who at that point had not suffered a single casualty, rashly followed the escaping civilians into the narrow streets of the city's slums. The cavalry wedged ahead of the infantry and quickly found they could not maneuver much on the rutted pavement nor turn about in passageways that were often less than a rod wide. Their comrades in the infantry could not get past the mounted men in front of them or smash through the masonry and corrugated steel walls around them. The citizens overturned handcarts in the streets and brought the soldiers' assault to an absolute halt deep within the man-made canyons of Garden City. Thousands of young boys climbed atop the tenement roofs and rained clay tiles and Molotov cocktails upon the trapped soldiers who had not been expecting a battle that day and were for the most part not dressed in full body armor. The five hundred sailors Father had left at the palace and those policemen left on patrol in the city raced to the southern barrios. Buoyed by the cheers of the delighted mob, these armed men climbed atop the barricades and attacked the City Guardsmen cavalry, pushing them backward onto the City Guardsmen infantry. Finding themselves suddenly thrust into a hopeless situation, as Selin's men would be four years later, the City Guardsmen did what defeated Pan-Polarians always do when they face other Pan-Polarians: they threw down their weapons and surrendered, knowing they would be able to strike a deal with their conquerors. The few City Guardsmen left outside the city saw how the action was unfolding and decided they too would rather be on the winning side than among those who were going to be condemned as traitors and possibly put to death. They at once became so dedicated to the emperor's cause they arrested Cleander, the man to whom they had sworn their undying fealty, and brought their former leader in chains to the Anthony ranch. At the first outburst of gunfire on the road, the emperor had run to the ranch house's main sleeping chamber and had hidden behind the bed. It necessarily fell to Father to take charge of the fallen chamberlain at the hacienda's front gate.

"Old friend," said Cleander, clasping the sleeve of Father's tunic with his manacled hands, "I need to speak to the emperor. People are out to overthrow him! Dion and the fuel factors are behind everything! You must help me, General Black."

"I have heard of a plot, sir," agreed Father, and shook Cleander's hands off his sleeve.

Father put Cleander in the care of his sailors and went into the villa's grand house to find the Concerned One. Father went to the door of the emperor's sleeping room and called to him. No one answered. Father had to shout forth his name and position before the emperor would chance a look at him. Everyone else in the royal entourage was hiding in other places inside the huge estate, leaving the emperor alone and terrified. He thought Father was there to kill him when he heard the general's footsteps at the bedroom threshold.

"Blackie!" he exclaimed as he glanced over the top of his bed. "I never would have expected it of you! Didn't I give you everything?!"

"My lord," said Father, "I am not here to harm you. I have come to return you to Garden City. The Mexican police and the populace have seized control of the city. You must, my lord, go to them and tell them you are their friend or they will think you have cast your lot with Cleander, and they will turn the Empire upside down."

"What of Cleander?" asked the Concerned One, who had again ducked his head from view.

"He is our prisoner, my lord," said Father. "The City Guardsmen have come back over to us."

"Have you killed him yet?" asked the Concerned One.

The emperor's courage—or whatever it was that ruled his heart—returned to him at the thought of dealing with his treacherous chamberlain. He stood fully upright and came from behind the bed.

"I think I should take care of him myself," said the Concerned One. "There would be justice in that."

He rubbed his hands together as he imagined Cleander's execution. Seconds after his great fright, the emperor had recalled that there was still pleasure to be had in the world.

"That is not of great importance at the moment, my lord," said Father. "You need to go to the city immediately and address the mob."

"You mean I'll have to give a speech?" asked the Concerned One, wishing the conversation would return to the subject of Cleander's execution. "I hate giving speeches. Give a speech and anything can happen: people can boo, they can say you are wrong, they can say so-and-so speaks better than you. You just never know."

"I heard you give a great speech once, my lord," said Father. "Your father, the blessed Mathias, had just died, and you were assuming solitary rule. You spoke to the armies on the Amur."

"Oh, that was ordinary politics," said the Concerned One, and sat on the bed. "This is an emergency," he whined. "When the subject is politics, I can say whatever I want. The words pour out of me then. It's nothing. It's theory; that's the word for it. If I learned nothing else from my father, I learned one can talk for hours on end about nothing when the subject is theoretical."

Father weighed asking him if he had not considered the death of Mathias an emergency.

"If it helps you, my lord," said Father, "you may think of this event as being a political meeting. Everyone's political future will depend on what you say to the people."

"You don't understand the pressures I am under," said the Concerned One. "You and your type have been out on the frontier all your careers, living it up among the natives, I imagine. I envy the easy life you have out there. No responsibilities. Only a little bit of warfare now and then to bother your day-to-day affairs. You have no appreciation of what I go through for you." He sighed and lay back on his gilded coverlets. "Are the people in a foul mood? I'll bet they're dangerous after this cold weather we've been having."

Father knew the people were starving and that afternoon the City Guardsmen had butchered thousands of their numbers, meaning they were in a fouler mood than the emperor could imagine. He did not feel he should tell the emperor that or he would never get the Concerned One back into the city. He told me he wished I had been there to tell him something clever he could say to persuade the emperor to do his duty. Father had to improvise on his own as he stood at attention at the foot of the gigantic bed. I must say he did quite well for a man lacking any inkling of how to be cunning.

"Your friends from the theater, my lord," said Father, "they tell me you are brilliant on the stage."

"Yes, yes I am," said the Concerned One, and pulled the coverlets over his eyes. "I am brilliant at everything. I am Luke Anthony, the Concerned One, the Father of His People."

"There, you have said it yourself, my lord," said Father. "You can easily do this. Lesser actors than you do it every day."

"I don't know," said the Concerned One, and sat upright on the edge of the bed. "I can say lines to a crowd. Here I will have to talk and think of things to say at the same time. That's very hard to do, Blackie. Professional actors only say what someone else has written for them."

"You only have to flatter the people, my lord," said Father. "Compliment them on their rioting. Tell them it was really well done. Tell them everything that has happened was Cleander's fault."

"They are his fault," said the Concerned One.

"Say you will get food for them as soon as possible, my lord, and that in the future everything will be better than in the past," continued Father.

"I suppose," huffed the Concerned One, and stood up. "I will do what I have to do. The responsibilities, Black, the responsibilities; they wear on me."

He and Father rode in the emperor's carriage back to the southern outskirts of the city. Squadrons of sailors and Mexican police ran alongside them to provide protection. Cleander was pulled behind their group by a long chain fastened about his neck. The Concerned One ordered one of his athlete chums to beat the chamberlain with a three-tailed whip the entire length of the four-mile journey. The usually immaculate Cleander was a bloody mess of stumbling rags long before he entered Garden City for the last time in his life.

At the city's edge, the still furious, ever-growing rabble met the group from the hacienda and showed the emperor little initial goodwill. Men in the crowd jeered him and shook bits of broken roof tile. The women held up their bleeding children who had been injured in the fight against the City Guardsmen. Father's Guardsmen had to push some civilians away from Cleander or they would have done away with him on the spot.

"Citizens!" exclaimed the Concerned One, and raised his hand to salute the mob.

This had been the single word Pius Anthony had used to quell a rebellion a generation earlier. The Concerned One made the same gesture his grandfather had, and his powerful voice echoed off the metal walls as dramatically as Pius's voice once had, but too much in the world had changed since his ancestor's time. The Concerned One's citizens needed more than appeals to patriotism to console them. Those few among the people who recognized the allusion to past glory moaned in disgust at the pretentious boy wearing the emperor's purple clothes. The unlettered majority asked if they could eat their citizenship. Father climbed from the carriage and demanded they be silent. He ordered the men in his command to call out to the people as he did.

"The emperor has food for you!" they and Father shouted, knowing full well the Concerned One did not. "Food! Enough for everyone!"

The crowd quieted down, giving the Concerned One an opportunity to begin again. He bit his handsome lower lip before he started, a calculated move that had never failed him before. The emperor blinked his eyes and conjured up a tear that trickled down his fair imperial cheek. The women in the mob, who had despised him seconds earlier, remarked how sympathetic he looked.

"My friends," he said, "we have been working day and night these past months, building the future of Pan-Polaria, making an Empire your children will live in, an Empire we have been so preoccupied with we have neglected some of the affairs of today. We had delegated authority to other men while we planned the future. We assumed they would serve the state as we have: with good faith and pure intentions. How bitterly we have been disappointed!

"Until yesterday, I was told by . . . a certain party"—he pointed to Cleander, and the crowd hissed as if on cue—"that our good citizens— you, my people—were being fed. I was deceived. My chamberlain, your chamberlain, was diverting the people's grain to . . ."

The Concerned One stopped because he had forgotten where the speculators said the grain was going. Father had to whisper to him, "Greece."

". . . to Greece," said the Concerned One, "the homeland of pirates and traitors!" (The crowd cheered.) "May posterity forgive us for allowing that cursed nation into our Empire. We will punish them for this offense against the mother of the world!" (The cheering grew louder.) "But first we will feed our people, and punish a certain party!"

The Concerned One ordered his guards to turn Cleander over to the people's judgment. The mob rushed forward singing songs of jubilation, and at once chopped the slender chamberlain to bits with weapons they had taken from the City Guardsmen. The roars of delight the populace bellowed forth rattled free rows of loosened tiles over the eaves of several buildings and knocked a dozen of the celebrants dead. At the time no one seemed to notice. Someone stuck Cleander's head on a pole and ran with the bloody trophy through the festive streets. The runner stopped at every prostitute he met and let her kiss the chamberlain's cold lips to show the contempt the least of Garden City's people had for Cleander, now that he was powerless and dead. Before midnight the runner had taken the head to every neighborhood in the city. In the early hours of the morning he put the head on display in the Field of Diversions, near the place Cleander had told Father he would one day mount Father's obligation. The body of the chamberlain, which the day before had housed the soul of one of the two grandest men on Earth, was thrown to the packs of half-wild dogs that roam the dry lakebeds that surround the city. The Concerned One had more things to say to the people after they had taken the chamberlain. The people did not let him say them. The joyous mob drew his carriage down the road to the palace gate before he could finish his speech. Each time he attempted to say something during his long, happy procession the cheering overwhelmed his words.

"What idiots I rule," he told Father as their vehicle reentered the palace grounds. "I could say 'Hey, hey, hey!' to them, and they would applaud me. I blame the foreign blood we have in the Empire, Blackie. I have noticed a similar decline in our dogs; we used to have good Pan-Polarian hunting dogs, and look at them now: they couldn't catch a dead rabbit. The new people, I tell you, have bred the brains clean out of our native North American stock. You should look into it. Write me a report. Not a report to me, mind you; send it to someone belonging to me."

"I will make an inquiry, my lord," said Father.

The Concerned One and his companions were roaring drunk for the following three days. When Father saw the emperor again, the Concerned One asked Father why he was still in Garden City.

"Aren't you governor of Turkey?" asked the Concerned One.

"Yes, my lord, I am," confessed Father.

"You should get back there then," said the emperor. "I have enough conspirators hanging about the capital as it is. I hardly need to be importing them in from the provinces."

As Father, the servants, and I returned to Tampico to catch a boat for Asia, we saw fleets of ships unloading grain at the docks. Days later the capital's markets were selling the previous fall's bumper harvest at bargain prices. Because there was soon food enough for everyone, everyone said they thought the Concerned One was the best emperor Pan-Polaria had ever had, in spite of the famine, the metal plagues, the new diseases, the conspiracies, the loss of much of the Empire's territory, and the other disasters that had befallen his reign. As the economy improved and the memories of hunger pangs faded, the people did not care that the Concerned One in the coming months would embark upon the worst murderous rampage of his reign. Everyone—excepting those he killed—said the emperor's little excesses did not bother them. The various plagues and the Concerned One's policies—or lack thereof—had left thousands of businesses in need of new owners and had opened up countless opportunities for those with the money to invest. The state welfare was working better than ever now that there were tens of millions of fewer bellies to fill. Pan-Polaria's enemies were far away and suffering similar disasters, and the all-conquering army still stood between them and what was left of the Empire. Nor were there any new taxes; what with the property the Concerned One was stealing from the people he murdered, the treasury's coffers were filling almost as quickly as the emperor and his friends could find ways to spend the new revenue.

For almost a year a large body of water would lie between our household and these happy times in the capital, and every day Father thanked Sophia of the Flowers for placing that expanse of water where she had.

XIII.

AD 2293

The news of our victory over Selin in the pass between Nicea and Eribulus moved more rapidly than we did. For sixteen days we marched to the northwest through Turkey and passed villages and towns that were become increasingly unstable after the people heard of Selin's defeat and beheld the small size of Father's force. For much of the journey several of our Boer troopers had to take turns carrying Father on a blanket. After passing dozens of likely resting places, we at last had to stop a while in a cluster of ragged pine trees near the place where the road swings sharply toward the city of Istanbul. The servants and I had to help Father from his blanket and help lay him on the high, cool grass. Medus rubbed the general's legs while Helen and I brought him some water to drink and to splash on his leathery face.

After we had rested for an hour, watching the birds above fly to where people no longer could, Father took from his tunic a last letter from Mr. Golden; its seal was broken but its contents were unopened. He handed it to me.

"It came to me at Nicea," he said. "My eyes would not let me read it. I can only read large print anymore."

"Was our rich 'friend' with Selin's army?" I asked as I looked at the missive that had been composed when our triumph had not seemed possible.

"Maybe he was in a rear area. He was not among the dead or the captives. Read his letter anyway," urged Father. "I am feeling old, Justa. You should humor me."

I read:

"'I had a conversation this day with my lord Abdul Selin which I would tell you of. He was this morning full of an account concerning a battle he fought near Lake Cyzicus—'"

"He means the battle he destroyed poor Brigadier Harriman in," commented Father.

"'—in the footsteps of Alexander, he there fought his way into Asia,'" I read. "'My Lord Selin's good fortune has put him in a generous mood, and I am today writing to you of a wonderful offer to you from him, the Turkish sirocco, the new King Arthur, the modern Napoleon whose special deity is the sun. The generous, manly, virtuous Selin has also bestowed upon this unworthy fellow the estates of two recently deceased gentlemen of your acquaintance.'"

"My family," whispered Father.

"'While he and I were in his tent,'" I read, "'and he was heaping reward upon reward on me, he happened to mention that you and I might know each other. "Why, yes," I said, "I believe my daughters were married to his late sons." "Have you had any recent conversations with General Black?" asked my lord Selin. "You know," I said, "although I have never been interested in politics, I think, if I am not mistaken, Black is somehow involved in this fracas, is he not?" My lord Selin then commenced a long and wondrous narrative describing the campaigns you and he waged together in the Great Plains, when he was the governor and you the stalwart soldier who rid his province of deserters. His eyes filled with tears as he recalled the happy times you and he had together in those days that are no more. "It is a pity," he said. "While he is my rival, I wish we could imitate the military discipline of that man." He was overcome with emotion for a moment. "If only," he said, "we could let the past be the past, and General Black could be with us when we go against the upstart Whiteman. We would just be soldiers again, fighting together as we did in the old days. We could save the Empire, he and I. I suppose that once I defeat the rest of his army he will get across the Euphrates with those scoundrels who led him into this error and will nevermore play a role in our glorious Empire." My love for you, my dear general, made me bold, and I dared to speak my heart in the presence of the great man. "It is carried to me by rumor," I said, "that the noble General Black may not flee to the heart of Asia, but might remain within the boundaries of our Eastern provinces. Rumor would even have it that I may be able to locate him." Would that you had been there to see the smile upon my lord Selin's face—'"

"I have seen that smile already," said Father. "Selin and the crocodile make pretty much the same expression when they're happy."

"Mr. Golden still lays the blather on thick," I commented. "I would pay to see his face when he learns his 'Lord Selin' has had to run for his life."

"That bit about my military discipline is from a letter Selin wrote to the Concerned One when I was in the emperor's good graces and Selin did not know where he stood," said Father. "Golden knows Selin likes to hear himself quoted. Selin must have imagined the Concerned One read anything written to him. Luke Anthony sometimes listened to that prostitute of his and that addle-headed giant; most times he followed his personal inclinations."

I read farther:

"'He forgot the dignity of his office and leapt forward to clasp my hand.'"

"Skip ahead beyond any heartfelt scenes," said Father.

"He goes on," I said. "Selin says he really loves you, wants to make you cospeaker of the Senate."

Father laughed regardless of the pain in his legs.

"Selin wants to know if Mr. Golden could contact you," I said, scanning through the letter. "Mr. Golden writes: 'Oh, yes, I can!' Oh no," I said as I read the ensuing words.

"What is it?" asked Father.

"Mr. Golden writes," I said, "that the late Brigadier Harriman betrayed you at Lake Cyzicus to save his wife and children in Garden City. Selin murdered them all anyway."

"Poor, poor Harriman," said Father.

"They have killed the Senators Caleb Coppola and Francis Penn," I said. "This is rich: Mr. Golden wants you to destroy any letters he has sent you. He writes, 'I would never, with my own hand, disparage the Empire or my lord Selin.' He claims a coconspirator allied with General Whiteman must have written some of the more malicious letters he sent you."

"I pity Golden also," said Father. "He thought he was backing the winning side. Selin will kill him too, in time. That greedy little chap will not share his realm with anyone. The fat fool Golden is already afraid."

"He wanted you to surrender to Selin," I said. "He writes he fears you would flee to the Chinese, perhaps form a government in exile."

I read aloud the last paragraph in the letter: "'You must go to the station north of Tarsus. Dress in the garb of a commoner, wrap a long coat around you, and get rid of your soldier's armor. A friend of mine will meet you on the road. He will take you to another friend of mine, one Nicholas Street—'"

"The assassin," said Father. "Our men found him dead among the fallen in the pass."

The letter concluded: "'This man's visage is darker than even yours; thus his somewhat forbidding face will be easily recognized. Perhaps you have heard of his exploits in the arena. Trust me, he is exactly the man for this mission. When he approaches you, draw back your coat and tell him your name. "What gives you the right to be here?" he will ask. Draw your sidearm and say to him, "This does." Surrender to him your weapon as a sign of your trust in the gracious Abdul Selin. Be assured that Mr. Street will straightaway give the weapon back to you. You will thereafter be brought to Selin's camp, where he and I will be overjoyed to see you.'"

"He ends there," I said.

"He couldn't resist mocking me, there at the last part," said Father. "Golden presumed I would surrender myself up to death. Are we fighting to rule subjects such as he?"

We brought out some bread and a little wine from our knapsacks. Helen spread a cloth on the grass in lieu of a dining table, and we ate our small repast in quiet moments of peace. Father remained lying on his back. With some help from Medus, he did manage to eat some crusts upon which he had asked Sophia's blessings.

"The news of our victory will soon overtake us," he said, and said nothing more till the servants had picked up the cloth.

While I went to tell the men we were about to begin marching again, Medus and Helen helped him stand, and he said something to them I did not catch.

"Come and have another drop of wine, sweetheart," said Helen, and she brought me the wine skin. "Drink up. We will be thirsty long before we get any more."

Father called me to his side. He had seated himself, after much effort, on a fallen tree trunk, and motioned toward the place he wanted me to sit.

"So, Justa, what do you think?" he asked me.

"Of what, sir?"

"Of everything," he said. "You should, I think, call me Father, and I will call you Daughter."

He kissed my cheek. The servants and the armed men were immediately at hand and could plainly see this brave gesture of affection he had never before granted me. I could not keep myself from crying as shamelessly as I had done when as a young girl I had witnessed the dying Mathias the Glistening.

"I think the world is a desolate place," I said, "if evil men like Selin and Golden can escape to prosper and good men like my father can give everything to the Empire, win every battle he fights, and yet gain nothing."

"I wouldn't know about that," he said. "Those things, as you know, are too deep for me. Right now, Daughter, my one regret is I never kept up my calligraphy. I had a wonderful hand when I was schoolboy. No telling where good calligraphy can take a man. I'll need it now that we no longer can type anything. Anyway, I did not give up everything. I did not give up you, Daughter," he said, and kissed my hand.

"I will give up myself," I said. "I will stay with you, Father, until the battle is finally and forever won."

"No, we will go to Amsterdam," I heard Father say. "We will ask for Samuel Van Coons in the marketplace, as I told you to do once before. There you will marry and have children, Daughter. That will be my final revenge upon Selin and his sort. The world will never be completely his as long as you and yours are in it. I will live as long as I can, and perhaps in time you will forgive me for the wrongs I have done you."

He called for the men to gather around him, and positioned the officers so they could relay his words to those in the seventeen thousand who were beyond the reach of his voice. Medus helped Father climb atop the tree stump, and from there he spoke to his command.

"My friends," he said, "no general could demand more from his troops than what you have already given me. You have won a great victory that will live on after you are gone, although the Empire you fought for will not.

"There is no Empire any longer, and no longer any emperor. Abdul Selin has escaped from our reach and is on his way back to Garden City to raise another army. Given his resources and that of his criminal family, he will gather enough men to keep himself in power in North America, but he will not make a force capable of sailing across the Atlantic and retaking the Empire's lands in this hemisphere. His other rival, General Whiteman, is stuck in Britain and Scandinavia. When his money runs out—and it soon will—he will wither away.

"I too must wither away, my friends, for I am already out of funds and can no longer pay you to fight more battles."

A murmur rippled through the men, although they were soon again quiet.

"You have won the battle, and I can only give you your freedom. I cannot give you more. There are no longer any battles left for you to win, not for you and not for me. There are only some angry factions fighting on the other side of the world. Their quarrels are meaningless to us. Whoever reigns in Garden City, he will only increase the suffering of those under him.

"Rather than continue to insert ourselves in their disputes, I propose we cross into Europe and begin the world anew. That land was the home to many of your ancestors. The new diseases have depopulated many areas and left the land open for settlement by new pioneers."

Most of the soldiers had traveled from Van City with their wives and children trailing behind them. To these families without homes, settling and farming, even in the primitive conditions of a world stricken by the new metal plague, sounded better than fighting more pointless battles.

"In Europe," said Father, "you will build a new nation and I will grow old. The Empire will pass away, and in a thousand years your descendants will read of it in a language that does not yet exist, and they will wonder if these things really were. And even if they think the story of our age is no more real than the tales of Camelot and Troy, those in ages hence will know who among us were villains and those who were loyal to the things they held dear."

I whispered to Father he should stop there, because I feared he might tell the story of the crocodile and harm the favorable opinion his men had of him.

The men voted to go on with us to that portion of Europe called the Low Countries, from whence the ancestors of the Boers had come six centuries before. As we marched through Istanbul the next day, the city that had held out for Father turned out to cheer us across the bridge over the Bosporus. Two days after we were gone, the city went over to the Muslim rebels from the nation's rural districts, and Turkey—as the rest of Asia had already done—left the Pan-Polarian Empire forever.

XIV

AD 2291–2292

We had been in Turkey for another ten months when Father was called to Garden City for the final time. The frontier had been kind to us; it had given us three full seasons of peace in spite of our deteriorating technological abilities, while in the capital city great changes had been taking place. Soon after Cleander's death the Senate had seated itself to hear the Concerned One speak upon a new agenda for the Empire he had told the senators he wished to announce within their hallowed chamber. The Concerned One was yet riding a wave of popular approval in the aftermath of the chamberlain's bloody downfall. The Senate was expecting him to use the moment to propose either a new campaign against the Chinese or to initiate a public rebuilding program. Every one of the distinguished gentlemen and ladies present was dressed in his or her ornate finery of silk and gold and sat on the plush seats hoping against experience that the Concerned One would at last emerge as the second Mathias they had long awaited. Their hopes should have been directed toward something else. The emperor entered that grand room wearing a ragged pair of denim shorts and a tattered straw hat that sat upon his head at a rakish angle; over his shoulder he carried a pole on the end of which was a hobo's kit tied into a red bandana. Into the Senate's sanctuary the Concerned One brought with him his gaggle of athlete friends along with his mistress Marcie Angelica and the huge wrestler Norman. Marcie was dressed in a manner similar to the emperor and had freckles painted on her nut-brown face. The nearly insensate Norman had on a pair of bib overalls, and was painted on his face and body with black greasepaint and bore in one hand a boat oar. None of the senators could bring himself to speak until the emperor had planted himself on the high throne directly in front of them. Those in the front row sat gaping as if under a spell; the ones in the back benches pretended to be looking at an interesting spot on the ceiling high above the emperor's head. Caleb Coppola, an elderly senator from a distinguished family—meaning his ancestors had toadied to generations of the very powerful better than almost anyone else—was the first to rise and speak.

"Welcome, Emperor Luke Anthony, the Concerned One, the Conqueror of Britain, the Friend of Peace, the—," he said, and was going to list the rest of the emperor's honorary names until the emperor held up a hand to signal him to stop.

"There is no Concerned One any longer," said the emperor. "Not in my current human form, anyway. He does, I know, live on among you citizens of Pan-Polaria in loving memory."

Mr. Coppola had served fifty years in the Senate. A man does not prosper in dangerous circumstances for that long without being able to shift his position when the ground beneath him shifts. He made a swift appraisal of the situation and said, "My old eyes have betrayed me. Who is it, my lord, that I am addressing?"

"Sometimes I am called the One Who Has Come," said the emperor. "Sometimes Mr. Hercules. Today I am appearing before you as Tom

Sawyer, one of my preferred earthly guises. Be not afraid, my friends. I may be the king of heaven, but as long as I am in human shape, I am much like any of you. Therefore, you may look upon me, and your eyes will not fall from their sockets, which they would do, I promise you, were I to assume one of my more awesome forms. Of course, even now I could crush all of you just by making a fist."

He flexed the muscles in his forearms to show them this was so.

"I see," said Senator Coppola, who was in fact doubting everything he was hearing and seeing.

The emperor explained that Marcie was now Huckleberry Finn, the boon companion of the fun-loving Tom. The giant Norman was, by the emperor's grace, the Negro Jim, but the senators were not to be offended by the presence of a slave; the emperor could, with a nod of his head, also make Norman resemble the king of Persia, if there still was a Persia and it still had a king—the emperor could not remember that morning.

"I thought it was only right to make him my companion after the cruel trick that was played on him," the emperor said.

"What trick was that, my lord?" asked Senator Coppola.

"When Huck pretended to be dead," said the emperor, much perturbed the senator did not know the story. "Have you not read the account written by Mr. Clemens?" he asked.

"I am very old. Many years have escaped me since I read of you in school. I had forgotten . . . ," said Senator Coppola.

He started to sit down, then quickly stood upright again.

"May I seat myself, my lord?" he asked.

The emperor allowed he might, but from that moment forward Coppola and the other people of the Empire would have to prostrate themselves whenever they were in the emperor's vicinity.

"I am a god now," he said. "The god, if one wants to quibble over titles. Gods have to be shown proper respect by you chaps who are someday going to be rotting corpses."

He paused to adjust his shorts, a garment that, much to the discomfort of the senators in the front rows, kept riding up on his beefy legs.

"Else I will have to destroy you," the emperor said. "I don't want to. Don't care if I do, either. The matter is entirely up to you. I am disconnected from your concerns."

He rose from his throne, and every senator fell upon his face in response. The emperor remembered something as he went toward the exit and returned to the throne platform to say, "I nearly forgot to tell you: there are going to be some big changes happening in your world soon."

The senators cautiously reseated themselves and listened.

"For instance," said the emperor, "Garden City is no more. No one can use that name any longer, unless he is referring to past events. You are currently living in the Mausoleum of the Concerned One, which I have named in honor of my former incarnation. I want the road signs, the coins, the rest of the what-you-call-thems changed as soon as you can manage it to reflect the city's new designation. I realize you are mortals and cannot do these things as quickly as I would want. You should also realize I can be a wrathful god when I am disappointed. Should you tarry at this assignment, I may have to take action to speed you at your task. Remember my history in the guise of the mighty Hercules: I have slain my own wife and children. Do you think I would hesitate to kill a roomful of old men?"

The signs were altered and new coins were minted two days later.

As he had told Father during our previous visit to the capital, the emperor/god had discovered Drummond's book upon the first twelve rulers of the Pan-Polarian Empire; the actions of his predecessors recorded therein had given the emperor countless new notions of governance. He would sit upon a balcony in the palace, killing flies for hours on end as his predecessor Timor had done, although the earlier emperor had used an energy ray to perform the deed and the man born Luke Anthony only had a prosaic swatter. The Emperors John and Juno had once had months of the years named after them, so the emperor/god who used to be the Concerned One renamed the entire year after his honorific titles: the Wild One, Lucky, Pius, Luke, Windy, Glistening, Canadian, Holy, Hercules, Roman, Trusting, and the Expected One replaced the traditional names of the twelve months. (The name of the last month became the title by which the emperor most often wanted to be addressed.) Because he had read how the emperor Cepheus had practiced every form of sexual depravity, the current emperor did him one better by keeping hundreds of young men in the palace whom he dressed in women's clothing and named after male and female body parts. He delighted in offending important visitors to the palace by kissing and fondling his peculiar new companions whenever he knew his guests would be watching. When he reread of how Darko had failed to fight the huge conflagration in the old capital city of Washington, the emperor was inspired to commit a still larger crime: he ordered the City Guardsmen to set the city ablaze and to protect only the palace and other public buildings. The flames they set destroyed most of central Garden City, some of which was centuries old. The former Christian church once known as the National Cathedral burned to ashes. The sacred Bell of Liberty, the most hallowed object in the Empire, was melted into a lump of bronze when the museum it was in was set aflame. The fire likewise destroyed the beautiful Temple of Peace, which many said was a sign that the Empire would never again know serene times and was also an incident that caused other citizens to ask why the Pan-Polarians had ever bothered to build a temple dedicated to peace. The emperor claimed the black wasteland the fire left in the heart of the city was now imperial property, and he proclaimed a day of thanksgiving because he had been given the chance to build a city worthy of himself.

"Now you will have more than a stadium to remember me by when I have ascended again onto Olympus," he told the Senate on a day he was dressed in his Hercules outfit.

On that same occasion he assured the senators they need not worry much about the homeless families the holocaust might have created; he had ordered the City Guardsmen to set the fires at night while the affected people were sleeping, and so most of the potentially dislocated had perished along with their homes.

"You are fortunate I think of these little details," the emperor told them.

The Concerned One—I still called him that in spite of his new titles—rarely spoke to the citizens not part of the government. He let Marcie go to the common people for him. On the occasion of one of her speeches she rode through the streets dressed as a warrior from some earlier age and astraddle an enormous black charger from which she proclaimed to the spectacle-hungry folk what glorious plans the emperor had for them. The tall, awe-inspiring concubine told them there would not only be public work projects to reconstruct the center of the city, there would be more athletic shows, and everyone would have double their usual dole allotments, simply because the emperor was so very fond of his people. She was an uncommonly good speaker for one of her background. She used short words the people understood, and she was loud. The people came to love the tall woman in a blonde wig, a woman they, like the emperor, now called "the Amazon"; they perhaps loved her more than they loved the emperor himself, as she was one of them, and was even more abusive of the wealthy than the Concerned One was. Rich and noble citizens despised her with a fury equal to the commoners' love. Marcie was lowborn, a woman and a whore, and she had the power to issue claims upon property and to kill anyone objecting to her methods. "See how they quiver before a woman!" she would proclaim from the back of her dreaded horse when she was preparing to pounce upon another victim. Once whatever prey she had selected was dead, she would use the same black horse to drag the dead man's body over the pavement, and she would ask the people, "What good are his titles today? Who now cares what the name of his great-grandfather was? Look at him: yesterday he had two hundred servants to bathe and feed him; today he is fed to us." Her supporters painted images of her on thousands of city walls; always they depicted her as the triumphant Hippolyte, the mythical queen of the Amazons, about to gut another cowering rich man. Other scribblers working under the cover of night would write "whore" or "murderer" underneath her pictures.

Garden City's graffiti artists were less kind to Marcie's consort, for many among them hated him for his corrupt government and for his lack of dignity and for his failure to respond to the destruction of our technologies and because—and I will put the matter in writing as delicately as I can—the Concerned One had developed a singular physical problem that made even him more ridiculous than he had been before. A certain embarrassing swelling (embarrassing to everyone else, but not to the emperor) had arisen in the area of the emperor's groin. No one had noted this peculiar growth while the Concerned One still wore his purple emperor's suits; when he went about dressed in the scanty fur kilt of Hercules or in Tom Sawyer's denim shorts, the condition was obvious to all who beheld him. On the occasion I first looked upon him after our return to Garden City, Helen and I were seated across from the imperial box in the Field of Diversions and from a considerable distance we could see more of the emperor's unseemly growth than any sane person would have wanted to behold. One of his matronly admirers near us blurted out, "He is the greatest man in the world! See how happy he is to look over the thousands of pretty girls he rules!" The fool woman had no idea what she was seeing. Something terrible had befallen the once achingly handsome son of Mathias; his face had reddened, and the tip of his nose had become bulbous since the time of Cleander's death. While he retained his massive, powerful figure, he no longer moved with his old speed when he fenced with his mates, and his skin was developing a rash that would slowly turn into clusters of open pustules. The graffiti artists drew obscene representations of the stricken emperor—most of which I cannot describe without sounding as puerile as the artists were—on the clean white walls of every new building the Concerned One erected. Even the supposedly sacred new Temple of Peace hosted grotesque caricatures of him. The joke among the irreverent scribblers in the city was that because of their pictures the Concerned One was truly building something for which he would be forever remembered.

The emperor/god forgot to welcome Father to the city for weeks after our arrival via Tampico. We learned immediately after we made port that the Concerned One had called the other leading men from the provinces into the capital, and was too busy harassing them to bother with Father at that time. While he was both evil and insane, the emperor must have had a few lucid moments when he recalled that Father had twice saved his useless life. I believe within his fevered mind there was a compartment that held Father to be a handy old patriot he could summon to duty in the most dangerous instances. As for the other generals, the Concerned One imagined they were constantly plotting against him. Some of them of course were, which to the Concerned One justified the threats and the occasional death sentences he apportioned to some of his other commanders. We in Father's household were meanwhile yet again left hanging in Garden City. Father had no official duties, and we had no inkling of whether he would be accepted as a friend or a foe when the emperor at last summoned him to the palace.

We did, as I have said, see the emperor from afar at the arena soon after our return from the East. On the occasion of the memorable Winter Festival games of that year the Concerned One fought as a modern gladiator against a man given a wooden sword to use against the emperor's steel one. The Concerned One had previously slain wild animals in athletic exhibitions on other occasions. This combat against humans was an innovation in his history of disgraceful conduct. Hunting is noble—or so most important men hold it to be so—but fighting other men for money is not. Crowds on the day of the emperor's fight filled the gigantic stadium to overflow capacity. For months before word had gone throughout what was left of the Empire that the Concerned One would debase himself in this fashion, and most of the citizens were eager to see him do so. The lower classes cheered the titled fool as he entered the arena in his golden armor; they threw fistfuls of carnations on him when he took a preliminary lap around the interior wall separating the adoring populace from the bloody artificial turf. The commoners screamed like a whole army of drunken Russians when the emperor commenced to whacking away at this opponent's wooden weapon with his metal blade. The sight offended the senators and governmental officials in attendance, but they too raised their hands and cheered because Marcie and a host of City Guardsmen were watching them to ascertain who among their number were not completely delighted. At the contest's end, the Concerned One spared his opponent's life after he had hacked only a few nasty gashes in the unlucky gladiator's chest and face.

For this victory, the professional athletes' guild awarded the emperor a bag of gold double-eagle coins that he brandished about the arena for everyone to see. The people clapped themselves to exhaustion in response to his heroism. Then, contrary to the normal order of convict matches followed by wild animal slaughter followed by athletic matches, the emperor's friends fought some matches against each other. It is a curious thing to recount, since this was the blood-soaked Field of Diversions we were in, yet none of the contestants in these fights of the Winter Games were really injured, as the contestants were—as they proudly shouted to the crowd before each mock duel—the emperor's companions and were above getting hurt. These favored athletes pulled their blows and put on great displays of false agony when anyone's weapon came within an arm's length of anyone else. They broke open packets of pig's blood to simulate wounds when they felt wounds were needed, and the crowd pretended to love their efforts. Everyone cheered and applauded as loudly as they had for the Concerned One. I wondered if any of the 180,000 present thought it ironic that in an era when almost no one else was safe, paid combatants fighting in the Field of Diversions were not injured by so much as a splinter in one of their fingers. The finale of the games was a shooting exhibition performed by the Concerned One and selected marksmen from within his circle. From the safety of the elevated walkway the emperor had used at previous shows, they shot dead a beautiful orange-and-black tiger imported from India, several tall birds, some wild goats that were as graceful as swifts when they frantically leapt in vain against the high arena walls, and lastly they shot a huge, leathery rhinoceros of a sort I had not seen before. (Some said it was an African unicorn, a description that only demonstrates how far Africa is from the glorious realms of mythology.) The emperor shot this last beast seven times and failed to kill it. The great wrinkly thing merely became more enraged the more he wounded it, until it became so angry it charged the carbon filament supports holding up the elevated ramp. The mighty creature bent one vertical beam cleanly in half, sending the emperor onto his imperial backside. The African "unicorn" might have torn the entire edifice down and trampled the Concerned One into the green plastic grass but for a squadron of City Guardsmen who charged into the arena and emptied their assault rifles into the furious animal. Hundreds of rounds were needed to send the beast from this world, and thirty Guardsmen were necessary to drag it to the center of the field, where the emperor/god posed with a foot propped atop his vanquished prey. Everyone declared aloud they had never seen a braver man than he. They screamed for a half an hour as he strutted about the enclosed battleground in his Hercules outfit. Women exposed their breasts to him in hopes of making his eyes linger on them an additional second. Poor men threw the last coins in their purses at the emperor's feet. (The Concerned One or someone in his circle had foreseen the possibility of this transpiring, and small boys were present to dash onto the turf and gather up the coins for the emperor's treasury.) Senators lowered their faces onto the concrete, swearing as they debased themselves that they were overawed by the emperor/god. My father the general missed all of this. During the first sword fight he had put a wet cloth over his head and had gone to sleep in the warm sunshine. The shouting of his neighbors covered the loud snoring he did while the emperor moved from victory to greater victory on the green surface below the towering grandstands. Father awoke upon hearing the trumpet call announcing the end of the spectacles. He declared to his legal wife the outing had exhausted him and he needed to go home and take a nap.

When someone in the palace at last remembered Father was in the city, a messenger brought the general a summons to meet with the emperor on the following afternoon. Since the heart of the city remained mostly windblown ashes, Father had to walk across a black wasteland to get to his interview. The remains of that man-made disaster turned Father's pristine white officer's uniform to a shade of dirty gray miles before he could reach the palace gateway. Yet he should not have bothered making the grim journey, as Father soon learned the trip would be for naught. The emperor/god's mortal parts were ill that day, and he was receiving no one. In a corridor near the emperor's living quarters Father did meet Marcie. She demanded to know who this dusty old man wandering about the home of a god was.

"We have met before, madam," he said. "I am General Peter Black, the governor of Turkey."

"Oh," she said, disappointed because he was not someone there to be executed, "the old Nestor."

"Pardon, madam?" said Father.

"Nestor, you dunce," she said. "You know: the elderly chap in the Greek book about Troy. He lived in the past, didn't he? The emperor calls you that."

"He summoned me," said Father.

"He won't be seeing anyone for a while," said Marcie. "Don't worry. He has no grievance against you. He likes you. It's the other army rats he is going to come down on. Some of those bastards will be a head shorter before this is over."

"Before what is over, madam?" asked Father.

"The transformation of the city, the blossoming of the earthly paradise, and the rest of it," she said, and pointed this way and that to show she was speaking of something that involved all of creation. "You should keep up with current events."

"Do you know why I am in Garden City?"

"In the Mausoleum of the Concerned One," she corrected him.

"Recalled from Turkey," suggested Father, for he could not force himself to say the absurd new name Luke Anthony had given the capital.

"He wants everyone of importance to remain in the Mausoleum of the Concerned One," she said. "They cannot conspire against him while they're right under his nose."

She told him to go home. The emperor would summon him again when he was feeling better. While he waited day after empty day for that interview to happen, Father learned he scarcely knew his legitimate wife after his many years of absence. While they lived together in the small house in the Field of Heroes, Father found their relationship had fared better when he was dwelling under a roof in distant Asia or in some other residence that was not near the capital. He awoke in the mornings to find her staring in disgust at his sun-blackened face and his gnarled soldier's hands. When she spoke to him during the daylight hours, she often as not reminded him of how much nobler her family had been than his before they two were married.

During the afternoon his wife would have her women friends over to gossip and sew floral designs on their clothing, flowers being the traditional symbols of Pan-Polarian nobility. If Father lingered there, the women sat in the front room staring in his direction, as if awaiting him to spring upon them like a wild beast. His wife's friends thought Father a vulgar rube on account of his coarse dining habits, for he was a soldier and soldiers must eat quickly when they have the opportunity. The same women thought he might be a foreigner because he pronounced his vs as though they were bs and elided his vowels; the society women asked (in not particularly polite fashion) if he had been reared in the Middle East since he spoke such terrible English.

When a prominent family in the neighborhood came over to visit—and one of them came nearly every day—Father found it easier to spend his hours of inaction in the small garden out back or by taking long walks to the city's bustling street markets. While he strolled through neighborhoods that were completely changed from his younger days, Father felt like a stranger in the city he had known briefly in his youth. He did not recognize the songs the street minstrels sang in the public places; the new tunes were filthy ditties in Spanish about the emperor's physical condition or about his harem of odd young men and not the old military ballads Father remembered.

There were theaters everywhere in the city, many more than when he had been a young man and people still had hologram sets and other electronic equipment. When he went inside some of these new establishments, he discovered that the actors he saw did not perform the old plays written in English and instead did outlandish deeds on stage such as mutilating themselves with daggers to please the drunken, sullen audiences; nor did Father understand why so many actors impersonated women and in front of hundreds of spectators did things with other men that would have earned them a trip to the mines had they done them in public thirty years before.

Every day on the streets there was some sort of native holiday; there were always long processions and the din of trumpets and drums. No one, however, could explain to Father what was being celebrated. Every city block seemed to contain a brothel that had blonde women hanging from its open windows. Every alley held naked beggars crouching in the winter cold as they pled for money or drugs. Father could not speak to many people on the streets in English (neither in the real sort nor in that of the army camps) or in Syntalk or even in the Spanish still common in the rest of Mexico; much of Garden City spoke either an obscure tongue from a far-away land, or they used a patois composed of dozens of different languages, only snatches of which could he comprehended. Father could no more have had a conversation with one of these citizens than he could with the sparrows feeding on the filth in the open sewers. The friends of Father's childhood were either long since dead or hiding from the modern world in remote country estates and hoping to die of old age before anyone discovered where they were or the new diseases or gangs got to them.

Father was only comfortable in Garden City whenever he came to visit Helen and me in our rented lodgings; while with us he could play dominoes against his servant Medus or listen as I read from Dickens and Jane Austen. I upbraided him during these frequent visits for rambling about the city unprotected. At that time groups of armed hoodlums were rampant in the often unpatrolled streets; these young thugs wore short hooded robes to hide themselves and had long knives they carried in their belts; everyone in our tenement building said these hooded youths ambushed their individual victims in swarms the way a pack of wolves falls upon a single deer and that a solitary person had no defense against them.

"Who would attack me?" was Father's response to my warnings. "Do I look like I have money?" he would ask.

"Sir, there are groups of wealthy youths who kill for the pleasure of killing. They think it a kind of sport. Money means nothing to them," I told him. "They care nothing of how you look."

Helen agreed with me. She told a gory story of a baker murdered in a street neighboring our flat to illustrate she knew what she was talking about.

"An old wives' tale," huffed Father. "People could not be so cruel . . . people who aren't emperor, I mean. I know the Pan-Polarians better than you provincial folk. I know they do not do such things."

"You haven't lived among them for forty-six years, sir," I told him. "The only Pan-Polarians you know are professional soldiers, and they only call themselves that."

"Aren't they citizens?" demanded Father.

"Some of them are," I allowed.

"Aren't my soldiers the same as these chaps loitering about here in Garden City?" he asked. "I admit there's not much order here. That's because no one has taken charge of the situation. Told them what they should be about. People are the same everywhere you go. I blame the city's leadership. Teach these people how to behave and some useful machine skills, and this town would whip itself into shape quite nicely."

I sighed at his ignorance. Both Medus and Helen did likewise; which was impudent of them, seeing as how they were hired servants, no matter how familiar they were to us. Happily, Father remained as unperceptive as he usually was and was not offended by anything they did.

"So you say, sir," I said. "You still should have a guard when you go walking."

He said the day he took orders from women would be the last day he walked anywhere. He continued to rove around the dangerous city as freely as a cloud scudding across a summer sky. The thieves he passed on the streets must have thought him a lunatic to roam about the disintegrating buildings looking like a character from an antique farce. His clothes were from some other historical era; his ragged hair, his odd speech, his sunburnt visage all declared him to be a penniless bumpkin in town to attend a festival or to beg alms. Garden City's legions of criminals consequently left him alone and sought victims elsewhere.

When Father was next summoned to the palace, the emperor was up and active, too active and much too furious to spare a word on General Black. Marcie had overseen yet another bloodletting upon several noble families. These executions of imaginary criminals had further convinced the emperor plotters were everywhere among the powerful. At the time Father arrived the emperor was abusing the ears of some goons among the City Guardsmen and some senior officers from the regular army who had let someone escape his mistress's clutches; even now, the emperor was shouting, even now this escapee was making plans to assassinate him. Father sat in the same antechamber he had sat in eleven years earlier when he had witnessed the murders of two innocent men and was splattered with their guiltless blood. This time a butler brought Father some food and drink while he listened to the muffled sounds filtering through the tall iron doors protecting the palace's interior. Most of the other provincial generals were inside those doors and enduring the full blast of the emperor's insane harangue. Some of them had been virtual prisoners in the palace since the time of Cleander's death. The Concerned One would have killed these long-term "guests" of his for conspiring against him while they were on the frontiers, except that he feared their replacements would be no more trustworthy. He figured the current generals were at least of a known quality, as imperial agents had spied upon them for years. The emperor told his captive generals each day he was a god—or at least a god in the image of a man—and he abused the military men for never showing him adequate reverence due a genuine deity. Some of them, the Concerned One observed, were slow to prostrate themselves to him. Only a few of them had memorized his honorific names. "Did you think I, a god, wouldn't notice?" Father heard him scream through the iron doors. Abdul Selin was among those the emperor made a special effort to browbeat. The smuggling and extortion rackets the enormous Selin clan had long practiced in their Tunisian homeland looked to an outsider like the emperor to be proof of a conspiracy of some sort; that the Selins were also members of an odd and highly secretive sun cult testified to some sort of sinister plot, or so it did in the emperor's opinion. As a criminal syndicate, a vast extended family, and a unique religious order, the Selins shielded themselves with triple layers of protection from any imperial agents attempting to penetrate their numbers. The Concerned One hated this pack of hairy little men infiltrating his military and civil administration. He feared them with an equal ardor, for the Selins were an enigma to him, as they were to everyone else within the Empire. For what he knew of them, killing one of their members, particularly a powerful member such as General Abdul Selin, might bring retaliation. Paralyzed by his fears, the emperor had to settle for bombarding the Selin clan with threats, hoping that might make them as frightened of him as he already was of them. I did not witness any of the sessions the emperor had with his generals. Drawing from what I had seen of him, I could imagine how a man of Abdul Selin's temperament took the hard words the mad emperor threw in his direction. Selin would not forget these constant dressing-downs, nor would he be one to forget that Father did not have to endure the humiliations visited upon him and the other commanders. That day at the palace would certainly not be one he would set aside in his mind after he met Father in the antechamber minutes after the emperor had yelled himself hoarse and had retired for the evening.

"So, Black," said Selin, bursting into the room and showing his very white teeth through the black tangle of his beard, "I see the emperor's favorite is allowed to sit out here and nibble cheese like a pet mouse while he screams at the rest of us!"

"I am hardly his favorite, sir," said Father, and brushed the crumbs off his face.

"Do you know what his oversized bitch called me today?" asked Selin, referring to Marcie. "That whore! The Concerned One, or whatever he calls himself these days, he lets the slut call me a hairy monkey!" (His small body tightened like a rope pulling a heavy weight when he thought of her.) "She put a collar on General Lamb and made him bark like a dog! 'Bark!' she says, and he did! She tries to put a collar on me, and I will snap her neck!"

Selin ripped a handful of wiry hair from his own beard to demonstrate his rage. Blood swelled from his face and down his chin, yet his glistening teeth remained fixed. Two of his family cronies, easily identified by the large sun-face decals they bore upon their military tunics, had followed Selin into the small room from the interior rooms; they quickly retreated behind the molded doors when they witnessed the mood of their clan leader.

"You really should control your anger, sir," said Father. "Look what you've done to your face. What must you be doing to your internal organs? My doctor tells me anger can cause ulcers and—"

Father did not continue because Selin had let go a shriek so terrible it made Father's ears buzz for several moments after the other man was again silent.

"You will know everything about my anger, someday!" Selin swore to him. "One day I will tear your heart out and eat it like I would an apple! First, I will roast you unto death over a campfire! I will stretch you on a wheel and peel your hide off! I will stick a glowing poker down your throat and make your lungs pop! You will beg me to bring the fatal blow!"

"Why do you say such things to me?" asked Father. "I am an old man. I saved your army for you."

"You . . . you . . . you ancient simpleton!" groaned Selin, and had to hold his hands over his abdomen, for an unnameable something had erupted inside him with such force his guts ached. "Someday I will teach you a final lesson!" he hissed at Father; then he hurried from the room to vent his fury on his hapless relatives, two of whom he would beat to death before the morning.

Because the Concerned One already had absolute power and the inclination to execute anyone at any moment, Father decided he had greater worries than what Selin was promising to do at some indefinite point in the future. Father reasoned the emperor was still very young and would be ruling long after he and Selin had gone to their separate versions of paradise. Everyone of importance had told Father that if the emperor died in the immediate future his successor would be either Fabian Clement or Patrick Herman Pretext, the leading lights in the Senate; the former was the greatest orator of the day, and the latter was a very old man everyone esteemed—using the low standards of our time—as an extremely distinguished man simply because he was so very old. Father thought the upper classes and the City Guardsmen would never support a provincial strongman of Selin's ilk. General Emile Lamb, the fellow Selin had seen bark like a dog, commanded the City Guardsmen at that juncture. Unlike his predecessors in that post, Lamb had little power and functioned under the close scrutiny of the emperor's spies. Everyone agreed he was a nobody. The other important office in the emperor's court, that of chamberlain, belonged to Able Einman, another weak functionary the emperor's men (and Marcie's) kept tied to a short rope. Thus there was no one in a position to challenge the Concerned One's rule, and should the son of Mathias eventually regain a portion of his long-absent sanity, Father believed Selin's animosity toward him could bring no one any harm, for power would long lie somewhere other than in the little Turk's hands.

Father did not know General Lamb was an associate of Selin's and like Selin a worshiper of Helios; they had attended the same private school when they were boys and had made a blood pact when they were young men at home in Tunis to help each other rise in the world when they were older. Lamb was obligated to do little while he was under the Concerned One's thumb in the capital. He was there fully employed in the job of keeping his head atop his shoulders. He nonetheless did somehow convince the emperor one night when the Concerned One was more intoxicated than usual to sign an order sending Selin back to the Great Plains. Selin there would be free from the emperor's outbursts and in control of the Empire's largest army. The little Turkish gangster slipped from Garden City in the middle of an otherwise uneventful night, the emperor's orders in hand. He flew north on the Pan American Highway in the company of ten thousand of his relatives, certain he would outlive the troubles to come and equally certain many of the men he left behind in the capital would not. If history were not a dunderhead, she would record Selin began his assent to absolute power that night he extracted himself from the fiasco that was taking place in Garden City and fled to his troops in the grasslands of the windy American plains.

When the spring of the emperor Luke Anthony's last year on Earth came slithering into the Mexican high country, the emperor/god decided the time had arrived for a grand ceremony involving the entire population to mark the refounding of Garden City as the Mausoleum of the Concerned One. He announced he would plow a furrow in the earth around the entire circumference of the capital to replant symbolically the city the Aztecs had founded but failed to name after the son of Mathias the Glistening. All of the leading citizens, including Father, and some three hundred thousand less prestigious folk, came to a cornfield beyond the southern suburbs to cheer on the divine sower of cities in this great endeavor. The Concerned One arrived in his Hercules outfit and riding atop a golden chariot. He gave an impromptu oration to the assembled, explaining that he had dealt with oxen before: he had captured the herds of Geryon and the Cretan bull when he was working for the late King Eurystheus. The crowd was very polite to him; only a few small boys snickered at the mad emperor's retelling of mythological tales from another civilization, and those impudent little imps were buried deep in the massive throng, in places the City Guardsmen could not single them out. The Concerned One posed behind his animal-driven plow for a team of photographers and artists while the latter drew sketches for a commemorative coin. Thirty minutes later, after a shout of encouragement from his City Guardsmen, the emperor cracked his whip over the broad backs of what must have been the fattest oxen in Mexico, and the plow inched forward. An hour into the wonderful task, the emperor/god and his entourage realized something they should have known before they began: plowing a furrow around a city containing twenty million residents was not a job to be accomplished in a single afternoon, and perhaps not in several weeks of sunny afternoons. (Imagine, some of the Guardsmen said, what the job would have been like a few years before, when there were forty million people in the city.) Furthermore, there were tree roots, hedges, roads, rivers, walls, and elevated aqueducts in the emperor's path, and none of these objects were as impressed with the Concerned One's divinity as he was. By the time the midday sun became the evening sunset, the emperor had not progressed far enough to be out of sight of his starting point. He kept running into a new obstacle every few steps and was repeatedly cursing his beleaguered City Guardsmen, who had to chop away at whatever was in the plow's path. The capital's leading men meanwhile grew red in the bright sunlight. Their wives fanned themselves and complained of the heat. My weary father had seen men plow before; he did not care to see another one, so he sat himself beneath an oak tree, and in its comfortable shade took a nap that lasted until after dark. The emperor by then was longing for his dinner more than for completing his monumental chore.

"Now that I have begun this menial job," he told the anxious, hungry crowd, "let us return to the affairs of state. These sturdy beasts"—he meant the fat, indolent oxen—"will, by my command, complete the circuit around the city on their own. Should they defy my wishes, let the world know I will return to destroy them!"

He and nearly everyone else went home to eat, leaving behind a detachment of City Guardsmen to continue plowing the endless furrow. The instant they were alone, the soldiers hit upon the ingenious idea of taking the plow out of the ground and dragging it along the surface of the earth so the steel triangle would meet much less resistance. Even under these new conditions, the soldiers still needed ten long days to drag the plow all the way around the city. Their completed furrow was a mere scratch across the topsoil, which, when one considers the fate of Mausoleum of the Concerned One, was a more fitting tribute to the new city than the City Guardsmen could have ever anticipated.

The emperor/god financed some additional athletic exhibitions to celebrate the great renaming of the city. To pay for these new shows the Concerned One committed a host of fresh murders and confiscated the property of his wealthy victims. In one nighttime purge he killed most of the living ex-speakers of the Senate, the Pedros brothers, Marcello and Samsung from the speculators' guild, and the reigning governor and tribune for the people in California. While he was at it, he executed his nephew Albert Anthony and his father's cousin Anne Kelbertson. These last two victims had been friends to the emperor's concubine Marcie, if a cold-hearted killer like Marcie Angelica could be said to have friends. That the Concerned One would kill members of his own family awoke a terrible new fear in the make-believe queen of the Amazons. The commander of the City Guardsmen, General Lamb, and the chamberlain Einman were quick to impress upon her the notion that anyone, absolutely anyone, could be the next to die. Einman attempted to sway her because he was as terrified of the mad emperor as everyone else was. Lamb, as I have said, was Abdul Selin's man in the imperial court and was eager to undermine the emperor any way he could. The Concerned One increased Marcie's anxiety when he put to death four members of his harem on the preposterous charge of having had sexual relations with the late Cleander, when everyone knew Cleander never had been affectionate with anyone; all four of these women had been close friends of the chief concubine before she rose in the world. The day following their executions the emperor killed every one of his long-time athlete comrades (save for Norman) because he said they had touched his godly body during wrestling matches and thus were no longer fit to live among the mortals.

"I had to turn them into gods," he explained to his City Guardsmen the morning he examined his friends' butchered corpses lying within one of his gardens. "They would not have been happy staying here after having gotten a feel for heaven."

Marcie did not have to be reminded she touched parts of the divine person every night.

"Whom will he murder tomorrow, my lady?" General Lamb must have whispered in her ear countless times. "A man who would kill his wife would give no thought to killing his mistress"—for General Lamb and Marcie both knew the emperor had killed his wife Barbara in 2288.

The byword of the Concerned One's rule—"I can, therefore I will"—became, in his last year on the throne, "I can do anything." He made noblemen dance naked for him in the palace gardens. Those few who refused to obey him would be thrown to wild beasts so they might amuse him as they perished. His dinner guests were each night forced to eat food mixed with human excrement while he watched and laughed at their distress. Among his retainers he kept at his elbow throughout his waking hours was an unspeakable young man he called "the Ass"; on those evenings simple torture did not lift the Concerned One's soul to the heights he wished to scale, he would watch while the Ass abused little boys and girls. The emperor was so pleased with this criminal he made him a priest in the new religion of the Living Hercules. At one dinner party while the Ass was performing for the Concerned One and his horrified guests, the degenerate performed acts of such piety the emperor took a pistol from a City Guardsman and sent his favorite to dwell in heaven with his athlete friends. "Such a great artist is wasted upon this world," said the Concerned One as he kicked the Ass's body to make certain he was completely gone. That summer the emperor declared bulls to be sacred and demanded followers of Invictus to sacrifice humans instead during their baptismal rites. Armed with his Herculean club he sometimes stalked the palace corridors on nights he could not sleep and would on impulse beat to death anyone he happened to meet. He would scream for hours over the dead like a lion roaring over its prey. In celebration of the longest day of the year he dressed a hundred deformed and crippled men in tight linen casings, laid them on the floor of his throne room, and while the City Guardsmen stood around the doomed men in a square the Concerned One shot the wretched men while they struggled against the tight clothing and their emperor screamed, "I'm killing Hera's snakes!" (The doomed men were not scholars and would not have known that the goddess Hera supposedly sent giant serpents to kill the infant Hercules in his cradle, although the young hero slew them first.) One autumn day in the fighters' school behind the Field of Diversions, the Concerned One heard someone in the crowd laugh while the athletes were training. He thought the bemused spectators were laughing at him; therefore he had his City Guardsmen seal the exits, sweep through the stands in formation, and kill everyone present.

Marcie did her best to keep him drunk as often as possible. When he was full of liquor, he became dull and inactive, and would not kill anyone until he slept off his stupor. It was unfortunate for the Empire that his athletic training kept him sober far too often, and there was no safety for any within the reach of his power.

Yet the common citizens continued to love their emperor through these long months of carnage. These were fat times for most of those in the city when compared to the years of famine and disease. While the money lasted and the trade routes within Mexico remained open, the public dole was more generous than it had been only months before. As I have said, the emperor's building projects in the city employed tens of thousands of formerly idle men. I have not yet observed that the standards of these projects were agreeably lax, and much could be built slipshod and more still could be stolen by those owning a construction contract. The new diseases and the emperor's whims had eliminated scads of property owners, and anyone with a little capital to invest in land or ships now had plenty of chances to take the places of the dead. The metal plagues had crippled the foreign powers as much as they had the Pan-Polarian Empire, and thus the remaining lands within the emperor's control remained secure, for the moment. New mines in western Mexico had given the Empire an apparently inexhaustible supply of gold and silver coin with which our merchants could import all the food, drink, clothing, and artisan-made luxury items our people could still consume. The speculators and the moneylenders ruling the Empire's trade from their market stalls in the city's central plaza grew as rich as the kings of most other nations. A man of wealth but of low birth, such as Father's patron Mr. Golden, could afford to buy a place in society his ancestors could not have dreamed of. Such men could now live in villas high in the cool, dry surrounding hills. They brought to their new homes small armies of servants and bodyguards, exactly as the aristocrats had done for centuries. Their wives could wear silk and turquoise like Egyptian princesses and have teams of Mexican servants stand beside them to sweep away the flies with fans made of gigantic feathers. It was almost as good as having air-conditioning back. Their children could grow to be as fat and as arrogant as the young aristocrats already were, while their merchant fathers wallowed in the myriad carnal delights of the privileged. In such almost golden times, the commoners were forgiving of the Concerned One's personal excesses. Such things did not harm them.

"Of course he does bad things in the palace," a woman living in the tenement apartment under Helen and me told me, "but he does them to the rich. Who cares what he does to those bastards? They have been robbing the world for a couple hundred years. Let them have a taste of the supper they've been serving to everybody else. Let him take his boot off their necks, and they would start bullying us again. The emperor is our defender. We need him more than ever now that we don't have the things we used to have. The machines, I mean."

The last time Father was summoned to the palace, the defender of the people, the man/god Hercules, the emperor of most of the northern world had let Marcie Angelica get him roaring drunk again. The Concerned One lay undressed on his vast bed, half conscious of everything near him in his candle-illuminated sleeping chamber. Rather than turn Father away another time, Marcie allowed Father to sit in the flickering light on a stool near the side of the bed.

"He has asked for you specifically," the concubine told Father. "Something about wolves."

The emperor heard her say "wolves," and he roused himself and shouted, "Where are they?!"

"They are not here, precious," said Marcie, and stroked the curly hair on his head. "Lie down. We are safe in the palace."

"Who's this?" he asked of Father.

"General Peter Black," she said. "You called for him."

"Old Blackie was a good sort," said the Concerned One, lying fully on his back once more. "I'm pretty certain I killed him years ago. Lined him up against the wall and shot him. This one is an imposter. Have the guards take care of him."

"No, precious," Marcie advised him. "This really is General Black. He has come from the East to visit us."

"Get a lamp in here!" ordered the emperor. "I need to see this with my own eyes. So many damned spies around."

A City Guardsman fetched a blazing oil lamp for him, and the Concerned One had the man hold the light to Father's face while the emperor rolled on his left side to have a clear look at his guest.

"Why, it is the old coot!" he announced. "Didn't Cleander find some way of bumping you off?" he asked.

"Apparently not, my lord," said Father.

"Have you seen any wolves about?" asked the Concerned One.

"Not in Garden City, my lord," said Father. "We have many in Asia."

"Could you get some for me, old boy?" asked the emperor, focused for the moment on this peculiar subject. "I want to shoot some in the Field of Diversions."

"I suppose I could, my lord," said Father. He glanced at Marcie and the soldier holding the lamp; both of them were old hands in the palace and had learned to keep a blank face when the Concerned One got to ranting. Father took his cue from them.

"Remember in Progress, way out there in Siberia, when we still had Siberia, before Daddy went to heaven," said the Concerned One, "how the wolves used to steal from the forest after sundown. I could see their gray heads moving in the night. Like they were floating in front of the undergrowth. They were terrible, weren't they, Blackie? I watched them from my window for hours before I went to sleep. They would wait and wait for their chance. I have to get rid of them. They've gotten into my dreams, you know. Take the Turkish divisions and go into Siberia and round them up. I will finish them one by one in the pure light of the arena."

Aiming at a target he alone could see, the emperor aimed an invisible rifle in the hushed bedroom air.

"Every wolf in Siberia, my lord?" said Father. "That would be a large project. There are so many. . . ."

"Because the goddamned Chinese protect them!" said the emperor with more feeling than twenty sane men would use in a year. "Round the Chinese up, too! Ha! That would be something! Speaking of China, do you know what they found there?" (He sat upright in his bed to tell Father this in a whisper.) "Merchants coming from that part of the world say they found . . . a whole flock of white ravens. Pure white, old man. When they found their nests, they cracked open the eggs and out came lizards! Little wiggling lizards! They say it's the end of the world. I have a woman from Egypt who saw the same thing in the sky. Not lizards; the end of the world, I mean. Even the damned stupid priests of something or other I have here in my capital saw an omen inside some albino calf they found. They cut it open, and there was nothing in there. Nothing."

"The mystics are always telling such tales, my lord," said Father, who believed in Sophia and nothing else.

"They tell tales because of the damned wolves!" said the emperor, and rolled onto his back. "They will tell them until every wolf is gone." (He ordered the City Guardsman away, and put an arm across his face to shield his eyes from the lamplight.) "What would you do, Black, if I let you do anything you wanted? Anything? I mean absolutely anything?"

Father did not have to reflect much upon the question.

"I would like to return to Turkey, my lord," he said. "I have a garden there, and I need to get my flowers in before the rains come."

"If you could do anything you wanted," asked the astonished emperor/god, "you would go back to Turkey and raise flowers?"

"Yes," said Father.

"Wouldn't we all?" whispered the emperor, and he rolled over on his stomach and fell back into a deep sleep.

Father would not speak to the Concerned One again. We saw him from afar three weeks later in the Field of Diversions when the emperor once more frolicked as a modern gladiator before the bloodthirsty thousands. These were the traditional Thanksgiving games of November, the occasion the Concerned One chose to stage the largest wild animal show Garden City had witnessed in her long and sanguinary history. Following his custom, the emperor climbed his elevated platform and with his rifle dispatched hundreds and hundreds of exotic animals that had more beauty and grace than he and his dying Empire ever would. The Concerned One spent the equivalent of a year's budget for the entire city on this one grotesque exhibition that took two full days to complete. For this one spectacle, our old acquaintance Mr. Golden and his friends in the market made millions on special importations from independent trading companies in Africa and South America. The frightful waste further proved to the emperor's supporters how much he loved them. To his detractors he proved again he remained the same monster he ever was, only now he was growing somewhat worse in appearance and manners. At the show's long-anticipated finale on the second day, the emperor slew a hippopotamus, a fat river horse from the Nile that could not protect itself from his bullets outside its muddy water; the emperor had to shoot the bewildered creature eleven times, making the entirety of its tough exterior bleed torrents of red before it collapsed. For once the crowd became disgusted with their hero. Some reckless boys sitting high in the cheap section booed loudly at the emperor as he climbed down from his platform to pose over the mutilated beast. The offended ruler glared into the stands. A few boys insulting him was to him the same as if the entire world had. As much as he wanted to, he could not kill 180,000 at one setting as he had massacred the smaller crowd at the fighters' school. To vent his wrath he snatched up the head of an emu he had killed earlier in the show and ran into the portion of the grandstands in which the senators were seated in their crisp, linen suits. He shook the severed bird's head at the prominent men and screamed, "I can do this to you just as easily!" The politicos did not quiet his rage by bowing their faces down to the cement arena steps. The emperor screamed at them and at the crowd as the people ran toward the exits before he could sic his City Guardsmen on them. At the palace that evening the emperor smashed the furniture in his dining hall, threw his golden crowns at the walls, abused his servants with his club, and committed the one crime he had previously avoided: he beat his concubine Marcie Angelica. The City Guardsmen commander, General Lamb, was watching from within the forest of a garden peristyle as the emperor slapped her face and dragged her by her hair about the inlaid marble floors. "Why didn't you stop them?!" Luke Anthony demanded of her each time he brought his fists down upon her. With every blow, Lamb could see the emperor bringing himself a little closer to his grave.

On the third day of December, two weeks after the emperor had threatened the city's leading men in the grandstands, a list of names appeared on certain letters that were passed about in the Senate and later appeared in the wealthiest households of the capital. The lists were said to have been stolen from the emperor's administrators. The capital's rumor mill said it showed those the Concerned One was about to declare offensive to his person. The Senators Pretext and Clement were on the list, as were Einman the chamberlain and Lamb the commander of the City Guardsmen. Marcie Angelica's name was written at the very top. After years of reflection, I have now decided these lists of the damned were forgeries. Before that date the Concerned One had consistently fallen upon those he killed without giving them any warning. No one had ever known him to do any thinking before he acted. Telling people they are soon to die would serve no purpose other than giving them a chance to flee. Agents of Lamb and his master Abdul Selin were, I expect, the true authors of the lists, as no one else would have profited from terrifying the city's wealthy and powerful. In the atmosphere of panic the documents had created, no one questioned their authenticity. Other and still more expansive lists somehow appeared in the city's plazas. Wealthy hostesses made copies and distributed them at dozens of early winter parties along with the candied pigeons and the raw oysters in their shells. By late December, every prominent family thought the emperor was preparing to destroy at least some of its members. Marcie Angelica also had seen her name on the fatal scrolls. In her mind and in the minds of the leading citizens, the only question was what they could do to the emperor before he slaughtered them.

On the last evening of the year, the Concerned One laid himself to sleep on his vast bed in the palace. For the first time in many days, he was feeling healthy and in good spirits. He had trained hard through the past two months. While the rest of the capital lived in constant dread, he was looking forward to the games he would be presiding over on the morrow. On that day, the first day of the new year, he would kill a hundred giant snakes and declare from his elevated seat in the Field of Diversions that the Pan-Polarian people would henceforth be known as "the people of the Expected One." He awoke after less than an hour of repose. Something was outside the window, perched atop the stone balcony and softly murmuring to him. He drew a gun from beneath his pillows and tiptoed across the floor to have a look. To his horror, as he drew near the arched window, he beheld a large, white owl, a bird of ill omen, slowing turning its head and making demon's chatter. The emperor/god dropped his weapon and ran shouting into the adjoining room, seeking the protection of his chief mistress.

"We have to leave here!" he told her and the giant Norman. "This room is cursed! Get a company of men! I have to sleep at the fighters' school!"

The City Guardsmen accompanied the imperial party to the fighters' school behind the larger arena known as the Field of Diversions. Marcie prepared for the emperor a little cot from the many the combatants rest upon before they fight on the artificial turf. In spite of her efforts to comfort him, the Concerned One remained unable to sleep.

"That owl has joined forces with the wolves!" he told his companions. "All of nature has turned against me!"

He had the soldiers lock himself, Marcie, and Norman in a foulsmelling concrete locker room in which the athletes wait before they are sent outside to fight and perhaps to perish. He asked for a warrior's meal: a thick steak of lion's meat and a bottle of the reddest and sweetest wine available, for he was not too frightened to lose his appetite. The Concerned One devoured the meat the soldiers grilled on a skewer and did not ask why the meat tasted much like beef, for he expected the Guardsmen would do him the small favor of hunting up a lion when their emperor needed a late-night snack. Ample glasses of the sweet wine followed the meal into his stomach. He accepted these from Marcie's hand, as he had done for the many years they had been together. When he had drunk himself into a stupor, she opened a compartment on a ring General Lamb had given her and dropped some poison into the last wine the Concerned One would ever drink. He drained the deadly glass as eagerly as he had the previous ones. A few moments later he put a hand to his forehead and sat on the cot Marcie had prepared for him.

"I think I will take a little nap after all," he said, and fell over backward, spilling wine across his lap.

Marcie and the giant wrestler waited over him as he snored. She put her ear to his chest, and clearly heard his steady pulse. She looked up at the wrestler with pleading eyes. Without having been asked, he put a pillow over the emperor's face to prevent him from calling out and with his other hand he wrapped a leather strap around the Concerned One's throat and strangled him by slowly twisting the strap tighter. In this sordid way did Luke Anthony, the Concerned One, the last of his line, die: insane, his skin corrupt with open sores, his dreams haunted by ghostly wolves, and his last two friends in the world his executioners. What a great disappointment it must have been to his immortal soul to realize his body was mortal after all! What a greater shock it must have been to him when he discovered his soul was not going to heaven to dwell in the company of Mathias the Glistening and the other gods!

Not knowing what they should do next, Marcie sent for General Lamb, and the commander of the City Guardsmen ordered the body buried beneath the floor of the school; then he sent out the happy news of the emperor's death to every aristocratic home in the city.

At dawn on New Year's Day, everyone was aware the Concerned One was gone. Senator Coppola, one of the men the emperor had supposedly been going to murder, asked and got a resolution from his fellow senators that Luke Anthony's body be exhumed and dragged on a hook through the capital's streets. Not only was this done, the people took turns attacking the corpse with hammers and knives as the City Guardsmen brought it past their doorsteps. He had been their champion while he lived; now that he was gone, the people wanted to be on the winning side far more than they desired to honor their former friend. The city's great men, on the other hand, had gone to bed quaking at the thought of what the emperor might do to them; they awoke unafraid of anything, now that the creature was dead. They gathered on the tall steps at the front of the Senate to proclaim their reborn joy to the equally brave crowds. Never had the air above the floating city of the Aztecs been so bruised with fine words as it was on that New Year's Day. Orator after wellborn orator came forward to hurl insults at the dead man. They made jokes relating to his gilded hair and beard, and mocked his physical condition. "He was more savage than Cepheus," the speakers said, "more perverse than Darko. As he did to his countless victims, let it be done to him and to his supporters." The Senate called for the immediate deaths of the late emperor's secret agents, and the City Guardsmen did as they demanded. As many of these agents were unknown, the Guardsmen necessarily had to kill many they only suspected of having been agents in order to get at those who were guilty. On that day of freedom, no one objected to their crude methods.

Patrick Herman Pretext, he of the distinguished profile and the owner of the longest and most silvery of patrician manes, paid the City Guardsmen twelve thousand dollars apiece, and they, out of a new sense of public obligation, made him the new emperor. He put on the purple robes and sent the men and women of Garden City back to their appointed tasks, though in Father's case, that meant he was sent to a new assignment. Pretext began a program of administrative reform designed to return the government to fiscal stability and to reestablish imperial control in the provinces. He freed those Luke Anthony had sent into exile and pardoned those sentenced to death. Everyone who was anyone gave him high marks for his magnanimous behavior on the throne, for his dignified mien at public ceremonies, and for the generous reception he gave to every petitioner. He ruled for three months before General Lamb and the City Guardsmen stabbed him to death while he slept.

Father and those of us in his household meanwhile sailed to the big island of Hawaii and to the Empire's last operative hydrogen gun on the slope of Mauna Kea. In that isolated spot, the metal plague had not yet reached and we could be launched into orbit. The technicians put us asleep, because we would not be able to stand the g-forces while awake; then we were placed into a container that rides suspended above an electromagnetic track for twenty-three miles up the mountain's long slope, gradually accelerating to liftoff speed, when the detachable hydrogen engines turn on and blast us above the Earth's atmosphere. We joined an ore barge in orbit, and rode it to our destination on Mars, where the metal plague had appeared, but would not destroy the mining colony for many months to come.

As was told at the story's beginning, the fool John Chrysalis back in Garden City would give twenty-five thousand dollars apiece to the Guardsmen to become emperor after Pretext was dead. That pretender reigned for the sixty-six days Abdul Selin needed to march from the Missouri; on the sixty-seventh day, the First of June, Selin ordered this would-be ruler hunted down inside the palace and disposed of, but one of Chrysalis's last guards performed this task for Selin before the Turk's men could reach the palace. Within four years of Selin's rise to absolute power in North America, every person named on the fraudulent lists of the Concerned One's victims would suffer the same fate as had befallen John Chrysalis. Even the cunning General Lamb, the giant Norman, Marcie the concubine, and Einman the chamberlain would go in front of a firing squad. There they would learn Selin and his vast family of criminals were not going to share what little was left of the Pan-Polarian Empire with anyone.

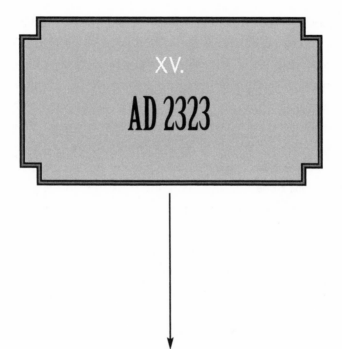

XV.

AD 2323

Thirty years have fled the Earth since Father defeated Selin in the pass between Nicea and Eribulus, and the past has long since blended into the present.

Selin returned to Garden City after his loss and patched together another, much smaller army. Within a year he had learned his other rival, Whiteman in Britain, had withered away after he was no longer able to pay his soldiers. Selin was thereafter left free to establish a new dictatorship in what was left of the Empire in North America. The ruling principle of his reign would be "Give everything to the army, and give the army to me and my family of criminals. Let the rest go to hell." He executed most of the prominent men remaining in the city for the sake of their property—property he needed to finance the army and their never-ending wars on North America's frontiers. Luke Anthony had been a careless madman, but Selin was as methodical as he was ruthless. While his insane predecessor had killed thousands as a sport, Selin killed hundreds of thousands out of what he construed to be necessity. He slew any who might stand against him and those he thought might someday be able to. No one in Garden City I have named in this account—save for the members of our household who were there but temporarily—would live to see the end of his eighteen-year rule. Selin raised up a new generation of leading citizens to become governors and legislators in the place of those he had killed. Before he departed this world for the land from which none return, Selin had already sent most of these younger men before him as scouts. Many of his administrators and officers naturally came from his enormous Turkish clan. Selin reasoned he could trust no one else in that troubled era. He did not trust them overmuch, and he retained the emperor's prerogative to kill any family members he thought too ambitious. Given the inclinations of his family, Selin would find many of his relatives too ambitious or otherwise defective, and he would have no choice but to eliminate them.

The sly Mr. Golden and the other market speculators survived as long as they were useful to the new emperor's ends. In time Selin would decide he needed their money more than he needed their fealty. Two years after Selin's ascension, a detachment of soldiers came to call upon Mr. Golden at his stately home high above the city. The fat, vulgar man had seen the armed men tramping up the pathway and went running with his family out the back door while his servants stalled the soldiers at the front of the estate. He did not realize the troopers had taken the precaution of surrounding the estate before they approached. They overtook Mr. Golden and his equally plump family in the sunny fields behind his house with its whitewashed walls and red tile roof. By evening Selin's men were strolling back down the hill, Mr. Golden's money in hand. The bodies of the fuel factor and his household were left hanging upside down from the arched gate in the front of their beautiful home.

Although by this time in history there was little in the way of technology that could be lost that was not already gone, the common people never favored Selin as they had the Concerned One, despite the fact that the latter man had presided over the loss of electricity and most of the Empire. The little Turk raised taxes, reduced the dole, devalued the currency in order to decrease the government's debt, cut back the athletic shows, and he was never slow to send in the army if the people ever rioted. Their disapproval of him gained the people nothing. The only power left belonged to the army and its leader. Those outside the army could weep salt tears to ease their troubles, and their tears no longer mattered to any but themselves.

For himself, Selin chose a quiet family life and hid his person within the safety of his very well-paid forces. He had no bad habits, not counting murder, and took no chances with his safety. He died of natural causes while campaigning against an uprising in that part of North America that once was called Texas.

During his time on the throne Selin would make war on rebels in Central America and proposed a new campaign on our traditional enemy, the Chinese, which was wishful thinking in an age when the Empire no longer had a navy; so he instead destroyed a hundred cities within Mexico and the American southwest for having supported either Father or Whiteman, and sent his army against any cults he suspected had a poor opinion of his own beloved sun religion. In the countryside around Garden City he put to death thousands of the indigenous farmers, as he thought the members of his clan should own their land. Two years into his rule, he declared the late Luke Anthony a god equal to the emperors before him. Taking into account every bad thing he did, I have to say Selin's greatest crime came at the end of his life, for on his deathbed he named his son his successor in power.

To be perfectly correct, I should say Selin named both his son Brass and Brass's little brother Gunter to succeed him, which is to say he nominated a lamb to serve with a wolf. The oldest son, known as the Hooded One for the manner of dress he made popular among his upper-class disciples, had his younger brother strangled within a year of their father's demise. For good measure and to impress upon everyone that he was answerable only to the army, the Hooded One murdered the other twenty thousand surviving members of the Selin clan his father had led. The Hooded One would have been a rare creature in any age; in his person were combined a madness worthy of Luke Anthony and the martial severity of his father. His six years as commander of the shrinking Empire were an extravaganza of public executions and private debauchery that will be the envy of tyrants for ages to come. To pay for his government he further devalued the currency and extended citizenship to every free inhabitant of the Empire. (Citizenship no longer brought an individual any political rights, since no one outside the army had any, but it did make everyone who owned it responsible for paying taxes.) The Hooded One's insane energy would, in time, make even the army weary, and Marcus Dross, a soldier of humble origins the Hooded One had set over the City Guardsmen, assassinated him and declared himself emperor. The army killed Mr. Dross after a few months of misrule and replaced him with a weird boy they found in a temple of the sun god, a boy who may or may not have been the Hooded One's natural son, but definitely was a devotee of the same cult the Selin clan had favored. The perverted child called himself Helios after the name the sun god is given in southern California, the spot in which the army had found him. Though the effeminate boy killed the wealthy and the poor as ably as any ruler who had served before him, Helios offended noble taste by dressing as a prostitute and practicing certain disgusting acts on the high steps in front of the palace. As much as his antics entertained the soldiers, their officers came to feel it was not proper, given the high standards the previous emperors had set, to have a sissy as their leader. After four years that he spent inside the palace grounds engaged in one continuous party, the army killed the odd boy and put on the throne the Hooded One's cousin, Alexander Selin, the last of the once vast family. He had reigned for only two years when the people native to the capital and to Mexico itself sacked the city and renamed it Mexico City. Over the past decades, there have been several pretenders in North America who have momentarily held a portion of what was once the Pan-Polarian Empire; none of them ruled for long or were able to expand into the separate nations and city-states the Empire has become. We in Europe heard of these would-be emperors only many months after they had been overthrown.

After we reached Europe when our army crossed the Bosporus, Father, Medus, Helen, and I journeyed through the newly separated states that had been provinces of the Empire to Amsterdam in what was again called the Netherlands. We found the man Samuel in the port district the day we arrived in that crowded city. He gave us the fifty thousand dollars in gold Father had set aside with him, which was money Father had gotten from Mr. Golden back when the fuel factor was buying army contracts. To speak in plain language, the money had been a bribe. Knowing that has not prevented us from using the ill-gotten cash as we would. There are no longer any fortunes in the world that are not ill gotten to some degree, and the dirty money Samuel handed to us was at least cleansed a bit by a father's love.

Amsterdam was and remains the largest and richest city on that portion of the northern coast. Political power had long resided elsewhere; during the years of the Empire, Amsterdam had learned to be content with presiding over the Empire's business in the northwest portion of the European mainland. The city was and is the corridor between the rich agricultural lands of the European coastal plain and points west. Whatever entered the city's port now had to do so via sailing ships, and the cargo they brought was unloaded on the piers and carried by animal caravans to cities that once had been linked by hyperfast railways and instantaneous communications. The terrible diseases that had only recently destroyed much of the world's population had lost much of their original power, and though Amsterdam's sanitation system could have used much improvement, the time of epidemics had passed. There was plenty to eat in the city—unless one wanted tropical fruit and chocolate—and, best of all, the people in the city did not know who we or Father were.

In the same market we met Samuel we purchased a tiny coffee shop. We bought and sold from the small room facing the street in the front of a one-story building. The servants and Father and I lived in the larger rooms behind the shop, where we also had a small enclosed garden and could escape the dust and noise at the other end of our home. From the rear of our garden we could see the city's famous harbor, which is not a large boast, considering as how the entire city seems to sit surrounded by water. In our new city we have done business with traders from every nation in creation, from the men in furs from Greenland to the brown men in turbans from lands south of China. We do not thrive. We do make more money than we spend and live as we want in the heart of the human anthill that we have come to accept as our hometown.

The permanent residents of Amsterdam are approximately half native Dutch and half refugees who landed there when the Empire collapsed. Both groups have become book lovers now that they have no other entertainment, and in addition to the city's many famous libraries, which are well stocked even if they are nothing compared to the imperial library that once existed in North Dakota, there are on every street book dealers who rent out copies of the world's literature they print in simple back-room presses. By law, the city makes a duplicate of every new manuscript a ship brings into the port, and the private dealers will pay visitors for the opportunity to do the same. At the time I settled into our shop I thought I would pass the rest of my life reading these books, caring for my aging father, and conversing with the ever-flowing river of strangers frequenting our shop.

Two years into our new stationary life my plans were interrupted after I met Jon, a native of the city and one a couple years my senior. He had been a fisherman since he was a boy of eight on one of the local vessels and had risen over the years to the rank of ship's captain; when I made his acquaintance he told me he was interested in leaving the sea and starting his own business in the city now that he had some money saved. Like many in the city, Jon was a Christian, a circumstance that made me leery of him, though—perhaps thanks to his religion—he had better manners than a sailor should have. After only a week of lingering about our shop and making inane conversation while he stole sidelong looks at me, he proposed he and I marry. I told him I was an old woman, nearly thirty, and marriage was out the question; I was content to run the coffee shop and read my books in the sunshine of our garden while Father snored away, dreaming of ancient battles. Jon insisted. Despite the futility of his petition, I admired him for not being easily discouraged. He believed Medus was my uncle, perhaps because he was dark like I am, and so Jon gave my father's batman a fat sack of gold and promised Helen—who Jon assumed was my aunt—he would treat me well. Father immediately liked Jon because the younger man listened to the old man's stories, even to the one about the Nile crocodile, and not once did Jon interrupt him. With all four of them teamed against me (and given his pleasing manners and looks) I gradually softened my position and allowed I might consent to be his wife, on the condition I have no children. I insisted upon that point even after we were wed and Jon quickly made me pregnant. I said to my husband after I had given birth to our first daughter that the great happiness I had found with him notwithstanding, this would be our only child. I told him the same after I had borne three more daughters and a son.

I have learned during the years of our marriage that Jon's religion is far more benign than I had once believed it to be. Given the new cults that had arisen in the last decades of the Pan-Polarian Empire and the general state of disbelief that preceded the Empire's decline, I am astonished it and the other old religions have not only survived but in fact thrive in the new world we are slowly building in Amsterdam and the other places like it. That it could go on when everything else that was our civilization has gone to dust is itself worthy of respect, though I admit I am not as firm a believer as my husband and our children are. I tell myself this religion is the gentler notions of philosophy, such as Mathias the Glistening preached, combined with everlasting hope, and still I have seen so much evil in this world that I sometimes doubt the efficacy of the works of either God or man. I sometimes continue to wonder if good shall really triumph over evil when the dust at last settles, for evil seems to me to be every bit as strong as the good, or at least it was in the Empire our ancestors built. I confess it is the subversive nature of the religion I find most appealing, and that is the thing that keeps me within the fold. I love going to church with my family and knowing we are raising them to offend the immoral order that ruled the Empire and its emperors, albeit that is not a very Christian sentiment for me to have.

In their later years, Helen and Medus also became Christers, in addition to everything else they already were. Helen remained a follower of Sophia, Anubis, Minit, and of some mystery cults that would never have had her as a member. The exclusive nature of her new faith was lost upon her. No matter how many times the priests explained she must give up her magic charms and secret herbs, she clung to them until her moment of death. With their pagan symbols hidden beneath their clothes, she and Medus were buried beside the church and were left facing Jerusalem in expectation of Christ's return. What God will make of my old maid, I cannot tell, but if He has a sense of humor I suspect He will take a liking to her in spite of everything else she was.

Father remained loyal to Sophia until his death. The old warrior became less active as the years passed, and most days he sat in the back-yard garden, lying blissfully in his lawn chair. He told us his stories again, and told them yet some more to his grandchildren when they arrived. On some days when he was feeling odd, he would call out to Harriman to bring up the light infantry, and then would look about sheepishly when he realized where he was. He practiced his calligraphy, as he told me he had wished he had done when he was younger; over a two-year period he copied out all of a large-print version of *David Copperfield* and was quite proud of his work. When Jon was not home, I would get out the odd costumes and paraphernalia that Sophia of the Flowers demands of her followers, and Father and I would act out the silly but heartfelt rituals of his faith. During Father's last year, Jon and I got him a small dog to keep him company in the garden, and the old man would hold the animal on his lap and tell it of the crocodile and of a crazed emperor who once ruled half the world. Father was holding the little dog the morning he went to sleep forever and drifted off to meet Sophia in paradise.

I named my son Peter after him. When the boy became older, I told him his namesake was a brave and honorable man, an anomaly in his time. I made my son swear while he held his mother's hand that, unlike his grandfather, he would never have anything to do with the military or politics. When our boy reached the age of sixteen, Jon purchased Peter an apprenticeship in a carpenter's shop. There our son learned the honest trade he practices today. We saw our children married to other families within our community, and I feel an un-Christian pride each time I see our lovely grandchildren and I know a part of Father lives on while the seed of Luke Anthony and that of Abdul Selin have been extinguished forever.

A merchant from Spain came by our shop yesterday and paid for his mocha with an old Pan-Polarian coin stamped with Luke Anthony's assumed name "the Expected One." On one side of the coin was the profile of the last of the Anthonys dressed in his silly Hercules getup. On the reverse was the image of the plow he had intended to push around Garden City. I had to laugh when I saw the pathetic moment preserved for the ages in metal.

"What is funny, madam?" the trader asked.

"Nothing, sir," I said. "Just that I knew him once. That is, my father did. Actually, I saw him many times; only once at close range."

"They say the Concerned One was a great leader," said the Spaniard. "The last one the Empire ever had."

"Who says that?" I asked.

"The people," he said. "They say the Concerned One gave the people in Garden City whatever they wanted."

"That is what a great leader does?" I asked. "He gives the people what they want?"

The Spaniard protested he was a simple merchant and did not wish to become involved in a philosophical debate.

"I was only repeating what others say, madam," he said. "That's everything I know: they say he was great."

"What do they say of his successor and of the ones who tried to come after him, sir?"

"Oh, I have heard plenty about Abdul Selin!" said the man. (He contorted his face at the mention of the name.) "He was a bad one, wasn't he? The people he had left under him had naught but higher taxes and war after he took the Concerned One's place. Now, I saw that character myself, madam. It was when I was bringing a shipment of wool into Garden City. He was fixing to march off to conquer somebody somewhere in the north at the head of his army. Looked as mean as a sick dog, he did. Good riddance when he took his last bow."

"What do you remember of the Concerned One's generals, sir?" I asked.

"Generals?" he said. "There were so many. I can't say any one of them comes to mind. . . ."

"What of General Peter Justice Black?" I asked. "He was a general under the Concerned One, under Mathias the Glistening, too. Under Pius Anthony he was a sergeant in the infantry."

"That's ancient history," said the Spaniard. "Black . . . Black . . ." He thought aloud over his coffee cup. "Yes, there was a saying about him: 'The African one is bad; the white one is worse; but the best is Black.'

"Or something like that. That was about him, wasn't it?" said the stranger.

"Yes, sir," I said, "they said that of him."

"Did you ever see that one, madam?" asked the Spaniard.

"I knew him well."

"Really? What sort of man was he?" he asked.

"General Black was a mixture of good and bad, as all men are," I said, and poured the Spaniard a free cup of mocha. "In him the good far outweighed the bad. He also was the last of his kind."

About the Author

THEODORE JUDSON is the author of *Fitzpatrick's War*, which was described by *Publishers Weekly* in a starred review as "a spectacular first foray into speculative fiction" and was selected as one of the seven best debuts of 2004. He lives in Fremont County, Wyoming.